LOVE SLAVE

LOVE SLAVE

JENNIFER SPIEGEL

UNBRIDLED BOOKS

This is a work of fiction. The names, characters, places and incidents are either the product of the author's imagination or are used fictitiously, and any resemblance to actual persons living or dead, business establishments, events, or locales is entirely coincidental.

Thank you to the journals and anthologies in which portions of *Love Slave* originally appeared. These include the following: *In Our Own Words: A Generation Defining Itself*, *Journal of Truth and Consequence*, *> kill author*, *Literary Lunch*, *Paradigm*, *Persona*, *The Scrambler*, and *Toasted Cheese*.

Unbridled Books

Library of Congress Cataloging-in-Publication Data

Spiegel, Jennifer.
Love slave / by Jennifer Spiegel.
p. cm.
ISBN 978-1-60953-082-2
I. Title.
PS3619.P539L68 2012
813'.6—dc23
2012010212

1 3 5 7 9 10 8 6 4 2

BOOK DESIGN BY SH·CV

First Printing

for Wendy and Melody

Subway's no way for a good man to go down.

Bernie Taupin

in Elton John's

"Mona Lisas and Mad Hatters"

LOVE SLAVE

PROLOGUE

Going Home with the Poets

New York City on Sunday, December 11, 1994

Madeline and I are walking home from the Nuyorican Poets Café, where these people with lousy day jobs, like waitressing or temping or sometimes dealing, read their poems, which are always about having really good sex or being a black woman.

We go there on Friday nights, always Friday nights, and we fold our legs beneath us on wooden floors, sipping cheap drinks and sweating under bare bulbs that make the place look ghoulish.

Next to us, the poets. Ahh, the poets! People of mystery, of magic, of words. We know they write quatrains and couplets on paper napkins at cafés on Sunday afternoons, stirring lattes, buttering croissants, consuming raspberry tarts—oh, we envy them their free verse!

Madeline and I, two in the morning, eye makeup black and thick, walk fast because we're in Alphabet City, which is like a suburb of the East Village but not really. We can handle the East Village freaks, but crack houses are another story.

Despite winter, I'm on fire—the kind of fire wrought by that rare and special combo of man and lyric together. Tonight, the poetry wasn't great—not great at all—but there was this one man, this one poet, a guy from Jamaica with dreadlocks, a black lanky body, and a somber long face. His poetry—sparse, unpretentious, not about being a poet—crawled over to me on the floor and punctured internal organs under a crystalline glare. It made me want to say something to him: *anything*.

In that moment, maybe like other moments before, I forgot my own paramour, my own backlash boyfriend, rarely present, rarely even imagined.

I forgot and no one reminded me, so I turned to this Jamaican poet with a searing, *easy* lust—I turned to him with famished, desperate eyes—and I listened to what people said: *Teaches high school English in Brooklyn. A cab driver, a bard.*

So I knew; I knew then he was both soulful and earthy.

I made my approach, touching his arm lightly. "Yours was the best."

He turned, his eyes lifting to mine, a honeyed Jamaican voice haunting his breath. "You are the only one who thinks so."

I do, I do, but I *do*.

It was like being thrown against the wall by a great gust of wind, and this is why I live in New York. This is why.

Now, walking fast with Madeline, I imagine this Jamaican poet/Brooklyn high school English teacher and me owning a loft in TriBeCa. In our loft, there'd only be a mattress. The room would be strewn with sheets, white and gauzy, blowing in a breeze that sallied through open windows offering up the scent of city, skin, and naan bread from the Indian restaurant below.

I think about meeting the Jamaican poet on corners at nightfall, how he'd see me coming and I'd see him standing there with his *I Don't Care* body posture—that lovely, lanky *I Don't Care* body posture—which would briefly, fleetingly, shift to reveal his thrill at seeing me walking toward him. I'd stare into his sleepy sad Jamaican poet face, and I'd probably have to weep just for the beauty of his poet approach.

Madeline, the only thing I've kept from a long string of temp jobs, points to a torn poster on the wet ground. "Glass Half Empty is playing at the Fedora on Friday."

Glass Half Empty plays there monthly, and we go religiously because, we say, when we analyze the situation over coffee at a diner or a Village café, it makes us feel like we have a community, and we know from our private dwellings—our beds and the places we stand alone, places in front of Xerox machines and other instruments of capitalist alienation—that we have no community, no community at all.

And this is what I want, what I need, what I choose. I temp, my lust is fruitless as temp lust always is, and whomever I love today will not be the person I love tomorrow.

And so: we watch Glass Half Empty play. It's the repetition of action, the sanctity of ceremony, the joy of the familiar. We need it to make us believe we are alive. To prove we *are*, indeed, alive.

I heard from some girl at Yaffa Café that the singer's wife died a year after they married and he still, seven years later, wears his wedding ring around a swollen finger. Though some may find this morbid, I think it beautiful. Perhaps he understands what it means to have loved and lost. Perhaps he *really* understands.

This time, in my head, it's the singer and me.

We're on a shag carpet because Rob is rather retro—a throwback to a time never had. It's the shag carpet, a messy apartment, a pizza on the coffee table. He probably bought this coffee table at a sidewalk sale on the Lower East Side one Saturday afternoon, after wandering for hours and hours in search of used CDs by Buffalo Springfield and old paperback novels with prices like seventy-nine cents on upper right-hand corners.

He's my kind of man, as the elastic of his Scooby-Doo boxers surely attests. I'm certain I'd be far happier with Rob than with my beautiful Jamaican poet. The poet would want profundity, and I am simple.

Madeline lets out a yelp of disgust, an *Ewhh!* a *Don't look now!*

Of course, I turn my head to the steps of NYU's business school—the *bane* of my existence—and, here's what I see: some guy getting a blow job, the girl not even visible.

Must I be privy to this? Did anyone hear me ask for such a sight?

Madeline and I look straight ahead, walking fast until we're well into Greenwich Village, which is where I live in somebody's basement with a guy named Tom who can't stand the sight of me because I once freaked when he left the keys in the lock on the outside of the door overnight. But he's in Greece for a year studying the Pythagorean Theorem, and his dad pays his rent.

By now we're obsessed with this most recent vision on our otherwise pure evening.

5

I remember how my mom responded when I told her that, one balmy summer day, when I was walking on Twelfth, I saw this guy taking a dump right on the street—right in the middle of the street—and how she couldn't believe I chose this existence, and I tried to tell her this is my life.

Mom, *this* is my life.

ONE

SPIN CYCLE

Saturday, January 7, 1995

Into my world he comes.

After I wake up early and write my column for two hours, I reward myself by doing laundry. "I'm trying to picture what you do during the day." I'm sitting next to a guy wearing orange pants in a grimy Laundromat on West Fourth at the beginning of a new, hopefully stunning, year. Saturday morning calls for wearing red sweatpants featuring Mickey Mouse on the left hip, dragging dirty clothes in a blue plastic basket with a broken handle five blocks to a slightly cheaper Laundromat than the one around the corner from my basement apartment, stuffing as much as humanly possible into a single machine, and relaxing while drinking deli coffee with half-and-half and eating a low-fat berry muffin while reading the *Times* as my laundry spins. This is the way it's been for over four years. Any variation and I'm thrown. Possibly made angry. Maybe I'll mope. I focus on the guy in orange pants. "You *have* to have another job. You can't be making it by playing a club once or twice a week." I look at him doubtfully, trying to quickly remember how much I weighed when I woke this morning. "Can you?" I blow on my coffee and suck in my stomach, which is tough when sitting down.

Kim, the Korean man who works behind the counter, adjusts the TV picture. We've known each other for as long as I've lived in the West Village. When it's only the two of us, he'll play an Anne Murray tape in his cassette player and sing out loud: *Could I have this dance for the rest of my life?* I pretend not to listen. This image is something I hold on to: the Korean man singing Anne Murray songs at the Laundromat on West Fourth.

I know who the guy in orange pants is. He's the lead singer of Glass Half Empty. Alternative rock, Manhattan scene. Madeline would be very, very envious. Jeff, however, wouldn't care. Out of nowhere, Rob Shachtley, rock 'n' roll singer, strolled into *my* Laundromat to do *his* laundry on a Saturday morning in the West Village. We spoke immediately, without shyness or formality. He said, *I recognize you from somewhere.* He recognized me from the audience. From the Fedora, Sin-é, the Cooler, the Mercury Lounge, other clubs. Madeline has a crush on Dave Stomps, the drummer. What began as Dave Stomps Watch turned into a weekend plan. Something to do, almost like commitment.

"I bet you're going to say you work with underprivileged kids, aren't you?" I cross my red legs. "Don't *even* say Teach for America." With two fingers, I pinch a fat cranberry on my muffin. "You work for Blockbuster Video, I know it. Admit it." I pop the berry into my mouth.

He looks around my age: thirty, thirty-one. He resembles Roy

Orbison, with thick-rimmed glasses, dark sideburns, and a slight but unobtrusive gut. He's a young, rather tall Roy Orbison. His clothes are mismatched and he probably got them in the East Village, which means they're pretty expensive. The white t-shirt he wears has the Burger King logo on it, but instead of *Burger King*, it says, *Burger Christ*. He's wearing East Village garb but he's doing his laundry in the West Village.

When I lived on the West Coast, girls asked each other, "Is he cute?" Back East, they ask, "Does he have money?" Looking at young Mr. Shachtley, I'm not sure how I'd respond. He's not drop-dead gorgeous, but—among certain girlfriends—I'd say, "I'd do him." He sings in an unknown band, but he dresses in trendy attire; he's not rich, but he's got spending money. A nice-looking guy who lives above the poverty line.

"Close, but no cigar." He eats sour-cream-and-onion potato chips. I hear them crunch in his mouth. "Catering. I cater."

"You're *divine*." I practically suckle the word. I mean it too. I mean it because I like his goofy hair, his slight but unobtrusive gut, and the way he eats potato chips at 8:30 in the morning. "Chips so early?"

"I haven't really gone to bed yet, so this is like a late dinner."

I lean forward. "What's the Burger Christ t-shirt all about? Are you trying to make a point?"

He leans forward too. "You know, usually I *am*, but this time I'm not." He smiles. "Does it make you uncomfortable?"

I look at his t-shirt. "I'm just wondering if there's a message I should be getting. I'm wondering if you're commenting on yourself, on contemporary life, or on Burger King. Which is it?"

He winks and clucks his tongue against the roof of his mouth. "Just remember me as the groovy guy with potato chips and mixed messages you met in the Laundromat. That's all."

"What do you wear when you cater?" I ask, imagining he has to wear something besides that t-shirt.

He doesn't stop munching. "Did you ever work in a movie theater in high school?"

He's killing me softly. "As a matter of fact, I did." How does he know? And should I ask for a chip?

"You remember the outfits?" When he tilts his head to the side, his hair shifts. Most people only dream of eating potato chips the way this guy is doing it.

I look at a water stain on the ceiling and envision the black vest and matching pants I wore at sixteen. I came home smelling of popcorn, the bottoms of my shoes tacky from cola. "There was a shiny strip of satin down the seam of each polyester leg."

Rob nods, excited. "That's what I wear." He stuffs more chips into his mouth.

"Wow." He's the lead singer of a rock 'n' roll band *and* he caters in black polyester. "Do you live around here?" I'm bold, an opportunist.

He shakes his head and brushes crumbs from his lips. "Nah. I stayed at Dave's house last night."

"Dave Stomps?" I nonchalantly ask as if I already know. I'm *in the know*. Dave, Dave Stomps, the drummer.

He clicks his tongue twice and points a finger at me. "Yep. Dave lives around the corner. Sometimes I stay over. I had to do laundry—a girl vomited on my leg last night."

"Gross." I look at his washer, the clothes spinning around in bright colors.

Rob scrunches up his nose. *"You have no idea."* He crumples the bag of chips into a ball and shoots it into a garbage bin loaded with used fabric-softener sheets. "I'm doing Dave's towels too. I really live in the East Village." He sucks in air. "What do you do?"

I sip coffee. "Columnist." I pause, deciding to try something out. Why shouldn't I? He's wearing orange pants, for God's sake. "I'm a writer for a hip paper with mass circulation."

His jaw drops open. "You write for the *Village Voice*?"

I can't hide the frustration. "No." I shake my head violently. "*New York Shock*. I write for *New York Shock* "

"Oh." He smiles. "I like *New York Shock*." He's possibly lying. "Who are you?"

"'Abscess.'"

Glittery eyes. "I *love* 'Abscess.'" He leans forward, looking like Rodin's *The Thinker*, but with clothes on. "I don't even know your name, 'Abscess' writer."

"Sybil Weatherfield." My name embarrasses me. Too pretty. I secretly like it.

Rob Shachtley extends his hand. "Nice to meet you, Sybil Weatherfield. Wow. 'Abscess.'" We shake. "You're like a celebrity."

Abscess—an open wound. Sounds a lot like *obsess*. "It's a neurotic little feature," I tell him. The racing of the mind, the bouncing off walls, the manifestations of cerebral overload . . .

Rob Shachtley stares at me the way people stare at newscasters at the mall, weathermen on the street.

"'Abscess' sold. There was practically a bidding war for it." I look him in the eye to see if he's buying this. I can't tell. "Not only did *New York Shock* want it, but so did a small college paper in Wyoming. The paper was called *Bitch and Moan, Stick and Stone.* Lots to grumble about in the boonies."

Rob, still leaning over like *The Thinker*, straightens, crosses one leg over the other, and looks at me strangely. No longer like I'm a lesser celebrity. For a second, he just stares. Under his gaze, I become self-conscious, aware of my physical appearance. I remember the recent trip to the gym, where they squeezed way more than an inch and gave me a percentage to keep with me, in my heart, perhaps to wear in writing on fine parchment inside a locket around my neck. I feel my medium height, my medium weight, the overall *average* quality of my presentation. I move a strand of brown hair behind an ear. It's brown hair I've described as *chestnut* on better days. I turn my hazel eyes to the ground—eyes I've called *gray* on my driver's license since gray suggests something stormy, smoky, enigmatic. Under Rob's scrutiny, I remember my fair but dry complexion, my pretty but unmemorable face, the scar on my forehead—the one I got when I ran into the dining room table at three. I raise my hazel eyes to his and see him hold me in his gaze. A baggy t-shirt covers a lot, but it doesn't mask certain aspects of the body. Mostly, when men look at me, I know what they see: a pretty girl they won't remember later. Rob's eyes hit the indentation on my forehead. They travel the length of my low-maintenance long hair. They pass over cheekbones, throat, clavicle. They pause over breasts, invisible but medium-sized. His eyes go down my legs, past the sharp angles of knees, and up again, pausing briefly once more—this time on lips. I blush but know he can't actually measure body fat; he can't detect the realities of skin and bone. I watch his face and see him assess the beauty. I see it. I've seen it before; I've seen men take in my appearance. I know it's an unspectacular beauty—it isn't breathtaking or earth-shattering. I look at Rob and wonder how long he'll hold on to his admiration. He speaks. "You know, you're divine too." And then he smiles, turning his eyes to the ground.

I blush.

He squints, looking at me through a line of eyelashes.

A few copies of *New York Shock* are scattered in the corner of a table people use to hold their coffees and put down their bleach. After a long moment, Rob Shachtley stands and walks over to the disarrayed pile.

He picks up *New York Shock*, which is like—I have to admit—picking up a little piece of me, even if it's a silly, sanctimonious, possibly offensive suggestion of who I am as a woman: effete, alone, brainy, bitter. He thumbs through last week's issue, arriving at my column. For a second, I think of snatching it away. I'm self-conscious about him seeing it, about him being made privy to my meditations. He spreads it open on his lap, lifts his index finger into the air, and says, "Two minutes."

And while he reads, I work on my low-fat berry muffin.

TWO

ABSCESS
SEND IN THE FREAKS

SYBIL WEATHERFIELD FOR *NEW YORK SHOCK*

From Friday, January 6, 1995

Random Manhattan freaks are my consolation, my comfort. Their presence *gnaws* at me like existentialist angst. Just when you think it's safe to go back in the water, there's a freak. Just when you're getting used to the conspicuous spending lifestyle, there's a freak. Freaks are reminders, cannonballs burning fire over our summers of love. When there's a freak on the street, it's always the winter of our discontent. Try being complacent about children fighting wars and the homeless living in paper bags when you run into a freak. Just try it.

A few unfair generalizations: freaks are people with "alternative" housing situations or toilet habits, a continuum of bad-hair days, a firsthand knowledge of what's open twenty-four hours and what's not, radical ideas about culture and religion and sexuality. Sometimes they're demarcated by body piercings, tattoos, combat boots, exposed undergarments, primary-color hair shades, or clothes that wouldn't work at a sales meeting for sporting goods.

You don't only come to New York for the bright lights, do you? You want the graphic apparition, the wake-up call, the embodiment of harsh reality in individuals at odds with the world. Isn't it nice to know *someone's* taking a stand against the status quo? I came to New York—in part—to witness that.

I look pretty normal. Average height, average weight. I had braces. I've been on Accutane. Diets have ravaged my insides. I don't wear two-piece swimsuits in public. I have pretty good cheekbones. Occasionally, I'll catch a man checking me out. I'm all for liposuction if one has the funds. I've flirted with getting a tattoo. I'd secretly like to wear a ring in my eyebrow. Maybe I'll get colored contact lenses someday.

I guess I just don't look like a freak. This has been a tough realization for me. I mean, I *feel* for freaks; I *empathize* with them. But I need to financially support myself too.

Actually, I'm jealous. There's something brave about nonconformity. Sure, you've got that whole contingent of spooky freaks out for attention. But there are *others*, others bent on creative eccentricity—those who dream of revolution, social upheaval. The heart of a freak *may* be a pure heart. This makes me believe grandeur is really possible.

Didn't you come to New York to find a *pure heart*?

When I first moved to Manhattan, a pigeon crapped on my head. Settling into the Village, everything made me very, very nervous. All those people, many of them hip. Fear of economic opportunity, ideological redundancy, philosophical paralysis, a multitude of fashion no-nos. What next? I knew I didn't belong. I had no AC and it was August. Because my linens were still packed, I slept flat on my back on a bare mattress—no doubt fraught with invisible bedbugs and body lice. It was so noisy you'd think the St. Patrick's Day Parade was taking place on a summer night on the street below. I missed every ex-boyfriend who'd ever cheated on me, and I desperately wanted my mommy.

When the sun finally rose on that fateful first Manhattan day, I went for a walk, determined to find the Strand Book Store and a good cup of coffee.

I sat on a bench near the dog run in Washington Square Park with an okay cup of decaf. While I watched the city dogs frolic like they were free in the Catskills, a pigeon took a dump on my head.

Befuddled and frightened, I headed home. I was on the verge of tears. New York hated me. The dogs were indifferent to my suffering. Even the birds despised my very presence. I trudged off, knowing the crap was hardening on my hair, knowing a shampoo polemic awaited me at home, if *home* it were. I tried to saunter; I waddled: crap on the brain.

Then, the freaks!

A guy with a stack of pancakes tattooed on the top of his bald head. Another dude with safety-pinned features and a t-shirt declaring, "I lie to women." A girl in a fuchsia wedding dress, carrying a boa constrictor.

After the deviants, I felt okay about the pigeon shitting on me.

Suddenly, with all the subtlety of a dog with gas, I knew the world and all it contains is absolutely, unreservedly, and utterly about things other than me—which made my bout of self-absorption seem insignificant.

Freaks say, "You are *not* the center of the world." A good freak points a finger at what's wrong with society. Freaks refuse to participate. Freaks are necessarily nonmyopic. Their deviation points to that from which they deviate.

If I love freaks so much, why do I still go to the Gap? Why do I shop at Banana Republic? Why haven't I even gotten a tattoo?

I'll tell you why. I'm a voyeur. New York isn't my porn flick; it's more like PBS. Like the glory days when I lived for *Sesame Street*, I'm learning to read. I want to get the subversion, the nihilism, the rejection. I just want to *get* it. I want to understand the landscape and, possibly, stand in the space between complacency and nihilism. Maybe cowardice prevents me from getting a tattoo of a stack of pancakes on the top of my shaved scalp. But the voyeur in me takes comfort in knowing someone, somewhere, is saying something about this old planet.

Send in the freaks. There ought to be freaks.

Oh.

Don't bother.

They're here.

THREE

New York Shock

Still Saturday, January 7, 1995

Carefully, ever so slowly, the paper falls slack in Rob's lap. It curves over his knee. With grave seriousness, he reaches for my eyes with his. "Freaks keep you here?"

I look out the window. Greenwich Village looks cold, blustery. The brownstones across the way are beautiful, idyllic, atmospheric. Sometimes I imagine hardwood floors, stair banisters, dried flowers in vases, wood-block cutting boards in kitchens. A wine rack with reds and whites, a big dog, a four-poster bed, an excellent collection of jazz CDs. Sometimes I imagine myself walking down West Fourth pushing a baby buggy. A woolly scarf covers my mouth. The baby wears footed pajamas.

A man in pink barrettes and a fur coat enters to do his laundry. Kim says hi while Rob and I have this quiet question between us. In the background, Anne Murray sings, *You needed me, you needed me.*

"This is my last year in New York," I say. "I'm thirty. I don't want to be thirty-one here." Already, four wiry gray hairs refuse to play the game, refuse to take part in *style*.

"I'm thirty-one," he says. "It's fine." He uncrosses his legs. *New York Shock* settles into its new position.

"I can't do it; I can't grow old here." I watch the man in barrettes empty a duffel bag.

"Then why don't you leave tomorrow?" Rob's voice is sardonic and sharp. "Or today?"

I'm taken aback by the tone of his voice. I've got my reasons. I'm here to be alone, to accept my liabilities, my neuroses. New York City is my internal state of mind made external. Everything it is on the *outside* is what's going on in my *inside*. Plus, the freaks. Don't forget the freaks. But I have to leave; I'm losing sleep, becoming lonely inside my own head. I'll go to a new city or town. I'll hide away my sorrows in suburbia and do things like plant tomatoes, give Christmas gifts to the mailman, and watch the rising price of gasoline. When I leave, I'll be ready to be alone in the presence of others. I point to his copy of *Shock*. "I've got the column."

Rob Shachtley, lead singer of Glass Half Empty, purses his lips, waits a second, then says, "Huh." He opens *Shock*. There's a sidebar inside, a sidebar for me. He arrives at it with his fingertips. At the top of the page, it says "Antibiotics." Every week, readers send in letters about my column. He flicks his fingers against the words. "You're a splash. You generate the mail, babe."

"I figure I'll stick around till 1996. Then I can be one of those writers who lives in New England or has a farm somewhere. Or a ranch. In Sundance. Or Vail. Didn't Hemingway die in Idaho?"

He remains silent for a second, looks at Kim, and then turns to me again. "You're not making it by just writing a weekly *New York Schlock* column, are you? You don't think that's gonna get you a ranch in Sundance, do you?"

"I temp," I divulge.

He gets up to check his machine. "You meet lots of struggling actors and actresses on the temping front?"

"Never. They all cater." I walk over to my washer. "What's the most interesting thing that's ever happened to you on the job?" Manhattan fodder for writers seeking the absurd.

Rob balances on the balls of his feet. "Once I catered a dinner at Kissinger's."

"Fascinating man," I say.

"Rack o' lamb with new potatoes. Rosemary something."

I squint, picturing it. "If at all possible, I'd avoid serving lamb."

"Old rich guys love it." Rob's machine stops spinning. These washers wind down without warning. No plaintive cry for attention, no wailing buzz, nothing. He starts the dance that takes place between washer and dryer. Nothing must touch the ground or it's over: you *lose*. "What's the most interesting thing that's happened to you while temping?"

I put my hands on my hips. "Wait—was it Kissinger or the lamb that was interesting?"

Rob holds wet pants in his hands and then whips them into the air to shake out creases. "The whole milieu, I guess." He exaggerates the pronouncement of *milieu*, moving his lips dramatically over its syllables. "The home, the study, the formality, the aura of the Cold War—not to mention the *lamb*." He decides to dry the pants after all, so he shoves them into the mouth of the appliance. "I'm not sure anyone was aware that the Soviet Union was now Russia, or that the Iron Curtain came down."

"I'm impressed by your use of the word *milieu*."

"Make your own assumptions." He shrugs. "Your turn. Tempting adventure?"

Back in my plastic chair, I swing my feet across the dirty floor like a kid. "Once I worked with a woman who was absolutely paranoid about her silicone breasts."

"This sounds good—I love breasts."

"Silicone ones?"

"They make me *a little* nervous," he admits, digging into his pocket for quarters.

"She was terrified that the end of the world would arrive—you know, the *Apocalypse*—and she'd be forced to flee to the mountains like the singing Von Trapps."

Rob walks over to me. "It could happen—"

"She said her biggest fear in life was that one silicone breast would collapse while she lived in the hills, and she'd be stuck with one perky and one deflated breast."

"Interesting visual." Rob sits next to me, his eyes faraway.

"I told her not to worry."

Rob leans back in his plastic chair. "I wonder how she'd get to the hills." He closes his eyes. "Was she a camper? Did she like hiking?"

I know more about this man than I let on. Rob Shachtley was married at twenty-four and, within a year, his wife died from a brain tumor. Seven years later, he still wears a wedding ring. I'm talking to him now and he's wearing a gold band. He sings sad songs about a girl in the sunshine with corn-colored hair, standing near doorways and windows and other open things. He sings about how she always looks like her twenty-three-year-old self and, no matter what he imagines her doing, whether playing with their imaginary children or pulling nylons over her imaginary knees, she's always twenty-three. The sad songs become angry ones. He sings about how he's being deprived of her old age, how he'll never see it, and the very thought makes him ill.

Grapevine, word on the street, hard-core analysis of Glass Half Empty lyrics.

Also, he has a reputation for being a sleaze.

"So, when are you guys playing next?" I ask.

"Friday, the twentieth. At the Fedora. Ten p.m." He sits up straight.

"I'll be there. With my friend Madeline." I look at Rob, staring at his orange pants, his Roy Orbison glasses. Rob Shachtley, lead singer.

"Who's she?" He walks over to the dryers, oblivious to my thoughts. "What does she do?"

"She stuffs envelopes at a human rights organization by day, and she's an ESL teacher in Queens by night. She teaches English to Romanians newly off the boat."

"Do they still arrive by boat?" He reaches into a dryer to touch his clothes.

"I'm not sure." I fold my arms across my chest. "I'll have to check."

"Is she an artist?"

"She's a great dabbler in the arts, but she wants to write."

"Who doesn't? Another middle-class college grad turned loose on the streets of New York, right?"

I almost tear up. "Yeah, that's her."

He leans back against a hot dryer. His machine stops. "U Mass, Amherst, 1988. Ask me something about Shakespeare. Go on—do it." He opens his dryer. "So, Sybil," he says, sounding like a caricature of himself, "do you want to get together after the show?" He drags out his clothes and begins to fold them.

"What would that entail?" I stop suddenly. "I have a boyfriend."

He dramatically drops his head to his chest. "I knew there was something you were holding back. I can always tell when people have secrets—"

I quickly say, "But we could still do something after the show—"

"Like me, you, and *him*?" He scrunches up his face.

"Yeah. Or me, you, him, and Madeline. Or just you and Madeline and me. Or just you and me, but before the show. Don't ruin a perfectly lovely conversation—"

"You said I was divine."

"I meant it." I sit down again. I have one more spin cycle.

"Why *before* the show and not *after*?" Rob stuffs his laundry supplies into a laundry bag. He struggles with a winter jacket. He's getting ready to leave.

I look out the Laundromat window. "I don't know." I meet Rob Shachtley's eyes. "I'm not sure. It doesn't make any sense."

He stands in front of me, a laundry bag thrown over his shoulder like Santa Claus about to deliver toys. "You want to be friends? Is that what you're saying? *The* Sybil Weatherfield of 'Abscess' wants to be *my* friend?"

I look at my hands. I feel small in my red sweatpants and old Doors t-shirt. "It's a brazen assumption." I'm embarrassed; he may be making fun of me. "I *never* suggest friendship with anyone. I haven't made a new friend in over two years. I spend all my time talking to office girls who are obsessed with their pets, many of them dead. I eat dinner on a TV tray and call it a night. I see movies alone, including *Interview with the Vampire*—"

"Enough!" Rob drops his laundry bag onto the floor. "I'll be your friend."

"Only if you want to," I add.

"Your name will be at the door on the twentieth." He bends over to pick up his bag. "You and *guest.* There are two weeks between then and now. That'll give me time to get over the fact that you're not interested in being my love slave. Or, it's time enough to dump the boyfriend."

Did he just say *love slave*? I think he did!

Rob Shachtley, widower at twenty-four, wearer of wedding ring binding him to a dead woman, moves outside. The door swings shut behind him. He raps on the glass above my head and draws a musical note with his finger on its dusty surface.

Then he walks away.

FOUR

THE DAILY GRIND

Wednesday, January 11, 1995

New *York Shock* is housed on the third floor of a shabby building about three blocks from the *Village Voice* near Astor Place; our people see their people every day. *Voice* staff eats lunch at Bowery hot spots; *Shock* staff packs peanut butter and jelly, tuna on rye. We don't mind, we insist. God knows, we're *such* a better paper.

We have our audience. Copies garnish NYU halls. East Village types take it on the subway, sometimes leaving pages open, inviting rumination from residents of other boroughs. People in Brooklyn make a point of getting it *hot*, so to speak, off the press. It's easy to find in Chelsea: splayed across plastic chairs in Laundromats, on tile floors near ATMs. One can pick it up on a TriBeCa street corner, but probably not anywhere near Gramercy Park. Those on the Upper West Side skim it, think about doing a weekend activity listed in the back but rarely follow through. Near Grand Central Station, Midtown folk read *Daily News* headlines, disregarding

Shock completely while drinking cups of coffee doused with whole milk and eating sugar-glazed donuts. SoHo citizens give it a quick glance if it's left behind on Dean and Deluca tables. No one from the Upper East Side has even heard of it.

The column, my column, bears my name, the day, the year: *Sybil Weatherfield, January 6, 1995.* A loaded name, a good year.

Despite my fame, one's gotta eat.

My poverty gives me the creeps. Haunted by thirty-thousand-dollar student loans, I lack knickknacks and the freedom to drink anything but water with dinner. Going out to eat *is* a problem. People talk about the great restaurants in New York; I wouldn't know. I don't shop on Fifth Avenue, never have. I eat canned tuna; name brands are treats, reserved for special occasions like Labor Day or Halloween. I'm thirty years old; don't think I'm unaware of this fact.

My short-lived boss calls out, "Ms. Weatherfield, could you come into the hall?"

I temp, therefore New York is.

Putting down *Shock*, I peek out of my cubicle. "Yes?"

"This goes in your in-box." Dapper as a butler, he waves a piece of paper at me.

I didn't know I *had* an in-box.

He holds the document out, and I grab. Just as I'm about to seize it, he snatches it away—forcing me to bob up and down. In my short skirt, I look like a city girl hailing a cab in a commercial for pantyhose.

Our eyes meet. A sly smile creeps out from behind his closed lips. A gas leak, a drippy faucet. Acid traces through my veins.

He lowers the paper again, offering it. I take the bait, making the reach. And just as I'm about to get contact, he pulls it away again!

This is a New York Shock.

It's like that guy in the opening credits of *Kung Fu* talking about snatching a pebble from his hands. Get the pebble, hit the road. I remember a peaceful Chinese man looking wisely upon David Carradine–as–Boy, a smooth pebble in his palm. The suggestion was parable, lesson, Grimms' fairy tale à la Asian Coming-of-Age story. Where is my satchel, my dusty sandals, my wide-brimmed hat to take with me as I wander the earth in search of knowledge, holiness, and righteousness?

Exasperated, I feel my cheeks sag and my frown lines deepen.

The man lowers that wretched memo/letter/fax cover sheet again.

Hell, no, says my face. I turn around, disgusted, and walk away. I'm a temp; irreverence is my luxury. If he wants me to see it badly enough, he'll put it on my desk.

I'm not, nor have I ever been, a full-time writer. If I don't go into the *New York Shock* offices at least twice a week, the staff forgets who I am.

Then I need to wear my *Shock* badge. It says, *It's Shocking, But True. I'm Sybil Weatherfield. I Write.*

Armed with a college degree from a good school in Southern California, I go—day by day—to different major corporations, time card in hand, job assignment in tote. This Renaissance woman punches a clock, earning big bucks for a temp agency and getting request upon request for Monday-morning returns. The good news is that I get to wear the same outfit over and over again. The bad news: no badge.

There are rules for a temp:

* Always—I mean, *always*—bring something to do in your spare time, but make sure it's not a book. You can use Microsoft Word to write that letter to your health insurance company you've been wanting to write, or you can figure out your monthly budget; but you can never, ever—not in a million fiscal years—open up a book and turn its delicate pages. That's a temping no-no. But know this, and know it well: it's better to keep busy than to sit around and twiddle your thumbs. Look industrious, not like a lazy ass.

* Don't go out of your way to look for projects. You may think it's your job to efficiently and quickly complete tasks and then chase after your transitory supervisors with a self-deprecatory willingness to complete a dozen more meaningless jobs, but it isn't. The truth of the matter is that your ephemeral superiors only want to keep you out of their hair. So do what they tell you and do it well, but that's it. One additional *Is there something else you'd like me to do?* is fine, but don't go overboard. Say no to displays of false humility.

* Don't be sexy. Dress professionally, not glamorously. Wear your glasses instead of your contacts. Part your hair in the middle. Go for the same rounded-toe, scuffed flats every sin-

gle day. You don't want to make anyone turn his or her head, and you don't want anyone to be jealous either.

★ If you're educated, let it slip unpretentiously. Read Charles Dickens in the break room. Accidentally leave your Picasso date book by the water fountain. Carry around copies of the *Economist*. Say intelligent things about the House of Representatives.

★ Be sure to mention you temp for a particular reason. You temp, but you really write. You temp, but you're also a cellist. You temp to save money for a trip to Florence to study art in monasteries. That sort of thing. Temping must *never* be an end in itself.

Why should you hint at your secret intelligence, your devotion to the classics, your plans to join the Peace Corps? People like smart temps, temps with goals. They don't like glamorous or buxom temps.

At least, these things work for me. And, yes, I have written more than one column on the job.

I get my temp assignment from my temp agency. I have a good working relationship with the girls who work there based on faux affection. They send me Christmas cards; I call for new assignments. We speak in hushed and gossipy tones about former employers, past johns. Over the phone, I scribble directions to floors on buildings near Penn Station, near Union Square. These addresses give bodies and faces to previously ghostly edifices.

New York, in the pretemping past, was mythical, intangible. Pinstripes on Wall Street, sweatshops in Chinatown, middle managers eating hot dogs while standing near vending carts. Corporate America eluded me.

But then, *then*: The early temping assignments. After hopping in place (skirt pushed high over hips) and squeezing into pantyhose a tad too small, I would push elevator buttons to dream-like floors, and I would step into offices occupied by men and women who crunched numbers and lived on Long Island, having gone to school in Florida. I knew that New York wasn't my Disneyland, my silent-film era. The ghosts diffused, vapor-like, reminiscent of Casper's upward flight.

Now I get my assignment, remember the rules, and do what needs to be done. I do it well, but without Great Expectations.

I'm meeting Madeline for lunch on a Bryant Park bench at 1:15. I rip my nylons in the elevator on the way down, so I have to take them off in the lobby bathroom and dump them in the paper-towel bin.

Walking past people in the park, I see Madeline Blue, whom I love.

She sits on a bench, legs crossed, an exposed ankle beating time to the Duran Duran song in her head. Her wrist is balanced on the edge of her seat so she can shake her cigarette free of ash. Her face is pouty, pale, slightly pitted from ancient acne. There's something sultry about her full lips, big eyes, and long lashes. She's sensuous like Morticia Adams, glamorous like Miss Piggy, commanding like Cher—a pretty girl, not a gorgeous one. She looks cynical but superstitious, like a woman who reads her horoscope, twists apple stems, and blows out birthday candles while making a wish. A world-weary cynic who loves puppies and kittens.

The pout: what does it mean? Is she unhappy? The lackadaisical swing in the ankle: liberal, loose? The cigarette between her fingers: blemishes, a past?

I see Madeline Blue, the only thing I've kept from temping.

The first thing I ever said to her, three years ago, was "Is that your real name?"

Keeping her fingers on her keyboard, her shoulders hunched in an arc, she looked up at me, the new temp at Rights International. "Yes." She went back to her computer screen. "I got lucky."

"It makes me think of the seventies," I said, touching human-rights papers on my new desk in the back office I would share with this girl.

Madeline typed as she spoke. "You're thinking of that Joni Mitchell album. *Blue*."

"*Madeline Blue*," I repeated. "How *Annie Hall*."

She stopped typing, pushed her chair out, and swiveled around. "Is *your* name real?"

"Yes."

"Because it sounds like a stage name."

Then we shared that back office for two months.

When I left Rights International, I revised my résumé. She examined it, her lips moving. "What are you *doing*?" she asked, having reviewed it.

Puzzled, I cocked my head. "What do you mean?"

"Your objective isn't 'to find a position that combines an expertise in rhetoric and composition with a desire to serve in public relations,'" she quoted. "Give me a break—"

"Sure, it is." I had a college degree, an internship at the state capitol.

"Sybil, you *write.* Remember?" She closed our back office door.

I had been in New York City for over a year. I temped and halfheartedly looked for a real job. I wrote goofy pieces that were published inconsistently. "Madeline," I began, "I need a *profession* already. I'm *aging.*"

Madeline Blue, with piercing eyes and blanched skin, whispered to me on my last day at Rights International, "Who says you need a profession?"

This was my epiphany. I crumpled up my résumé; I kept temping; *Shock* hired me shortly thereafter. I temp; I write; I live in New York. I have no real profession.

From the Bryant Park bench, she turns her head and sees me. Her lips make an *o* and smoke rises in artful curls and rings, like she's an expert at this cigarette thing. "What took you so long?" she calls out.

"Sorry. I had a pantyhose mishap as I was leaving."

Madeline looks at my legs. "But you're not *wearing* pantyhose."

"I ripped them in the elevator." I sit down and dig through my stuff. It's freezing, but we're desperate for fresh air, a shining sun.

"You threw them out?" She scrunches up her face. "Surely you could still use them for *something.*"

"Like what? Puppet-making?"

"To wear under pants?" she suggests. "What do you have to eat?"

"Fruit cocktail."

"That's all?" Madeline swishes her ankle violently.

"I'm on a diet. Where's your lunch?"

"Are you yacking again?" Her face turns red, and she's accusatory. "You're yacking, aren't you?"

"I'm not, I swear." Only once. Last night, after I ate a pint of Ben and Jerry's Chunky Monkey because of alienation, desperation, tragedy, sorrow, loss, life, death, and a rerun of *Seinfeld* that I had never seen before. It was quick and clean. I flushed the toilet and waited for *ER*.

Madeline makes a point of doing nostril tricks with the noxious fumes. "Drink the syrup at the bottom of your fruit cocktail for nourishment, why don't you."

"Where's *your* lunch?" I tip my Tupperware, wedging my spoon under a pineapple slice.

"I ate at ten. I was starving."

"Oh."

We sit there in silence, staring at people. Across the way, a homeless man rummages through garbage. Others rush around, a little sweaty despite winter. Then, for a while, we discuss low-income housing and the cost of public transportation. *Bad, bad, bad*, we agree.

I tell her about my boss and his snatch-this-memo-from-my-hand trick. She sighs and rolls her eyes. "Look in the mail room, Sybil. That's where the real people are."

Twenty minutes later, I offer a suggestion. "Let's sit on the lions in front of the library and drink hot cocoa."

"I can't." Madeline tosses straight hair out of her face. She irons her brown locks—she literally *irons* her hair. I assume other people use special gadgets and tools to straighten coiled tresses. Not Madeline. No gels called "Wavy Be Gone." No foamy formulas in her medicine cabinet declaring "Out, Frizz, Out!" Madeline pulls the ironing board out from behind her bed—the one she got at a yard sale in Park Slope—and spreads her mane across it.

I squint, unused to hearing zany Madeline refuse anything along the lines of sitting on the Bryant Park lions while sipping cocoa. "What do you mean, you *can't*?"

"I just can't."

"Why not?" I'm incensed.

"I'm not wearing any underwear."

I certainly didn't expect this. "What?"

"I never do." She drinks her Coke with nonchalance.

"Oh." I stare out at the park and the pigeons. "Well."

"How's Jeff?" she asks suddenly.

My boyfriend. "Oh, fine." I spin my Diet Pepsi around, making sure it still doesn't have any calories.

"Sybil. There's something I've gotta tell you." She smashes her cigarette into the ground under the bench and pulls her coat around her legs. Without warning, she's grim.

"What?"

"I've accepted a job teaching in Guatemala beginning in October. I'm leaving."

Twice, my mouth opens and closes. "Madeline, you *can't*."

She looks into her lap and pulls her fingers out of her gloves. "Sybil, we knew that, sooner or later, one of us was going to get out. I thought it would be you." Lifting her eyes to mine, she says, "We can't go on doing *nothing*."

"We're doing *something*. We're doing *something*." I get flushed, panicky, ill. "You teach. You're a great teacher. I write—because of you. You made me. You can't go—I can't do this without you. I can't stay here. It's just biding time—"

She shakes her head. "Till what?"

My voice cracks. "I don't know." I bite my lip. "Why do you want to go? Why would you want to leave me?"

Madeline Blue stands. She pulls her coat around her and arranges a hat on top of her head. "Because, Sybil." Her eyes are glassy with tears. "*I don't like my life*." She leans over, kisses me on the cheek, straightens, and says, "Bye, Kitty." She walks away through Bryant Park, heading to Rights International, where human rights are fought for on a daily basis.

I return to my temp job, my cubicle, my copy of *New York Shock*. I finish the day in a flurry of administrative know-how. On my way home, I stop at Mohammed's Gourmet, my neighborhood deli, to buy ice cream.

I pay my favorite Mexican immigrant nearly four bucks, which is a perfect binge price. A pint of Ben and Jerry's is the ideal binge: consumable in one sitting, contains countable calories, pricey for ice cream but cheap for an act of desperation.

I'm embarrassed because my immigrant friend can tell I'm alone. He knows that sometimes I eat like a deer, feeding on trees, grazing on grass. At other times, I clear shelves. In the morning, coming back from the gym, I buy a mango. Later, after work, after undisclosed disappointments, it's chocolate brownie pie.

Ask no questions, my Mexican friend. Yes, I'm alone. Yes, I'm not what I appear to be. Hand over the New York Super Fudge

Chunk, buddy. Put it in a paper bag. I don't need the neighbors talking.

When I get home, I unplug the phone. I'm going to eat the whole damn thing. Nothing will be left. I think: *Do it. Do it now.*

So I do it. I push in a spoon. I work it under the cream. I like the texture. I like the taste. It's better than any friendship with a woman, better than any man's love. It's better.

I'm alone, alone at last. I turn to "Abscess." I have this column; that's what I have. In it, I say everything. I say it all. It sounds crazy, but I don't care.

Sybil Weatherfield at the top of the page. Sounds theatrical, tripping with melodious syllables. A poem, a folk song, something to count instead of sheep. Other things should be attached. *Sybil Weatherfield, Lady-in-Waiting.* Maybe I'm a lady-in-waiting. Or I could be *Sybil Weatherfield, Writing in the Tradition of Jane Austen and Those Crazy Brontë Sisters.* Jane and her *Sense and Sensibility*, her *Pride and Prejudice*, that goofy girl with her genteel writing: we've abandoned her. Forget propriety and manners. We've got *Sin and Sensuality, Death and Duplicity.* As for Charlotte and Emily: *Wuthering Heights*, you say? We're talking *Washington Heights*, honey. Sybil's name sounds regal, but she's not noble. Add *Punchy and Pretentious* to the budding list of titles, fine examples of clever and descriptive alliteration.

I study my tabloid. I meditate on my terrain. I eat ice cream.

Exposés on the hard-core history of Chinatown, on where to find the Italian mafia should you be looking, on male escort services, on supermodel love, on the poetry of Henry Rollins, on what members of the underground (*What underground?*) do during the day, on Katie Couric sightings, on dog-run politics—these garnish our pages. We take polls on how many times New Yorkers have been victimized by a pigeon undertaking a waste management project. The mayor is a constant target. Celebrity-club christenings are frequent. Anecdotal columns are favored.

Me. That's me. "Abscess" is my column: a wound that doesn't heal.

And so we arrive joyously, enthusiastically, ecstatically, at my personal contribution to the alternative press. *Sybil Weatherfield*, my moniker. The year, a red line in time indicating where I am at thirty years of age, what I do at the beginning of 1995, maybe a good year, but possibly a year to forget in the maelstrom of years, of decades, of sweeping changes in the lifetime of a woman poised to write another into love.

That said, I have little in the way of expectation.

FIVE

ANTIBIOTICS 1

FROM *NEW YORK SHOCK*

From Friday, January 13, 1995

I like you; I really do. But the fact that you laud this segment of society while admitting that you shop at the Gap and are worried about the job market suggests to me one of two things: extreme spinelessness or insincerity.

—Joe, East Village

You're a coward. Be a freak, or change the subject.

—Sue, SoHo

Bite the bullet, girlfriend. Forget the flapjacks. Get a waffle on your ass.

—Vic, Chelsea

You and your romantic idealism, Weatherfield. It's dumb.

—Terry, the Bronx

SIX

Café Michelangelo

Friday, January 20, 1995

The Fedora is under a trendy restaurant called Without Delay on Lafayette. Without Delay is gold, black, aquamarine—possibly Turkish, Mediterranean, Moroccan, something Greek. The floors are mosaic; the salads are big, the people pretty.

I've never actually eaten there, but I've been to the Fedora a number of times.

In contrast to the nouveau riche Delay, the Fedora is swanky. Narrow tables clutter a charcoal-gray nightclub. As one leaves WD to enter the Fedora via a dark staircase, a girl in a very tight t-shirt stands poised to stamp hands. The Fedora serves drinks and finger food. I fantasize regularly about the stuffed potato skins and fried mozzarella. Up front, there's a stage: inelegant, unglamorous, made for the music.

The place is packed. Madeline and I sit down at a narrow table in the middle of the club.

"I'm excited." She wears a silver top, loose and shimmery, with what looks like black silk pajama bottoms.

"Don't do anything weird when we talk to him. *If* we talk to him." I'm in my going-out Gap dress. Dramatic, the color of charcoal, tight. I'm okay with "tight" tonight, because I've barely eaten all day. Disturbing things are appetizing to me about now. Goose liver. Beets.

"Of course we'll talk to him. Your name was at the door, wasn't it? He didn't forget, did he?" A waitress squeezes by. "I'll have a gin and tonic," Madeline says to her.

"Diet Coke for me." I scan the room with a fake smile on my face, my elbows on the table. By the stairs, a skinny guy sells Glass Half Empty's one and only CD, which both Madeline and I already own. The skinny guy is always around, always selling CDs. If our eyes meet at shows, I turn away in embarrassment. I feel *caught*; I feel like a *groupie.* I *hate* that feeling, because while it denotes repetition and belonging, it also suggests patheticness and nowhere-else-to-go-ness. I'm thankful that he hardly pays attention to me. Tonight I try looking warm, comfortable, and sophisticated, but it's hard, because I think I'm supposed to do something special with my hands. "What should I do? Should I be doing something? Am I supposed to go backstage and look for him?"

"Go up to that guy over there." Madeline tosses her head back quickly in the direction of the bouncer standing by the stage. He's bald, tough, and tattooed; he looks like a pirate. "Say, *I'm with the band.* Ask him if you can go backstage. See what he says."

I try it out. "I'm with the band."

"Try again," she says. "Deeper, more confidence."

"*I'm with the band*," I repeat an octave lower. When I see a blank expression from Madeline, I add, "*Damn it*."

In that secret, sudden way that men have when they approach girls in bars, Rob joins us, sitting down at my side. "You made it!" He smiles hugely. We're like long-lost friends. I have this inexplicable desire to embrace him passionately and plant a wet one on his lips.

He thrusts his hand out toward Madeline. "You must be Madeline."

She doesn't shake, but rather places her fingertips into his palm as if this were a Merchant Ivory film. "Charmed, I'm sure."

Yikes! Is Madeline trying to put on the sex appeal with Rob Shachtley, whose wife died only seven years ago?

"Likewise." He kisses her where the Fedora girl left a glow-in-the-dark stamp.

Sexual tension?

He turns to me. "I have to go, but do you two want to hook up after the show? Coffee? A drink? Truth or Dare?"

"Yeah, let's," I say as Madeline lights a cigarette.

"It'll take me a while to get out of here, so I'll meet you." He stands. "I'll sing you a song. What do you want me to sing for you, Sybil Weatherfield?"

I know there's something I should be doing with my hands. "'Sister Golden Hair'? 'Rhinestone Cowboy'?" I hesitate, staring at the ceiling. "I got it. 'Rhiannon.'"

"Let me think." He puts his index finger to his lips and closes his eyes. He opens them. "Uh, no. When I sing a Beatles song, it's for you." When he smiles, I blush. Second time he's made me blush.

Madeline drags on her cigarette while we agree, over loud music, to meet at Café Michelangelo on Bleecker.

"Listen for the Beatles," he tells me, leaving. "That'll be for you."

Before he gets out of earshot, I call after him, "Hey, Rob?"

"Yeah?" He turns his body around. The girls nearby watch him walk. The music seems to blare.

The girls *stare* at him. He doesn't seem to notice. He *must* notice. "Who's the skinny guy who always sells CDs at the shows?" I ask, pointing to the stairs. It's just an excuse to talk to him. Realizing this, I feel silly and self-conscious. I tell myself I have a boyfriend. I tell myself Madeline doesn't detect anything out of the ordinary. I tell myself I'm really interested in the mysterious identity of the skinny guy by the stairs.

Rob, looking past the audience, checks out the skinny guy. "Oh, Greg. Sound engineer/manager/record producer extraordinaire." He lowers his eyes to mine. "Dave's wife's little brother. He comes in from Boston a couple times a month." He pauses. "He does the flyers."

"They're great flyers," I say.

The machinations of rock 'n' roll. When he turns away and I find myself looking at him like the other girls, I blush again. I check out Madeline.

She watches him too. "He's fatter up close."

"You think? I don't think so. Maybe a little." Now I'm so red that I probably look like I'm about to die from a rash.

Glass Half Empty takes the stage: Rob Shachtley in a pink suit with a guitar and Dave Stomps in a black suit at drums. They look like an overturned box of Good & Plenty.

Listening to rock 'n' roll is like scratching a bug bite till it bleeds. Just when Madeline and I master blasé, he breaks into "Love Me Do." I remember in the Laundromat how he said I didn't want to be his love slave. That's what he said.

Am I being pursued? What does he want from me? I don't want to be just another groupie, just another girl.

I listen, trying to look unmoved. My cheeks can't redden. No standing on my chair. It's a rock 'n' roll moment, and anyone who's ever had one knows it's precious: a flash, a split second, like a Korean launderer, a nonfat berry muffin. It's like a memory of picking apples in an orchard or putting your cat in a stroller when you're three. A rock 'n' roll moment is about being there and not somewhere else, missing it.

The show ends when Rob summons up images of a wraith-like woman sipping from the Fountain of Youth at gunpoint.

The lights come on, Madeline places money under a glass, and we walk through the Fedora to exit. People press in and smile at someone visible just over our shoulders. It's easy to be claustrophobic now. I've lost whatever it was I had, and now there's an odd sensation that, in the midst of my efforts to get out of the Fedora with Madeline Blue—who will always be cooler than I, even in pajama bottoms—I'm somehow *off*.

"Good set," Madeline says on the street.

Fedoraphobic, I draw my jacket tightly around me. "It's freezing."

We walk west. "What do you know about Dave?" she asks.

"Nothing. Only what you know."

As we pass Washington Square Park, about ten homeless guys create a gauntlet for us to walk through. "Smoke? Smoke? Smoke?" We keep going.

Café Michelangelo is muted and dim, the colors of peacock feathers and the Italian Renaissance. Furnished in antiques, it's a torrent of curled iron chair legs, round marble tables, and stained wooden fixtures spread beneath mirrors, long and thin, short and stout, beveled, opaque, and crystal-clear. A veritable house of mirrors on Mona Lisa muted-color walls, Sistine Chapel ceilings. The dessert case is bright with cheesecakes lit up like a lost ark, chocolate layer cakes unsliced behind translucence. Just sitting on a hard-backed chair with a red velvet cushion makes me want to sip espresso and talk about Plato.

Rob arrives twenty minutes after us. "Dave's doing the dirty work." He hangs his coat on the back of his chair. "Kissing girls, speaking to *Entertainment Tonight*. John Tesh is full of questions this evening."

Our waiter has an Italian accent. Madeline haggles with him over the ingredients of a caffé Americano, which isn't on the menu. "I'm *desperate* for one," she whines. "It's *only* espresso and water." When he leaves, having agreed to try his best to make one, she expels air from her lungs. "He's *gorgeous.* God, is he gorgeous." She puts her chin in her hands and whines, "I don't know what I'm going to do."

Rob and I don't comment. When the waiter returns for our orders, Rob says, "German chocolate cheesecake."

I study the menu. My stomach growls, but I doubt anyone hears.

"What do you want, Sybil?" Madeline puts her menu on top of Rob's.

I feel her staring. "Probably just a drink."

"What have you eaten today?" She glares at me with hot eyes.

The waiter freezes over his pad of paper. Rob doesn't move either.

"I don't remember." Okay, so I had one cup of dried cereal, a few slurps of skim milk, alfalfa sprouts with a splash of balsamic vinegar, and an orange. Quartered.

"Get a salad," says Madeline. "Sybil's like Kafka's 'hunger artist.'"

"I'm broke—"

"We'll split one—"

"I don't have any money."

Rob breaks in, apparently sensing discord. He picks up a menu, opens it, and scans. "You like goat cheese?" He peeks out from behind the menu. "Goat cheese and sun-dried tomatoes?"

"Yes, but—I just want coffee." I shake my head decisively.

Rob points to something on the menu, showing our poor waiter. To me, he says, "I'm buying."

"You didn't have to do that," I say when the waiter walks away.

"I'm a rock star." He raises his eyebrows and leans forward. "I've got the money."

Madeline, deadpan but delighted, says, "She starves herself all day." She smiles in my direction and adds, "You need the protein."

"Thank you for sharing with our new friend." I'm mortified.

Rob leans back. "Let's get it all out on the table so we can be done with it."

The waiter brings us iced water. "I'll be right back with your caffé Americano," he tells Madeline. She winks. We watch him go.

"Who wants to start?" asks Rob happily; he's downright cheery.

"Madeline wants to know about Dave Stomps," I say. "Tell us if he's happily married."

Rob, looking resigned, as if he gets this often, eyes Madeline, who may be doing her own blushing now. "I have very little to say. He *is* happily married, and they have a nine-month-old daughter."

Madeline *definitely* blushes. "Okay," she says. The waiter puts down her caffé Americano. "Okay." She tosses that ironed hair over her shoulder.

Rob looks around the table. "Favorite book? Favorite movie?"

"Hemingway's *A Moveable Feast*." Madeline examines her drink for accuracy. "I always wanted to be an expatriate."

"You *are* an expatriate," I say.

Books and movies are mentioned (*Crime and Punishment, The Graduate*), hometowns are acknowledged (only Rob is from nearby with Providence, Rhode Island). A nod to God, a political stance (some kind of amalgam of multiculturalism, democracy, and moral relativism), a sexual preference (heterosexual!). All of us have seen *The Rocky Horror Picture Show*, but none of us cares. Madeline has done acid, Rob's been married, and I've taken ice-skating lessons. Two of us have seen *Stomp*, and all three of us have seen Blue Man Group. We can all sing the theme to *The Love Boat*. My first concert was Captain and Tennille, Madeline's was David Lee Roth, but Rob's was the Moody Blues.

We *are* the freakin' world.

Our long-suffering waiter presents my salad, which is huge. Madeline steals a bite of my baguette. "And we were all English majors," I say, going for the salad. With great deliberation, I have to eat as if I'm not overly anxious, as if I haven't been thinking about sun-dried tomatoes and goat cheese all day. I have to tell myself to put my fork down occasionally, take little breaks, act carefree as opposed to behaving like a stray dog hovering over leftovers in an alley behind a grocery store. It's like having a Beatles song sung to you by the lead singer of a small rock 'n' roll band. These things happen. No need to gobble down the greens. No need to color wildly.

Rob sighs. "If we're *really* going to be friends—if this isn't just a one-night thing—we shouldn't spend too much time on character sketches, on histories." He sips his drink. "It's way too easy and sad and self-indulgent to get mired in the past. We'll become sentimental."

Madeline bristles. "Rob, we're sentimental girls. You *must* know that."

"It'll weigh you down." He looks solemn. "The eighties are over. You can't celebrate them for the rest of your lives. Sentimentality is *evil*. Nostalgia is forgetful. Reagan was president when Wham! made it big."

Still bristling, Madeline leans in. "Excuse me, but aren't *you* the one wearing your wedding ring after seven years of being a widower?"

I quickly say, "I have a BA from UCLA. I'm from San Diego—"

Rob covers his ring finger with his right hand. "I know people talk."

Madeline's voice returns to a normal pitch. "I'm sorry. I shouldn't have said that."

"Yeah, I still wear the ring." His eyes dash between us.

I reach out and touch his arm. I remove my hand, embarrassed by the gesture.

"So I'm sentimental too." He regains some lost composure and scolds us with his finger. "But it's fucked in the head—it's no way to live."

Madeline straightens. "I went to Berkeley, I'm from D.C., and I believe in a higher being." She isn't religious, but she expects to become so later, when she has kids.

"It sounds like you're trying to be P.C. about God." I pop a tomato into my mouth.

"I am," she admits.

Rob puts his napkin on the table. He adjusts his Roy Orbison glasses on the bridge of his nose. "Your borough? Your 'hood?"

"I live five minutes from here, off Greenwich Ave., near Benji's Quesadillas." I throw my thumb over my shoulder. Then I return to spreading goat cheese on a baguette. My Beautiful Baguette.

Madeline crosses her arms in front of her chest. "Brooklyn. Fort Green, but I say Park Slope. With a girl who doesn't look anyone in the eye. I think she has A.D.D."

Rob turns east. "I live above Bombay Café on Sixth between First and Second."

"We like Indian *a lot*, Rob." Madeline drains her water and looks for the waiter.

Rob asks, "What's something you want to do but probably never will?"

Madeline and I are dumbfounded. There are so many things. It's part of being sentimental. One romanticizes a bittersweet past while craving an unrealizable future. "You go first," I tell him.

"I'd like to play Madison Square Garden," he says.

"It's not out of the question." Madeline tilts her head.

"I'm upset about missing Woodstock. Even Live Aid," he adds. "I missed them all."

"What was it you said about nostalgia?" Madeline cocks her head.

I fold my arms on top of the table. "I'd like something *really, truly, completely* unique to happen to me—something utterly unexpected—"

Madeline stretches her hand out and quickly grabs Rob's wrist. "Get ready."

Rob eyes the twisted fabric of his sleeve clasped between her fingers. "For what?"

As if I weren't even there, Madeline whispers, "Sybil's grandeur riff—"

I roll my eyes. "Not fair. Not fair at all."

Madeline lets go of his wrist. "After a well-articulated discourse on the need for *grandeur,* we will be treated to a soliloquy on why Sybil Weatherfield will soon be leaving New York City for greener, *grander* pastures."

I look around, putting my fork down because I genuinely want to stop eating now. "Madeline is misrepresenting me." I melodramatically twist my body around in her direction. "Why are you misrepresenting me?"

"Sybil," she begins, "he said he wants to get it *all* on the table."

Rob flips both hands over, his palms up, his fingers moving as if to say *bring it on.* "Give me the riff. I wanna hear the riff."

A theatrical silence hangs over our Michelangelo table of ornate iron and cool marble. Quite lovely for a monologue on grandeur, really. Both of them stare at me. I stare at them. Okay, I'll do it. "I just want the extraordinary," I say to Rob, appealing to Rob, elucidating for Rob. "I mean, here I am. I'll never know what it was like to be a flapper. I'll never live in New Orleans in the French Quarter. I'll never walk around my French Quarter hotel room in a slip, fanning myself in front of an old fan with those metal blades spinning like an ancient propeller on a rusty plane. I'll never do those things. I just want something *grand* to happen." My face heats up. "You know?"

Rob, the rock 'n' roll prophet who first appeared in a Burger Christ t-shirt, spouting off knowing words about love slaves, says, "That sentimentality really *will* kill you." He speaks with his mouth full of cheesecake. "Maybe something grand is happening right now."

I look at the mushed-up cheesecake in his mouth. "But maybe it isn't," I say.

He looks at me intently. "I'm the one in a band called Glass Half Empty, Sybil Weatherfield."

"Madeline hasn't told us her unrealizable dreams yet." I turn to her, sweating.

"And you didn't give us the I'm–leaving–New York follow-up." She chomps on an ice cube. "I don't think I'll ever hike the Appalachian Trail, though."

I swing around to face her. "I never knew you wanted to."

"Well, I do," she says. "Preferably with a man I love who owns a two-man sleeping bag and good raingear."

"And a dog," I say. "You forgot the dog. A golden retriever?"

Rob, who barely even knows me, says, "I doubt you'll ever leave Manhattan, Sybil." It's after two in the morning, and Rob rips his paper napkin into tiny pieces. For a while, we're quiet. Rob fixes his eyes on me. "Do you love your boyfriend?"

Straight out, just like that.

"Do I *love* my boyfriend?" I repeat.

"Yes, do you *love* your boyfriend?"

"Jeff's a good man."

"We've probably heard enough clichés for one night," he says.

Madeline, at this very moment, makes herself known. She loudly puts down her empty caffé Americano cup, and it vibrates in its saucer, china moving against china. She tries to stop it with her fingers. "Sorry."

I blink. "We each bring our own expertise to the table, Jeff and I. I don't know if it's really about love." Madeline gazes into her water glass, Rob stares intently, and I pontificate. "It's like we're each solving for *x*. That's exactly how it is. We're solving for *x*."

Rob lets out a huge sigh. "I've always hated math."

"That's sex without love, though, isn't it?" Madeline chimes in. "It definitely doesn't fit into your *grandeur* plan, your longing for the *extraordinary*—"

"Thanks, girlfriend." I look at my watch. "It's been lovely, folks." I reach for my bag. "I have to give Jeff credit. He's decent. He's decent to me." I pull out a ten. "He's a decent man. We act like we're in love." I finish my water. "It's nice to have someone treat you so *decently*. He never approaches me as if he were just solving for *x*. I really appreciate the decency."

Madeline pulls out a cigarette for the street. "Snuffy and Sybil enjoy the pretense of a committed, *decent* relationship. What's love got to do with it? Huh, Sybil?"

I flutter my eyelids in her direction. "Touché."

Madeline provides a wry viewing of her pearly whites.

Rob grabs the check, pushing away my ten. "I'll treat for Indian tomorrow."

"Rain check, babe." Madeline bats her lashes. "Platonic-male-friend plans."

Rob looks at me.

"You mean *gay-male-friend plans*," I say with a touch of mean.

Why would I go for dinner with him after this deluge of the personal? I don't know, but I say, "I'd like that very much."

On the sidewalk, we exchange kisses on cheeks like we're Europeans and not sad kids on a wintry Manhattan night. Madeline and I walk off together, heading to my Village basement, content with the combative quality of our conversation. "Six o'clock tomorrow at Bombay Café, then?" Rob calls after us.

"Six o'clock," I say.

SEVEN

Bombay Café

Saturday, January 21, 1995

I walk to Sixth Street between First and Second Avenues on a chilly Saturday evening to meet Rob Shachtley at Bombay Café for Indian. I wander down Eighth, looking in storefront windows at clothes for drag queens and prom girls. Outsiders and aberrants congregate on sidewalks bridging West and East Village. Strangely, the bridge is marked by funky shoe shops: everywhere spiked heels, black leather boots, slippers Barbie might wear with high heels and pink fuzz on the toes. Once I bought a pair of fishnet stockings around here for a Halloween party. Once Madeline pierced her belly button somewhere on Eighth. When she arrived at my apartment afterward, she said she did it because she was becoming sexually insignificant. Then she told me about the sign hanging over the table as she got pierced: *A nipple is a nipple is a nipple.*

Whatever.

On St. Mark's Place, having crossed from west to east, I pass pizza joints, gritty comic-book vendors, lingerie "boutiques," dimly lit taverns, used-CD shops, tattoo parlors, and gift stores for the criminally insane. I make a right on Second, a left on Sixth. A young man clad in a secondhand vintage suit and a winter coat huddles under an awning. Sitar music twangs, beckons, floats onto the street. Indian men and women stand outside restaurants, summoning my presence with sweeping, welcoming hand gestures. The aroma of tandoori escapes from behind them. Saris, musicians, and exotic spice claim the neighborhood. Rob, seeing me, points to the sign above his head and mouths, "Bombay Café."

Bombay Café, indeed.

"The Guptas saved us a table." He kisses my cheek. We step down a few stairs into the restaurant, and he leads the way. In the window, sitar and tabla players recline on pink pillows and perform weepy, melancholy melodies. When we sit, a pot of hot tea arrives instantly, along with papadom and chutney. The decor is elegant in pinkish hues. There is, however, one bizarre oddity: a disco ball suspended overhead.

"Who are the Guptas?" I spread a pink napkin over my lap. Licorice-scented steam spirals away from the tea. I dip a piece of papadom into mango chutney.

Rob spoons cilantro and mint onto his plate. "The Guptas own the place—they're my landlords."

"Where is it that you live, exactly?"

"I rent a one-bedroom above the restaurant."

I look around. "Are they here now?"

"Shankar is right there." He points to a woman in a gold-and-blue sari. "That's Shankar Devi Gupta." He twists his neck around.

"And Chunilal Gupta is near the kitchen." A tall Indian man in an expensive suit guards a swinging door.

My eyes tour the busy restaurant. "How long have you lived here?"

"Six, six and a half years." Rob opens his menu.

"Wow." I chomp on papadom, thinking. "Why did you move here, Rob?" I really want to ask if he moved here when his wife died.

A waiter whom Rob knows arrives, and they talk. Then Rob says, "We'll start with *pakoras*, and then we'll have—" He opens his palm to me.

"You order for us; I don't know. I like everything." I inhale fennel.

He lists naan, tikka, saag.

When the waiter leaves, I muster up courage. "Why did you come to New York?"

He plays with his fork and knife, and looks into my eyes. "I had to get out of Providence." He smiles a sweet sad smile. "My mother was there. I had a wife buried in the suburbs. Dave was newly married. We had big ideas about being a New York band." He opens his hands. "So here I am." He pours us tea. "You?"

My cheeks burn scarlet. Rob sees it and looks into his plate. "You're coloring."

"Sorry." I burn brighter.

"You really don't have to apologize." He folds his arms on top of the table. He's a relaxed guy. I really don't feel like binging and purging under such hassle-free conditions. Then he says, "I'm up for the grandeur riff."

If I become a joke, I'll binge. I will not be mocked. I cross my arms on top of the table too, and take a deep breath. "A friend from UCLA knew these two old gay Broadway stars who lived in New York in the fifties when it was *grand*—that's the word they used. *Grand*. They said people danced in the streets." I pause to sip tea. "After they told us that, I would always envision old gay Broadway stars in top hats with canes, like something out of *Victor/Victoria*, dancing in the middle of the streets. The streets were always wet, and the old guys were always launching into numbers straight out of *An American in Paris*." I blot my lips with my napkin. "So I decided I should get in on that *grandeur* thing—see if there were something to it." I shrug my shoulders. "You know, Woody Allen, Holden Caulfield, James Dean, miscellaneous freaks on Eighth—those were my reasons. Plus, I heard the pizza was good." I put my hands in my lap. "That's the whole thing. There's nothing more to it." I pause. "Really." And this is true.

Rob removes his hands from the table and cocks his head. "You must have a history, right? Some driving force?"

"I thought you didn't really want to talk about that—"

Rob hems, haws. "I mean, what drives a girl to seek grandeur in the Big City?"

"Oh, Rob," I say, "it's an old story, you know that." I look away, blurry-eyed. "I pictured dense Woody Allen conversations in ticket lines for foreign films—"

"That's a scene from his movie, Syb—"

"I'd run across Holden Caulfield in Central Park, feeding ducks or watching the carousel. James Dean would be walking down slick and rainy—*slick* and *rainy*—streets near Times Square with his hands in his pockets and a cigarette dangling between his lips—"

"Did you know that Holden is missing in action in another Salinger story?" Rob whispers. For some reason, I reach out and touch his wrist.

"And James Dean is dead," I say quietly. "I *hate* his death." It sounds a little dramatic, but I like it.

"Your conception of *grandeur* is made up wholly of clichés. And impossibilities." Rob blinks. "And I don't know about the freaks. *What about the freaks?*"

"Hard to explain." I look at the disco ball hanging from the ceiling. Also hard to explain. "Even though my jacket is from the Burlington Coat Factory in Jersey, which may suggest I'm a big dork or, at least, somewhat provincial, there's something stark and sincere about having freaks around. I like to be surrounded by weird people."

We're silent. I'm tongue-tied for the moment. The candle flame dances in his glasses. He's pensive, contemplative. "You don't know what you want," he finally whispers. He laughs, and I'm embarrassed. But he's not cruel; there's no cruelty when he puts one hand on top of mine. "*Grandeur. Freaks.* You're coming; you're going. What's the deal, Sybil Weatherfield? And when are you leaving town? Aren't you leaving soon?"

James Dean is dead and Woody Allen fell into "disrepute" and Salinger is a hermit. I write "Abscess," which is completely devoted to my disappointments. I binge and purge intermittently since I'm neither gorgeous nor hard-bodied. I've been doing it since my midtwenties, when my good intentions failed, when disenchantment set in. I turn to Rob, who waits for an explanation.

The pakoras arrive. Thank God for pakoras!

"Madeline's leaving—did I tell you? Says she doesn't like her life." I put a pakora on my plate.

"I don't think you mentioned it," he says, pulling his hand away.

"I'm not a big fan of mine either." I smile, trying to sound detached. I dip a pakora into a sauce. "I figure I can go somewhere else, exercise my intellectual liabilities in another town, bitch about grandeur elsewhere." I touch my hair. "I like it here, Rob. But I'm *tired*. Of my own *tiresomeness*." I smile at him. "You know?"

"Intellectual liabilities?" He raises his eyebrows.

"Do you like smart girls?"

He doesn't hesitate for one second. "They're better than dumb ones." Then Rob eats without speaking. In silence, forks and knives hit plates. When he puts down his silverware, he asks, "Why are you so exhausted?"

I have to think about it, because thinking too much really *does* tire me out. "This'll sound silly."

"Try me. I've got on a Mickey Mouse watch. When I'm home alone, I put peanut butter and raisins on celery sticks, call it 'ants on a log,' and eat it joyfully in front of the TV. I can handle silly, Syb."

"I'm tired of myself, I guess."

At this point, Madeline would be rolling her eyes and calling me a drama queen. But I continue, "Despite the people all over the place, I find that I'm almost always alone. And despite the bigness of the Apple, we all know our own worlds are really small." I pause, picturing the basement I share with Tom, who's in Greece for the year. "When I get out of bed in the morning, I'm practically out the door. If I take a running jump across the hall, I'm in

Brooklyn." I smirk and shake my head. "There's just no getting away from me." I look into his eyes to measure my melodrama. "*I'm just so tired.*" I stop talking, then add one final thing. "I guess I'm lonely too."

He stares intently. Though the melodrama barometer is rising, he's okay. He's listening. Quietly he says, "I've never met anyone like you."

"Of course you have," I say. "And that's the problem." I look into my lap. *"You've met many people just like me."*

From somewhere in the restaurant, song breaks out. "Happy Birthday" invades our intimate dining space. The waiters and waitresses encircle a table, lights dim, the disco ball descends, beginning to spin. Glitter and shine cascade around as a birthday serenade to someone named Paco fills the room. More waiters and waitresses arrive with sparklers, illuminating the darkened restaurant and casting a reflection on Rob's glasses. The disco ball twirls while everyone sings, "Happy birthday to you."

Rob sings too, not loudly but well—keeping his eyes on mine the whole time.

When the song ends, hands shield ignited sparklers as waiters and waitresses retreat. Someone shouts, "And many more." Everyone claps, and the disco ball ascends. Gradually the lighting adjusts, leaving only soft shadows.

"I forgot to tell you," he says, "every birthday gets the star treatment. Weekends can see up to twelve on a single night."

Basmati rice and flatbreads arrive with a spinachy chicken dish in a kettle. "Let's not be formal." He dishes out saag. As we eat, hands brushing against each other as if we were playing the xylophone and zither, inhibition fades. Mrs. Gupta sends over gulab jamun for dessert. There's no bill.

He spoons into his dessert. "Is there anything good about your life?"

I squint. "My columns are good. They're pretty funny." I wink. "Who knew I was so funny?" I laugh aloud. "What about you? What's good in your life?"

"The band could turn into something. I think it will." When he's done with the gulab jamun, he declares, "Well, since your ideas of grandeur were always illusory, never even remotely possible, it sounds like you've briefly settled on a life of voyeurism in which you feel rebellious because you appreciate nihilistic displays of sedition on the streets of Manhattan." He smiles widely, apparently proud of his speech-making abilities. "So now, ever loveless and continually trapped between delusions of grandeur and the punk-rock scene, you're planning on going away with your metaphoric tail between your metaphoric legs."

I purse my lips. "Well put." I scan the mesh of low lights, pink tones, and Indian cuisine.

"Come see my apartment," he says.

Past the disco ball and out the door, he calls to me over his shoulder, "Wait. Godot may be upstairs." I frown, following.

Once outside Bombay Café, one immediately enters a side door and climbs a flight of narrow royal-blue steps; the first door on the right—the one with the peeling paint—is Rob's. He puts the key in the lock, swings it open, flicks on the lights, and shouts, "Voilà!"

The smell of Indian food saturates the apartment. Entering, I hug myself and look around. Rob throws his keys on the kitchen counter. The kitchen isn't separate, but tile floor demarcates the space. He opens the refrigerator. "I have milk and beer. Coffee."

"Tap water is fine." I step forward, curious about his dwelling.

Wedding photos on the wall, a shoebox of Legos on the floor, *National Geographic* on the coffee table. Impressive cleanliness throughout. I walk into his kitchen and reach for the fridge door. "May I?"

Rob hands me a glass of water. "Yeah. Why?"

"I like to see what people eat."

He looks at me as if I were nuts. "Sure. Go ahead."

Milk, beer, ketchup, butter, strawberry jelly, processed lunch meat. I go for the freezer. Frozen pizza, three Lean Cuisines, a pint of ice cream, and frozen broccoli.

Rob leans against the sink, watching me. "So? Is it okay?"

"Food interests me."

He squints. "Yeah?"

I have my back to him. "Yeah."

He seems to remember something. "You're not going to puke, are you?"

I shut the freezer. "Don't worry about it. I like your apartment. It's clean—"

Just then, we hear "Happy Birthday" from below. "Sorry," Rob mouths. "It can ruin the mood. Good thing we weren't having sex. So what were we saying about puking?" He walks around the counter. "Are you bulimic? Anorexic?"

"Happy Birthday" ends. "Neither—I just binge a little." Then I lie: "But I rarely purge—once or twice, maybe." I stare into his eyes; he doesn't believe me. I continue, "Look at me. I'm not super skinny. It's no big deal, Rob. Do I look sick? My period hasn't stopped. I've never chewed up a cookie and then spit it out, just to get the taste." I fake a laugh. "So hurling appeals to me slightly." This scrutiny is problematic. I toss something out: "People say you sleep around. Like *constantly*."

Rob is not easily undone. "I always practice safe sex."

My neck itches. Rob's heater hisses in the corner like an old vaporizer.

He runs his fingers through his hair. "Are you using that Jeff guy for something?"

It's another birthday below.

"Jeff's a great guy." I look at the magazine covers on the table. "He's a great guy—he's like a good temp job." My words embarrass me as soon as I say them.

"So we're *both* practicing safe sex." He laughs. The room is warm, almost hot—the way apartments get in the winter. He takes off his jacket.

I look at his suit: like the Burger Christ shirt, it speaks. Ambiguously retro, polyester blend, rock star-gangster, used sophisticate. What does it say? "So what are you going to do with your life, Rob?"

"Sing." He drinks water. "I have a lot of songs to sing."

We talk about the Guptas, about how they first went to Canada and then moved to New York. He tells me how their seventeen-year-old son, Sunil, is going to Columbia in the fall. He has stories about the little girl, Sonali. The most Americanized and the most fascinated by Rob's life as a lead singer of a rock 'n' roll band, she sometimes comes into his apartment, sits on his furniture, drinks orange soda, and wants to know what he was like as a kid.

And then, even though Rob decried sentimentality, dwelling on the past, his and mine, that's what we talk about. His vintage suit sleeves rolled up, my shoes off. Lives unfold until it's late. No one gets weepy, but Rob suddenly stands, knocking his ironic suit jacket to the floor. "I hate this shit," he says. "Naval-gazing, myopic, self-absorbed nonsense."

"That's a little strong, don't you think?"

"You can sleep on the couch." He takes off his glasses, rubbing his eyes. "You and I—we'll be good friends. I can tell. Let's not be disposable, though. I won't treat you like a one-night stand, and you don't treat me like a delusion of grandeur." The glow from the street illuminates the darkened room. "Deal?" He hands me a blanket and pillow.

"Deal." I watch him move toward his bedroom in the dark.

I scan my surroundings. He has postered walls (the Coneheads, Sha-Na-Na, and the Sistine Chapel). Books, furniture, organized as if he's been around women, a wife. The heater pumps steam into the apartment, and spices creep out of vents and through floorboards.

Under the coffee table, I see a big book. I drag it out. I span my palm across the book's cover. A scrapbook. Opening its Beatles gift-wrapping paper cover, I find pages with dates: dates from the past, one after another, not ordered but pasted next to magazine pictures and newspaper articles. Each date makes an announcement. I flip through its leaves, each carefully collaged, an accumulation of history, of rock 'n' roll history. Timelines, announcements of births, marriages, and obituaries dot the margins. Rob has saved concert-ticket stubs and album reviews. Turning pages, there's Led Zeppelin in London, Pink Floyd at the Berlin Wall. Mick Jagger next to Roger Daltrey, Bono singing with B. B. King. David Bowie wears a wig; Aretha Franklin puckers her lips. Creedence Clearwater Revival, Neil Young, Lindsey Buckingham, Joe Cocker. I pore over the book. It takes me an hour to look through everything, and I leave articles unread. I draw my fingers over ticket stubs, Rob's claim on history: Rob's insistence on narrative continuity and his rejection of disposability.

Nostalgic, after all.

EIGHT

This Is What I Do

Wednesday, January 25, 1995

This is what I do.

I set my alarm for 5:30 a.m., and that's when I wake. I go to a gym on Seventh Ave., where beautiful gay men and single women without makeup work out. I always look like hell—steamy glasses, cellulite on thighs, hair wild but not sexy.

Every morning, it's the same. "Hi," I shyly mutter to the guy at the front desk.

"How are you?" he asks. I don't know his name, but I think he's straight.

"Fine, thanks. And you?"

"Great." He takes the ferry in from Staten Island at four in the morning. He told this to me once while he checked my account for late fees. Last month, he mentioned he was an actor when I stopped at reception to see if my sunglasses were found in the lockers.

It bothers me that this is all we have. That he's just another potentially gay man and I'm just another unglamorous woman who works out before my job.

This is what I do.

I work out. I dread wasting time, so I read a book or watch CNN while on the Stairmaster. I read the entirety of *The Satanic Verses* on exercise equipment over the course of several days; this is a mild source of pride for me.

Afterward I go home and eat measured portions of breakfast food. If one serving equals three-fourths of a cup of dried cereal, by God, I'm eating three-fourths of a cup of dried cereal. At the start of the day, I have no problems with food; food is my friend. While eating bran flakes, I envision myself showing other women how it's done on *The Richard Simmons Show*.

Then I go to my temp job. If I walk, I listen to a tape. Maybe *Godspell*, maybe Van Morrison. This will leave me feeling lonesome and tragic. I'll resort to daydreams—standard, weary daydreams. Once they were good. Back in the eighties.

In September, at Bendix, Madeline looked at me over wheat germ and declared, "Even my fantasies bore me."

Usually I imagine being the wife or gorgeous girlfriend of a monogamous guitar player, a really excellent one—as good as Jimi Hendrix, Jimmy Page, or the Edge. We're always on the road. I like to think of us in airports, wearing dark glasses and carrying duffel bags. We're typically off to London, Paris, or Rome. We usually have to avoid millions of cameras because everyone is dying to see us, and the lights are blinding. We hold hands tightly, moving quickly, not saying much. The paparazzi go wild. In my ear, "Day by Day."

At my temporary office, I flip on the lights, the computer, the printer. I follow the temp rules, trying to find time to write. Sometimes I have flashes of self-importance. Sometimes Jeff Simon calls.

Jeff's a financial analyst who looks like a soap star. He's cute. In fact, he's *really* cute, categorically *dashing*. The guy has dark brown hair, classic good looks like Ralph Lauren Polo ads, and a snuggly but manly wardrobe of taupe pants and black turtlenecks. A regular Pierce Brosnan. A great jaw. During the week, he's at the World Trade Center. On weekends, maybe the Hamptons. In tweed sport coats, he attends Sunday brunches. Muffins and mimosas.

He likes the fact that his girlfriend lives in squalor. When I tell this to Madeline, she says, "You do *not* live in squalor, Sybil. Dream on."

It's nice to be a financial analyst, and it's nice to say that your girlfriend is a writer in the Village, but the squalor part is best. Waking up in the middle of the night in a single bed, the girl pressed against the wall like a sexy Eliza Doolittle/cockney-street-urchin-cum-Audrey Hepburn, the train rumbling beneath the floor, he wonders, "How *did* I get so lucky?" He leaves before daybreak; we rarely wake together.

In my Village abode, Jeff gloats over the knee-high fridge, the cans of tuna on the shelf. He likes the toilet-paper rolls behind my bed. He's fond of the desk made from an old door retrieved from the garbage.

What an interesting bohemian/writer girl! Doors for desks, tuna for dinner!

He isn't a bad guy, this Jeff Simon. He isn't *that* removed from the middle class. He enjoys dipping into the lives of the less fortunate. Who'd better be artists.

How I feel about him: he'll eat McDonald's on road trips. He keeps talking about going to the Grand Ole Opry in the summer. Despite his lunches at the Yale Club, he'll touch my face, saying he wants to see me, asking no questions.

This is what I do.

I get wind of free food at work. Actually, let me be frank: I keep a lookout for it—my ears are open; they're *burning.* I'm not looking to gossip by the water cooler. I don't care about the nitty-gritty details of the lives of these people—I'm a temp. Here today, gone tomorrow. I just want to know who has the chicken wings, who brought in the cinnamon buns with the sugar-glaze frosting shit.

My good intentions, the measured cereal, the Stairmaster antics: gone! It happens around 10:30 in the morning. When I'm done checking my e-mail. Right before I try to figure out how to do a spreadsheet in Excel. A spreadsheet? Excel? *Um, I don't think so!* I'm a writer, a temp, the potential love interest of an excellent, monogamous guitar player!

Free shortcake in the house!

A baker's dozen is really thirteen? Thirteen sesame-seed bagels with real cream cheese, please!

This may be a way to save money: eat everything in sight in order to avoid grocery shopping later. I search out office leftovers, the remains of business lunches, someone's box of chocolate doughnuts. I climb stairs, wander back halls, look carefree, lie about what I last ate. When I run into the events coordinator or the human resources woman, I say I haven't eaten in *days.* I pretend I'm *starved.*

Then I find what I'm looking for. Forget the measured three-fourths of a cup of dried cereal. Forget the gym and the actor, gay or straight. I eat like there's no tomorrow. I love minimuffins and cold quiche, roast-beef or turkey sandwich halves, trays of stuffed mushrooms. I'll be there for shrimp cocktail, little pizzas, miniegg-rolls. You name it.

Afterward I go back to my office with my head hung low.

When the day is done, I go home to my basement apartment, look at my mail, maybe watch TV. Perhaps I'll balance my checkbook, call Madeline, or make gazpacho (I did it once!). Perhaps I'll ralph. If I'm good, I'll write. Additional flashes of self-importance are likely.

Sometimes Jeff calls. "Meet me at my office."

Before I go, I undress and weigh myself on the scale I keep in the fireplace. My bedroom is the living room, which is also the dining room. It opens onto the street. Between Tom and me, only a kitchen exists. But Tom is in Greece, so I stand around naked till I reassemble the Sybil Presentation, the exhibition of Bohemian Writer Living in Squalor whom I take to Jeff Simon's office in lower Manhattan.

Subways, pigeons, scary business suits, escalators, and elevators. Everyone looks busy. I greet Jeff with a kiss, reminding my lips to pucker.

Jeff usually sits at his desk. I read magazines like I'm at a doctor's office, or I talk to investment bankers about their vacation plans. They're frequently about to take off for Bermuda. Sometimes I massage Jeff's shoulders while he's on the computer. He gets into it and moves around, rolling his body under my hands, and for some reason, this irritates me more than actually having *sex* with him. It's like—and I know this sounds goofy—I'm devouring free food. When I'm kneading his shoulders and he's responding to my touch, I feel as if I'm consuming chocolate pie. Stuffing it in.

Wasted calories.

This is no time for judgment; this is what I do.

Even though I was a glutton at lunch, we go for dinner. With Jeff, it's *dining*. He knows the good places, and sometimes a good place is where he wants to go. Usually I say, "I'll just get a drink." Yet another sad misfortune of my life. Just when someone's willing to take me to Lutèce or One if by Land, I have to bow out because I ate a dozen cheese puffs at four. I never plan ahead. I never hold out. Good things come to those who wait? Hah!

If it's a weeknight, he may come back to my place.

If it's a weekend, I may go to his place on Central Park West.

It's Jeff Simon's apartment I'm after. Jeff and I met on a blind date. He made dinner for mutual friends and me.

"Is this your place?" I first said to him, setting a plate of tinfoil-wrapped burned cookie bars that took me all afternoon to make down on an immaculate counter in a drop-dead gorgeous loft apartment overlooking Central Park. A huge picture window framed the park, and the room was sectioned off by strategically placed pieces of furniture to indicate a kitchen, dining room, and living room. A giant wood-block table stood in the middle of the kitchen, something I've always loved. Copper pots and pans hung over the sink and counters; the couch matched Jeff's pants; maroon pillows rested on a taupe sofa. ("It's fawn, mushroom," he said, describing the color.) Lit candles—golden, mustard-yellow—

were on a table. The only bedroom was a loft upstairs. The entire place was dimly lit except for candle- and city light.

I felt like Lily Bart in *The House of Mirth*, not like myself one lousy bit.

"Yeah, I bought it last year." He served us chicken and squash.

"I brought chocolate rocks for dessert," I announced over chardonnay.

"I'll make coffee," he said. "Since those are my favorite."

He ate three hockey pucks, and I decided to stay with him for that. A man who took what I had to offer, no matter how little it was! Sweet Jeff Simon!

We've been dating for six months. We're accessories in picturesque lives, trappings in visions of bohemia and the Stock Exchange. We say nice things to each other. When we have sex, we are more than decent to one another. He's a kind man. Jeff Simon and I are *kind* lovers.

This is not the world I imagined, the world I set out for, the world I even admire. My friends used to talk about a love that makes one stagger. No one told me about disappointment. No one mentioned necessity.

And Jeff Simon, in his approach to my naked body, is kind when it comes to disappointment and necessity. Jeff doesn't retch like me or perpetually mourn like Rob or spout off biting, erudite witticisms like Madeline. Rather, he kindly solves for *x*, never telling me I'm an equation with a number missing. He is a *kind* lover, and for this, I like him.

If I'm alone, if Jeff has never been over, I read before bed. One of the reasons I hate work so much is that it cuts into my reading time. I've got Tolstoy on my shelves, Shakespeare too.

I pray when the lights go out. Like my fantasies, these prayers are standard and weary. I know what I'm praying for, and I know for whom I pray. To whom I pray, I do not know. I pray and I pray and I pray.

This is what I do.

NINE

ABSCESS

SARTRE WAS WRONG AND I HAVE THE SCARS TO PROVE IT

SYBIL WEATHERFIELD FOR *NEW YORK SHOCK*

From Friday, January 27, 1995

I have several fears in life, all revolving around Michelle Pfeiffer.

I first became aware of this during a Ms. Pfeiffer movie preview. At the sight of her elfin cover-girl features, I threw an entire bucket of hot buttered popcorn into the air, and it rained snack food until the film began. The well-dressed man next to me said, "What's wrong?"

What to say? Where to begin?

Frankie and Johnny scares me because running a dishrag over a diner counter as if that's your lot in life is a tad unsettling for one who envisions guest appearances on *Oprah.*

Batman Returns chills me to the bone because, prior to becoming Catwoman, Pfeiffer is a frumpy secretary who can do nothing but let out a big sigh of utter despair when she walks into her Gotham apartment. Though she has a ton of felines, she's all alone. How many of us can hope to be transformed into Catwoman? And, if it happened, could we fit into the catsuit?

I turned to my movie date. "What makes you think something's wrong?"

In truth, I'm afraid. I'm afraid of walking into my own apartment, switching on the lights, and realizing I'm all alone. I don't even have any cats.

My secret fears, articulated by Pfeiffer transmogrifications, go deeper. They become metaphysical, *eschatological* statements on heaven, on hell.

Sartre was wrong, and I have the scars to prove it.

Hell isn't about spending eternity in a small room with people you hate. Though that would be very bad.

This'll be hard, but try—*try*—not to laugh.

I discovered a few gray hairs. I couldn't remember if I was supposed to pull them or let them fester. The late-night runs to BBQ on Second Ave. with my Kate Moss roommate were catching up with me. Turned out I had a fat ass. Then I began financing Kate Moss's boyfriend's toilet-paper habit. He wouldn't stop using.

A radio station announced it would sell tickets to a one-night-only Pearl Jam concert. I just had to call the station's toll-free number.

Don't let me lose you here.

I really, really, *really* wanted these tickets. I wasn't even that big of a fan. My aspirations were simple. I wanted an evening out. I wanted to revel in flannel and angst. I wanted something *singular, profound, unique.* Can't you understand?

The station would sell tickets until they were gone, beginning Friday night with a break from midnight till Saturday morning.

Friday night arrived, so I dialed the number.

Busy.

Hmm.

I pushed redial.

Still busy. Redial again. Busy again. Redial one more time. Busy still. One for the Gipper. Busy. One for Aunt Mae. Fucking busy. Five just because. Busy, busy, busy, busy, busy . . .

It's crucial you stick with me. I'm a girl with a past. I've camped out for Duran Duran tickets. I have a framed picture of James Dean on my mantel like he's one of the family. I've etched men's names into my skin with razor blades. When *Rick* heals, I'll write *Mike.*

Something in my head clicked. The nerve in my brain that's supposed to control erratic redial behavior had been severed. I lost it, becoming a slave to redial. Death was imminent. Eminent. Imminent. That nerve was disengaged too.

Then I knew. Everything—*everything*—hinged on this one single thing. Nothing else mattered: not my student loans, not my crush on a Trekkie, not my failure to save the world, not my secret desire to frequent places like the Bowery Bar—*nothing.*

The only thing that mattered was this: *I needed Pearl Jam tickets.* They represented the whole of my life.

This is a horrible thing to know.

Sartre was wrong about that business of being stuck in a room without an exit. Hell is pushing redial over and over and *over* in pursuit of Pearl Jam tickets.

Desperation is not about the loss of lovers, dips into alcoholic oblivion, or bad SAT scores. What can be worse than the self-loathing of realizing that the entirety of your existence can be summed up by your desire for and inability to obtain *Pearl Jam tickets*?

Now I was dealing with God. That's right. God had gotten involved. I prayed. I knew he had abandoned me too. I tried to make a deal. *Dear God,* I began, *no more chocolate.* I'd offer to give up sex, but I wasn't having any. *Dear God, I know you hate me, but please, God, please. Let me have a lousy pair of tickets. Show me that you haven't abandoned me. Tickets, God. Not money, not power, not Johnny Depp. Just two Pearl Jam tickets. Let me get my way once. Let me see Eddie.*

I went over the details of my life. I took subways. I drank cappuccino in trendy cafés named after European composers. I knew where to buy my bagels. I knew the place to walk my dog. I had gay friends. I lied about listening to Howard Stern. I voted Democratic. I was for cheap sex, cheap beer, and low-income housing. I lived in the Village and I didn't eat red meat and I smoked when I drank and I was open-minded, user-friendly, acquiescent, accommodating, compliant. . . .

As evening approached, it took everything in me to put the receiver down. It rang—my mother! I burst into tears. When I told her what I was doing (it was now Saturday), she said, "Go for a walk."

On the streets, I only stopped once by a pay phone to try again. Near Astor Place—my head pounding, my nose running—I held my arms up to the heavens and said, "For the love of God, somebody *please* help me!"

Okay, so I never did that. But people *do.*

I went home and baked a potato. While baking, my skin grazed the grill, searing the fleshy web between thumb and index finger on my right hand. I lovingly put the wound to my mouth. I ran my tongue over it. I tasted it, savored it: my war wound. My Pearl Jam scar. *Little Eddie.*

Everyone should have a scar like this.

I have no moral to offer. I know nothing. I don't even know when my next dentist appointment is. But I should've been listening to the Stones on this one. The radio station only played Top Forty hits, and everyone was having his or her five minutes of fame at my expense. But the Stones said it best: *you can't always get what you want.*

I think they said something about getting what you need.

That scar is an emblem—my crest. Acknowledging I'll never be Catwoman, it attests to hope. Want big things. Go for more than a nice evening out. Eschew defining bliss in terms of concert tickets. Fear not Michelle Pfeiffer. Know hell for what it is.

TEN

ANTIBIOTICS 2

FROM *NEW YORK SHOCK*

From Friday, February 3, 1995

Get *one* cat. Not *many*—just *one*.

—Denise, Chelsea

FYI: That razor blade thing wouldn't work. They don't heal like that. Your wrist would be positively thrashed.

—Chad, Brooklyn

ELEVEN

HEY JUDE

Wednesday, March 1, 1995

Early in the day, someone tried to kill me.

Temporarily jobless, I took comfort in a megabookstore. There's nothing like a Barnes and Noble to soothe the lonely, the unemployed. I checked out the magazines, the travel guides. I returned some of my newer-looking books, pretending they were gifts I didn't want, and I bought *In the Kitchen with Rosie*. Perhaps I'd learn to cook.

When I left, I casually strolled along Sixth Avenue, minding my own business. An Audi slowed next to me, its window rolled down. I didn't look, in case someone was dumping a body. Then an unidentifiable object came flying out and hit the wall behind me. The Audi sped away. Since bodies thud rather than break into a million pieces, I glanced back: a beer bottle, brown liquid, shards of broken glass.

Then I got a cup of coffee at Dalton's, where I thought Henry Rollins of Rollins Band was behind me in line. I walked to Washington Square Park, thinking about Rollins and his many tattoos. This led me down a thought trajectory of body parts ending with contemplation of my own dry hands. *Excruciatingly* dry hands. My knuckles are weather maps, proclaiming winter with tiny cuts. This made me think about my caffeine intake, which a San Diego friend links with the increase of lines around my mouth. Bad news. At the park, I sat down on a bench to read *New York Shock*, which featured an interesting article on independent film. My day, in a nutshell.

Tonight Rob Shachtley and Jeff Simon will meet for the first time.

Glass Half Empty is playing at Sin-é, and Jeff, Madeline, and I are attending. Sin-é is a small Irish venue that typically hosts acoustic acts. Tucked onto St. Mark's Place between First Ave. and Avenue A, it doesn't serve alcohol.

Jeff, arm around my waist, holds the door open for me. Entering, I scan the room, smiling, removing my jacket, looking for Rob. A little wooden table in front is marked with a paper sign that says, "Reserved." I'm with the band. "Over there," I say, grabbing Jeff's arm.

We wait for Rob and Madeline to arrive, barely speaking to each other.

I'm thankful that Rob comes over soon.

I stay seated, but Jeff jumps to his feet and extends his hand. I feel old. Do we do that now? Must we stand?

And yet, I notice, Rob knows how to handle this. I see him there, from where I sit. In slow motion, Rob reaches out and touches Jeff in perfect, congruous meeting mannerisms.

"Jeff Simon." Jeff grips Rob's hand with both of his.

"Rob Shachtley." Rob pumps their colliding appendages up and down.

Ugh. Sybil Weatherfield. Sit down. I consider pulling on Jeff's handsome herringbone jacket, but this is his thing, his arena. Rob, garbed in rock 'n' roll regalia—a dark purple suit, thick-rimmed black glasses, and messy hair—meets Jeff in this decidedly manly moment. They grasp hands, puff out their chests, and look into one another's eyes.

I pull out a chair. "Rob, sit. Join us, friend."

He leans over and kisses me on the cheek. "There's an opening act. Valerie Hart. Does cover songs." Rob looks at us. "So I can sit." He settles into the chair, looking at my boyfriend. "Jeff, I've heard great things about you."

I find myself reaching out and adjusting one of Rob's purple lapels.

"Sybil says nice things about you too." Jeff grins at me.

Madeline, in her crazy kid's winter jacket with fake fur bordering the hood and sleeves, rushes in. She's out of breath. "Kitten!" She pinches my cheek and kisses both Jeff and Rob.

"Parakeet!" Rob exclaims.

Madeline sits and opens her canvas bag. "I have something for everyone!"

"This is fabulous," Rob says.

Madeline lays two newspaper-wrapped lumps down on the table. "For Rob and Sybil, bread." She hands us each a loaf. "I baked this afternoon. Still warm." She pulls her scarf off her neck. "I was pretending I lived in a small town. I opened my window, imagined the pigeons were bluebirds, and talked to myself about heading into the barn to collect eggs and milk the cows."

I start to unwrap mine. "That's lovely, Madeline. May I smell it?"

"Of course, Kitten." She digs into the canvas bag again. Madeline's keys, cigarettes, and nutty Hollywood-starlet sunglasses are on the table. "I didn't have time to wrap yours, Snuffy." That's her nickname for Jeff. "For you, Chianti." She pulls out a miniature bottle, the kind served on airplanes. "Since you're a man of taste, I thought this would appeal to you. I got it from a hotel fridge in Philly—I've been saving it for the right occasion." She smiles and slides it over. Jeff turns the bottle in his hands. "It's aged—I've had it since last year."

"You're so considerate." Jeff winks at her; she blushes, lowering her eyes.

"If you opened it now, Jeff, we could all take a gulp." I look around the table for acquiescence, but there are no takers.

"No." Madeline shakes her head, annoyed. "Jeff should save it. Pour it into one glass. Make pasta. Sip it slowly before winter ends."

"How idyllic." I breathe deeply, looking at the three people with me at the small wooden table. I feel strange, like we're playing a game, Duck-Duck-Goose. I should speak, act like a girlfriend. I rest my hand on Jeff's arm. "I'll make dinner for you soon."

Jeff puts his hand on top of mine. He holds it there. I'm hyper-aware of both Madeline's and Rob's eyes on us. Madeline jams her things back into the canvas bag, and Rob pushes his chair away from the table, which causes it to screech against the floor. Our drinks arrive.

"How did you spend your day?" Madeline asks.

"I sat on a bench in Washington Square Park." My hand slips off Jeff. "I think I saw Henry Rollins at Dalton's. He had on combat boots—"

"I once spent the night in the park." Rob says, pulling his chair in again.

Madeline licks latte froth from her lips. "What happened?" she asks Rob.

"I shared a bench with a one-eyed crack addict named Pip."

I picture it: it's dark, but the arch is lit up, the lights reaching up Fifth. A one-eyed crack addict on a bench with Rob in a vintage suit.

He continues, "We just sat there, Pip and I, talking. It was three a.m. Pip occasionally smoked crack." He pauses. "He had on this black sweatshirt with big silver letters, big silver letters right across his chest. Guess what the letters spelled," Rob says. "Guess."

"What?" Jeff leans over his espresso drink.

Rob is visibly riveted by his own story. His voice becomes a whisper. His sudden intensity pulls me in until I'm picturing the one-eyed crack addict radiant under the illuminated arch—Washington Square with its scattered beams of light, the nearby streetlights and random cigarette tips glowing in the dark. When I envision the scene, I'm mesmerized by their poses, their bodies slightly curled while they sit on the bench, bending toward each other, in the still of the Manhattan night. Rob uses his index finger to write on his chest. "P-I-P. *Pip*."

Everyone laughs. All I can say is "Rob, I *love* this story."

Rob swigs his water, chomps on ice, and nods his head madly. "Like that, huh?"

"It's lovely." I'm wistful, dazed. "It's a *lovely* story."

"He was a sad fuck in the park, Sybil." Madeline isn't seduced by the imagery. "How tragic is that?"

Rob taps my arm. "Syb, he was a *freak*—existentialist angst was *everywhere*."

I grab his purple sleeve, oblivious to the others around us. "Did you feel the pang, Rob? Wasn't that a moment of truth in the heart of the black night? Did you ever see him again?" I squint and reluctantly let go of his wrist.

"Actually, I did." He checks out Valerie Hart setting up her equipment. "About a year later, same place." Rob clearly enunciates each word. "I said, 'Hey, Pip!'" Rob looks into my eyes. "The guy jumped out of his skin. He had no idea who the hell I was or how I knew his name."

Suddenly I'm sad. "He didn't know who you were?"

"Look at you two—all moony over a homeless crack addict who fried his brain so much he couldn't remember one day from the next. Those are the very people who make me want to get the hell out of here and never come back." Madeline pulls her big canvas bag onto the table. "Last winter, at Coney Island, Sybil and I paid three bucks to see a two-headed baby. That was when I thought appreciating deeply disturbing things made me a happy camper. The two-headed baby would surely cheer us up."

"What did it look like?" Rob asks, diverting his attention from the one-eyed crack addict named Pip to the two-headed baby. "What did the baby look like?"

"Like a rat or a bunch of grapes," I announce. "Who could tell with all that formaldehyde?" I put my hand on top of Madeline's bag. "Madeline, why do you make it sound so bad? We had fun; don't say we didn't—"

"I'm not. Really, I'm not. You know I look *forward* to our acts of voyeurism. You know what they mean to me." She turns to Rob and Jeff. "This year, we're going to the annual hot-dog-eating contest on the Fourth of July. They have one every year at Coney Island—to see who can eat the most wieners." She looks at me. "We had a fight after the two-headed baby?" Everyone turns to her. "You remember?"

"What fight?" I say.

She's irritated. "We were playing that game where you name two people and you have to say which one you'd rather sleep with, like Howard Stern or Fabio. We figured out that you wanted to sleep with Willem Dafoe and I wanted to sleep with Aidan Quinn, so we got in a fight over who had the best chance of doing so—"

I turn red. I can't believe she's bringing this up. I glare at her, hoping she'll stop. "I don't remember."

Jeff has an amused but fake smile on his face. Rob is fascinated and wide-eyed.

"Sounds like a silly game," I say, hoping to forget—though now I remember.

Madeline's voice reaches an angry pitch. "You said you saw Willem on Houston and Broadway once, across from the Angelika, so it was more likely that you'd get to sleep with him than it was that I'd sleep with Aidan, who probably wasn't in New York very often. That's what you said. Willem probably lived here—"

I suck air in through my nostrils. "I don't remember." I turn to Jeff. "At *all*."

"Jeff doesn't care," Madeline says. "Do you?"

"No," he whispers.

Madeline addresses Rob. "Would you care?"

Rob looks around systematically, taking each of us in. "Probably." He sits back in his chair and adjusts his purple tie. "I mean, it's Willem *Dafoe*." He pauses meaningfully. "Had she said someone like Mel Gibson or Brad Pitt, it would be okay. You can deal with those guys. But Willem *Dafoe*. What do you do with *that*?" He shakes his head, furrowing his eyebrows. "Obviously, something's going on there—"

"Rob," Jeff interjects, "what were you doing spending the night in the park?"

There's an odd moment of silence; the rest of us straighten. "Yeah, Rob, what *were* you doing spending the night in the park?" Madeline asks.

Rob takes a long drink. "You know?" He looks into space. "I don't recall."

"You don't *recall*?" Jeff is surprised.

"Unfortunately, no."

So I'm thinking he *does* recall; he just doesn't want to *tell*. Kicked out. Some girl. Could've made it home, but didn't. Got sidetracked in Washington Square Park.

It's March, and I've spent a lot of time with Rob Shachtley. There have been films at the Angelika, the Quad, the Film Forum. *Strawberry and Chocolate* in late January, *Shallow Grave* in February. I agreed to see *The Brady Bunch Movie*, so he took me to *Before the Rain* near Lincoln Center. We've had nights of chicken korma and beef vindaloo. He's come to my basement apartment, seen my trunk/coffee table, touched the black felt curtains I can't afford to replace.

When I look at him, I see a collage. Part street urchin, part immigrant, part family man, he lives in the grubby-chic part of town—the section subject to criticism, hip to cultural aches, and testy in the interplay between decline (shot veins, drunks in bars, whorish girls) and ascension (cutting-edge painting, alternative rock, underground prose, disdain for racism). That's where he lives.

I know he likes coffee from Store 24. I know he doesn't mind the smell of sidewalks in summer because walking down them makes him feel alive when usually he feels dead. I know Dave Stomps is his closest friend. I know he can't believe cancer killed his wife.

I've told him stuff: how I'm broke, how I have neither love nor money. I've apologized for living in Greenwich Village, where I pay nearly double the rent Madeline pays in Brooklyn because it's important to me that I live there and not anywhere else. Not even the East Village. I'm a West Village girl, because I like cleanliness, quaintness, and the company of educated gay men over experimental artists with scary histories. I'm secretly bourgeois, haunted by credit-card debt without any experience whatsoever of track marks. I like the pretension involved with literary history and Saturday-afternoon cafés filled with chocolate croissants and yuppies reading the *New York Times*. He knows I'm weary, shell-shocked, starving, and sad. He knows I always point to my neighborhood and say, "But look where I live."

I suppose I have secrets still. It's only March. And about him, there's a certain blankness, a black hole.

Before we knew each other, I'd sit down at a table in the Fedora and be drawn into the buzz, the web of gossip, the speculations about the characters of Rob and Dave. That's how I learned that Rob was a widower. And a sleaze. A widower and a sleaze. Say it ten times fast.

The girls: they'd talk. "He's a widower and a sleaze," they'd say.

The story went that Rob would pick up a smitten girl at a show, go back to her place (never his), sleep with her, and leave while it was still dark.

Now I hear nothing. No one tells me a thing. Since I'm with the band.

But, if I imagine the old scenario, I imagine him bending over the body of a naked sleeping dumb girl, tying his shoes. Black shoes. A crimson velvet suit already on. Maybe he leaves a mint on the pillow. Never cash. But I know he really carries mints.

They, the girls, always said he never spent the entire night. They said he wore his wedding ring the whole damn time.

"I think we had a gig in the West Village," Rob says. "I'm not really sure."

Valerie Hart, guitar strapped onto lithe body, sits in front of us on a rustic three-legged stool. She breaks into "All Along the Watchtower."

While she sings, I see myself high up in a tower, a modern-day Rapunzel, cursed but not beautiful. I dwell on Jeff, guiltily—shyly drifting over our sex life. *Lives*. Plural. We're convenient, obvious garnishes on already-full plates. At the end of Valerie's set, we clap sincerely.

Out of left field, Jeff says, "I don't think I've ever spent the night on a bench—"

Madeline, pulling her eyes reluctantly off the now-empty stage, says, "That's the problem with New York. No matter what you do, there's always someone who's done *more*. No matter how much fun you're having, there's always someone having *more* fun—"

"I should go." Rob stands. "Sorry to be rude. It was a pleasure." He turns to Jeff. Again with the handshaking routine. He leaves, kissing Madeline and me on the cheeks.

"How much time before Rob plays?" Jeff drums his fingers on the table.

"A while," I say. "Twenty minutes. A half hour."

"They take forever." Madeline switches chairs to sit where Rob sat.

"I'm going to run across the street." He pushes his chair back. "Gum."

I reach for the coat hanging on the back of my chair. "I can go with you."

"No." He puts his hands up in protest. "I want a little fresh air."

"Yeah, me too." Madeline winks. "I'm gonna have a smoke in a sec."

"Okay, sweetheart," I say. *Sweetheart!*

When he leaves, Madeline is on me like an attack dog. "So what's going on? You're introducing your new boyfriend to your old one?" Meanwhile, Dave Stomps moves behind us on the stage.

Madeline stares at Dave for a minute. I wave. He waves. Madeline waves. She's back on me. "Don't you think this is a little weird? Suddenly Rob's your new best friend."

I squint in righteous indignation. "There's nothing going on. We're friends."

"If that's the story you're sticking with."

"We're *friends*, Madeline."

"Really?"

"We click. I need friends. Don't make me give him up." We speak in hurried, rushed tones, aware that time is of the essence.

"You like him?" she whispers.

"I do." I look for him. Rob bends over by a speaker, tilting it to see underneath. "Madeline," I look around maniacally, "we don't have time to discuss this. Why can't he just be my friend?"

"Friends with a man?"

We leave it at that. Rob approaches and sits down.

Madeline stands. "I'm going for a smoke." She turns and leaves. "When I get back, we're going to be ironic bitches again—we're going to deliver scathing opinions on just about everything." She nods in Rob's direction. "On you too." Then she walks away.

Rob sits. "I have a minute." He checks out Sin-é. "Where's the stud?"

"Gum. He wanted gum." I smile. "Jeff likes Dentyne."

Rob juts out his chin and nods. "He seems like a nice guy."

I catch the waitress's eye and point to my coffee cup. "He is."

Rob puts his elbows on the table and twists an empty glass around. He does this for a long time—till the waitress brings my coffee and takes the empty glass from his hands. "Well, I guess I hate him. But he seems like a *great* guy—what's the word? A *decent* one." He reaches over to take a sip of my coffee. "I mean, I'm sure he opens the door for you every time."

"Rob," I say dryly, as if I haven't noticed that *Rob is jealous*.

"I'm being unfair?"

I nod. "Definitely."

"Sorry."

Rob grabs my hand and holds it. "There's probably more there than meets the eye."

I leave my hand in his. Dave does a drum roll. "You're confusing me," I whisper, looking at my hand in his.

He looks at our fingers touching. "I'm sorry. I was wrong—I don't hate him."

Jeff comes in, smelling like cinnamon. "Gum?" he says to Rob, standing over us.

"No, thanks." We slowly pull our hands away from each other. Rob stands and pushes in his chair.

Dave sidles over and grabs Rob in a headlock. "We need you for a sec."

Rob gives me a smile, and then he moves to kiss me good-bye on the cheek. Into my ear, he whispers, "The Beatles song is always for you."

Alone at the table with Jeff, I watch Rob and Dave make a few final adjustments. "So that's Rob," I say.

"Nice kid." Jeff rolls a gum wrapper into a little ball and tosses it toward the center of the table. "You said his wife died?"

"Yeah. Seven years ago. Brain tumor."

"Sad." He picks up my loaf of bread. "What's he going to do?"

"What do you mean?" I rest my hands on the table. "I think he's doing it."

"This doesn't seem like a real life—" Jeff cracks his gum. "Plus, it was *seven* years ago."

"This is a real life." I feel my cheeks redden. "Some people really *hurt*—seven years can feel like yesterday."

Jeff puts down the bread and reaches out to touch my arm. "I mean, what does he *want*? What's he doing with his life?"

My skin is hot. Why does everyone keep asking me what everyone wants? I shake my head. "I don't know. I have no clue. Rob would probably like a record deal. I'd like to write the Great American Novel. I suppose both of us will eventually settle down with different people and have 2.5 children apiece. I don't know, Jeff; I don't know—"

"Relax, Sybil. You're a little defensive." He caresses my arm. "Lighten up."

I blow air through my lips. "Jeff, isn't there such a thing as just *living*? Some people exist without having definitive plans. Must there always be a *plan*? Why can't Rob just do what he's doing?" I look at his fingers moving across my arm. "Do you and I have a plan, Jeff?"

His fingers freeze. He whispers, "Would you like one?"

I look into his eyes. They are, after all, the eyes of a kind man. I see it in the smoky centers, the soft sable pupils. He waits for me to speak, waits for me to love him. "No," I say, and he removes his hand from my arm. "But, Jeff." I see I've hurt him. He withdraws, sitting up straight and resuming his status as stoic beauty. "It's the *plan* that bothers me. It's not you—I like what we have."

We have nothing.

"Okay." He smiles at me, distant now.

Madeline arrives, sitting down heavily. "Can I have a stick of gum, Snuffy? I don't want to stink—especially if Rob comes over and sings to me." Jeff hands her a stick of gum.

Glass Half Empty begins playing late, around 11:30. Rob sings well. His voice is tinny, like an echo in a cave, sweet and sour, the fifties but now. I spy on Jeff, who sways gently next to me. I sneak a glance at Madeline, who casts forlorn eyes on Dave Stomps. Rob is playful, bouncy, a showman, a sudden songster. After five songs, he croons into the mike, "We're not a cover band, but we play the Beatles."

Then, with confession in his voice and flourish in his gesture, he sings "Hey Jude."

I suck in the song, hungry for messages. So what if Jude is a guy? Rob speaks in metaphors—a man acquainted with figurative language. He's well-read, allegorical, allusive, symbolic. I rise and fall with each note, letting Jeff Simon touch me gently on my shoulder, wondering if anyone knows this is for me. Do they know? Can they tell? Jeff's hand on me is weightless. I don't feel it. Madeline sings along. I'm naked, a woman sung to, burdened by lyrics he didn't write but spreads like gospel.

When he finishes, it's like putting my clothes back on after a sordid night.

We say good-night to Glass Half Empty.

"I *really* enjoyed the show," Jeff says.

"I'm glad we finally met," Rob answers.

And they shake hands again.

TWELVE

ABSCESS
THE MISSING TAMPON STORY

SYBIL WEATHERFIELD FOR *NEW YORK SHOCK*

From Friday, March 17, 1995

Taste is for the birds; let's get real.

Once upon a time, at a very dull temp job, nature called. Bored out of my skull, the only things I looked forward to were frequent trips to the bathroom and Diet Coke with lunch.

Alone in the toilet, finding my tampon string proved impossible. Well, I couldn't exactly spend the entire day searching. Though I had a date later, there'd be time to look after—quote unquote—"work." Until then, in the words of the great Rolling Stones, let it bleed.

I got home at 6:24 p.m., and I had to be out the door at 7:15 to meet a guy on the Upper West Side for a movie: no champagne toast at the Rainbow Room, no poached salmon at Le Cirque. Well, I *did* eat a big lunch. This would be our second date. I didn't really want to eat in front of him anyway.

I headed into my bathroom, the lavatory, the loo. Searched. Nothing. Nada. Zilch.

I'm not in touch with my body. I'd rather take a pass, thank you very much.

Once, when I was in Atlantic City trying to communicate with God through gambling, a friend of mine who doesn't wear underwear declared, "I think I just got my period." We'd been walking along the boardwalk, discussing things like sitcom television and the future of rap music. Seagulls landed on wooden planks, gobbled stray puffs of corn, touched off again, disappearing into the majestic New Jersey horizon.

I looked for the Taj Mahal casino. "There are *millions* of hotels around—they carry tampons." Where's Donald Trump when you need him?

"I'll be fine. I'll use toilet paper."

"Huh?"

The squeamish are thinking, *This is more than I need to know.* But it isn't.

"I *know* my body, and I can just roll up toilet paper," she said.

Is this the part of the dream where I say to myself, *Wake up, wake up, wake up*?

Apparently she performed an origami-toilet paper trick in the restroom. Afterward we obsessed about slots and blackjack. Then we ate a big, honkin' buffet (breaded chicken, do-it-yourself tostadas, peach cobbler, antipasto salad) before driving home at eight.

This story takes on whole new meaning when you remember she doesn't wear underwear.

Imagine knowing your body so well. *Don't make me!*

So, at 6:30 p.m., pre-date, I wasn't exactly pulling out the dental mirrors.

Having failed to find anything, I called my friend who doesn't wear underwear. "Show Stopper [not her real name], dire straits. I can't find the string from the tampon I stuck in this morning. I'm gonna die of toxic shock any moment."

Show Stopper was quiet.
Then, "Aren't you bleeding all over?"

"No, it's the end."

"I'll tell you what you have to do."

"What?" I stood in front of the full-length mirror I'd bought at Woolworth's.

"Go touch your cervix."

"What?" I scowled. "I don't even know where my cervix is."

"Go look, Sybil. You'll feel better. You'll see how small it is and how a tampon couldn't possibly fit through there."

"So it's not just floating around my body?" I had a fistful of my own hair in my hand.

"No, you took it out. You don't remember."

"I'd remember, Show Stopper. I never lose anything, not even my keys."

"Go touch your cervix."

"If I don't call tomorrow, I'm dead."

We hung up. I dragged my feet into the loo. With dread, I searched for my cervix. I was just a little too Presbyterian for this.

Alas, no string! And about this cervix . . . *Wake up, wake up, wake up.*

I decided to call my mom to say good-bye. It was now 7:01 p.m. I put on lipstick, just in case I had to run.

"Are you sure you didn't take it out at work?" she asked.

"I'm sure."

"And you're sure you put it in?"

"Yes, I totally remember."

"What's the name of that doctor friend of yours?"

"Julie?"

My mom sighed. "Call her to come over to take a look. She can pull it out."

I let these words sink in. "Mom, I'd rather die."

"Well, honey, I don't know what else to tell you."

"Let's face it. I'm gonna die." I grabbed my purse and stuck a granola bar in for the subway. "I love you. I love Dad. 'Bye."

"This is good-bye?"

"This is good-bye." I kicked off my heels and slipped on a pair of slinky black boots. "Burn my letters."

Out the door and onto the subway headed uptown by 7:15, feeling like Marlo Thomas. I was a regular city slicker, urban legend, mover and shaker, just a little sore from searching for my cervix.

My date was waiting on Broadway and Sixty-eighth. "It's going to rain," he said. "We'd better get inside."

In the theater, we hiked up on an array of escalators. "You want a drink? Candy?" Boy Toy [not his real name] asked.

"No, I'm okay. Thanks." I don't like to binge so early in the relationship.

I don't remember how long we sat there or what we said. The movie began. I was so preoccupied with the missing tampon that I couldn't concentrate on the story. I could only picture myself dead, in bed, in the morning. My roommate Elevator Music [not his real name] would find me when he came home from work. Earlier, he would've thought I was just sleeping in. At the autopsy, they'd discover the tampon. By then, it would've migrated to my brain.

Cause of death: *Missing Tampon.*

After the movie, it was pouring. Boy Toy lived farther north. Walking to the subway station, we held newspapers over our heads. "Wet," he said.

"Yep," I answered.

"It was good seeing you," he added.

"Good seeing you too," I agreed.

"Well, 'bye." Water dripped off the corners of his newspaper. The sky crackled and growled. Around us, people in rain jackets opened umbrellas. The streets smelled like wet dog, human feces, and fried egg.

"'Bye." I'm sick and tired of dating men who don't take me home. So what if I'll be fine? Don't we live in New York Fucking City? Isn't it raining? Isn't it past ten? I'm wearing heels, for God's sake! Just once, it would be nice to have some guy escort me back to my place. Even if it's out of his way.

Whoops. I slipped into the present tense. Sorry.

I made my way into the bowels of the New York City subway system, where getting raped or killed is always a possibility. Maybe I'd die of toxic shock while waiting for the 1 or 9.

But I made it home. Because I could. Because I was strong, independent, a career girl, et cetera. At 11:21 p.m., I searched for the tampon again. No luck. I got into bed and slept amazingly well.

In the morning, much to my surprise, I was alive. At work, I did something gross. Sucking in air, pushing back sleeves, I examined garbage. I rummaged through disgusting oddities, pretending I was an archaeologist in Egypt. Digging and exploring, I saw it. *There,* in its original wrapper, was the tampon dispenser. I pulled the fucker out of its plastic tomb. Wrapped decently, in all its glory, was its defective cotton self. I was never wearing a tampon at all!

Boy Toy and I didn't go out again. I look back nostalgically at the way he kindly offered me candy and covered my hair with newspapers in the rain. But cervixes, caverns, gaping wounds, things that bleed—they stood between us. And I'm still not in touch with my body.

THIRTEEN

ANTIBIOTICS 3

FROM *NEW YORK SHOCK*

From Friday, March 24, 1995

You're the Indiana Jones of Feminine Hygiene.

—Cari, West Village

I'd like to know more about communicating with God through gambling.

—Tina, West Village

FOURTEEN

Cows

Wednesday, April 5, 1995

I sit on my bed, *Shock* copies all around. I reach out and press the button, listening to the answering-machine message one more time: "Sybil, it's Fred." Fred is my managing editor at *New York Shock*. I like this man. He gets the prize for being my all-time favorite boss, but he thinks I'm a little *out there*. Plus, he won't introduce me to his children. "Personally, I think the tampon column is gross, but people—the women—are loving it. *God bless the women.* Nine out of ten calls and letters are from the ladies. Do an ob-gyn bit. I know it's been done, but you and stirrups. What do you know about nuns?" Fred's a middle-aged family man. "How old were you when you started to shave?" The machine cuts him off. He calls back. "Anyway, it's good. Sick and wrong, but *good*."

Sick and wrong, but good.

People have been telling me I'm good for a while. When they say this, they're always talking about my writing.

In third grade, I presented my parents with an orange construction-paper pumpkin with a curly green stem. Written in black Magic Marker in loopy handwriting across its unlined surface, a whimsical tale unfolded across the space of three not-so-bad paragraphs. There was a witch named Shara in the story, and she had a black cat, because witches do. They rode through the raven-colored night on a broomstick, dodging falling stars. Shara cast witchy spells and blended purple potions and smelly brews. Of course, she was a good witch. She often moonlighted as the Tooth Fairy, giving her second cousin the night off.

All through elementary school, whenever I got new stationery, I pulled out a piece of scented or decorated paper along with its matching envelope, and I wrote myself a long letter. I did this because I was a collector, and I wanted to save the pretty new stationery with the kitten design or the Monet at Giverny print on the cover. I'd tell myself a little bit about me. I'd write instructions on the sealed envelope: *To a Girl with Blond Hair and Blue Eyes, Open This on Your Thirtieth Birthday*. Which, at the time, seemed like a million years away.

My hair turned brown in junior high; my eyes are not blue anymore. I'm thirty. I opened the letter some months ago, and in it, I had written, *I want to be a writer*. I was only ten when I said that. I don't know where this came from—I don't know what made me think it was something I could do.

I never expressed the desire to be a veterinarian, which all the other kids seemed to want to do. Horses were okay.

In high school, I coedited an underground newspaper called

What's Up? No remaining copies exist, and that's fine—we were in it for the money. Sometimes I reviewed books, labeling them "riveting" and "groundbreaking."

Living in a dorm room as a college girl, I had a mirror-and-desk combo. I'd darken the room except for the lone lightbulb hanging above the desk, illuminating the space like a flashlight in a cave. While I did homework, I could look myself in the eye. I could tell myself off; I could sing myself songs; I could close my eyes and hope I'd go away. I'd wear UCLA sweatpants, but my feet would always be bare and a little dirty. I'd drink a can of Diet Dr. Pepper, watching myself as I took a swig, pretending I was a lush, pretending I was Dorothy Parker or maybe Ernest Hemingway in Spain and my aluminum can was actually a wineskin. Suddenly, even in my sloppiness, I was beautiful. The props helped: I was a wordsmith, a linguist, *a writer.* I'd play New Romantic rock 'n' roll that Lord Byron and Percy Bysshe Shelley would have liked had they been alive.

And I'd write. I'd spend hours under that bulb, choosing words with the deliberation necessary for treading water: a synchronization of gesture, a concentration of energy. Stories about girls obsessed with bad boys, stories about bad boys ignoring obsessed girls. The setting was always a dorm; the kids were always sad. But articulate—obsessed, articulate girls and bad, articulate boys. Either way, sad.

A poem was published in the undergrad literary journal, and my parents and brother drove up to L.A. to hear it at a UCLA reading. This is the poem:

Cows

I like cows because they wear bells
and what can be more pleasant
than the sound of a moo
a brilliant sound
for a beast with soft spotted skin
and udders that are almost human.

I don't like chickens
those wild chickens
because they flutter
God, they flutter
like nervous wrecks
and their hearts beat so fast.
Where are the calm cows?
Get the chickens off the dance floor
and let us dance
in the moonlit barnyard
to music from the fifties.

After the UCLA reading, we ate dinner at the Cheesecake Hut in Santa Monica. I wore a backless, acid-washed denim dress. Very sexy, except I looked flat as a board. I had a boyfriend, another tortured poet, but he wasn't around. He had some bad-boy things to which he had to attend. The UCLA editors misspelled *Weatherfield* in the journal, christening me *Sybil Wetherfield*, but I didn't care. I was very happy, and my parents were very proud. Cows today, sonnets tomorrow.

Now, in early April, I still like that poem, though real poets have told me—in nice ways—it sucks. But the chickens still get me. I read it, and the chickens still make me smile. Oh, I like those fluttering chickens. Boy, I like them a lot.

Now, in early April, I'm a columnist. Sometimes, after I see whether or not I've won the Lotto on the Saturday-night news (I buy *one* Lotto ticket, because I'm convinced that winning has more to do with divine intervention than with odds), I'll write out elaborate and colorful scenarios, sketch out complex and psychologically damaged characters, list bold words and vibrant phrases I like (*pomegranate, red crab legs, suction cup, lordly*). I have pipe dreams of novels; these have replaced letters to myself. Someday I'll write one.

FIFTEEN

Struggling Artistes

Friday, April 7, 1995

Directly across the street from Benji's Quesadillas in the West Village, there's a coffee shop called the Gay Purée. If I'm going somewhere and I'm in a hurry, that's where I eat dinner. Despite whatever its name may suggest, it's a diner catering to old men with newspapers and business types wanting egg sandwiches to go; on the counters, glass dishes display stale seven-layer cakes.

It's Friday night at eight, and "The Missing Tampon Story," already old, lies open before Rob Shachtley, dressed in gold lamé. He eats coleslaw in our Gay Purée booth.

I pick at my turkey club and pickle spear. "What they say about the newspaper business is so true." I tap "Abscess" with a finger. "That's old news. I'm on to something else already." I'm telling him he should ignore this column.

"This is about Jeff?" He looks up from *New York Shock*.

"Yeah." I yawn and stretch my arms on the back of the red vinyl booth. "Do I need to explain?"

"So where is he?" he asks between bites. "I'm pretty sure he'd walk you home if it were raining. Plus, Jeff's kinda astute—he could tell if you were upset about something."

I trace a fry through a patch of salt. "Jeff's the tampon. He's the *tampon*, Rob."

He eats another bite slowly, staring at me. His jaw moves in small circles, his eyes fixed on mine. He swallows and wipes his mouth. "Jeff's the *tampon*?"

"Doesn't it make *some* sense?" I tilt my head. "Just a little?"

Rob thinks. "Well, in a crazy way."

I turn red. This is Sybil Weatherfield at her best: analytical, quirky, sardonic, gloomy. "Think about it, Rob—it's *perfect*! The tampon's a great metaphor for our hapless, utilitarian relationship." I pause. "You need 'em, but don't like 'em. In fact, out of sight, out of mind. Downright gross. In this case, altogether unnecessary. And where was it after all that?" I look at him victoriously. "In the *garbage*!" I fold my arms across my chest. "The tampon was in the *garbage* the whole time!"

It appears that Rob is speechless. He takes another bite of the now-soupy coleslaw. He finishes his iced tea. When he finally speaks, an ice cube rattles around his mouth, smacking into his teeth. "The way your mind works . . ." He trails off, the ice cube making his cheek bulge. I watch him carefully, because my cerebral deliberations are a sensitive subject. "What does Jeff think when he reads this? Or how about your roommate? *Elevator Music*, for God's sake! Or *Show Stopper*? What does Madeline think about this?" He makes sucking noises with a straw at the bottom of his glass. "And why am I never in 'Abscess'?" More slurping. "I should be in 'Abscess.' You've never—not even once—written about me."

From the diner window, I see that Benji's Quesadillas across the street is a happening place. Young couples clutch each other in some hilarious shared joke as they pass my front door. The bars on my basement windows remind me of Laverne and Shirley's apartment in Milwaukee. I leave Rob inside the Gay Purée to remember a time when a visiting friend from California slept on my old couch for a week. I remember how she heard a guy puke outside my window, retching fiercely, bending over, emptying an obscene blend onto my walkway—and I slept through it, unable to decipher his sounds from other New York sounds that lull me to sleep: the rumble of the subway through my walls, the click-clack of high heels, laughing young women drunk on margaritas. I look at my brownstone, where intoxicated yuppies sometimes urinate in my doorway on weekends. I smell it on Saturday mornings when I leave to grocery shop at the A&P. My mind sifts through the details—

"What do these people think?" Rob interrupts my nomadic hovering over West Village sidewalks. "Are you hurting them with what you write?"

I prickle. "*Hurting* them? You think I'm *hurting* them?"

Rob fidgets, adjusting his glasses on the bridge of his nose, brushing his hair back. "Well, I don't know. You tell me."

"Madeline doesn't care." I stop. "And Tom's in Greece—" My voice is a screech.

"Don't get crazy, Syb—"

"Jeff thinks it's all fiction." I put my hands on the table. "That's what I tell him."

The waitress takes away our plates. "Two coffees." Rob looks up at her.

"Often, it *is* all fiction."

"He doesn't wonder why you never have a boyfriend in your column? He doesn't wonder where his presence is? I mean, I wonder about mine. How come he doesn't wonder about his?"

I look at my fingernails. "You know how it is. I'm protecting our privacy." I smile. "We're like rock stars."

"He doesn't wonder why your love life is *always* bad?"

I twist the ring around my finger. "I'm very funny. He thinks I'm very funny. I make him laugh." I run my tongue over my lips. "I can say whatever I want. As long I'm funny." I picture Jeff walking somewhere in the Financial District, London Fog belt slapping against his long legs. He whistles. *New York Shock* is tucked under his arm. He can't wait to read what his bohemian-living-in-squalor girlfriend has to say now. Will she attack a time-honored tradition? Will she be uncouth, distasteful, *naughty*? Jeff Simon rides the elevator high; he snaps his fingers as he parades past the receptionist from the Bronx; when he enters his glass-walled office, he closes the heavy glass door behind him. Spreading the paper across his big desk, he reads with a grin. But the grin freezes. It congeals because he wonders things. *Why is she so unhappy, so desperate, so* unmerciful*?* And, finally, he thinks: *She Doesn't Love Me*.

Rob closes *Shock*. "I hope you're not hurting anyone." He folds the paper carefully. "You can be *acerbic*."

The waitress puts down the coffees. I'm stung. Rob slides over a bowl of creamers.

"Maybe that's why I never write about you." I pull a spoon through my lips. "I don't want to hurt you."

We sit silently, trying to figure out what I mean.

There's this moment, this delicate second between us—like when I knew he was jealous at Sin-é. We feel a *difference* in how we feel about each other in contrast to how we feel about others.

I continue, "I don't think I'm *hurting* Jeff, am I?"

Rob speaks softly. "I don't know, Syb."

"Rob, we're artists." I'm smug and ironic. "You know that." This week, *Shock* features a section on performance art: its sociological and philosophical impact on modernity. "Anything for my art." I blow on the coffee. "My artistic agenda makes sense of my temping and all the crap that goes with it." I smirk but sound gloomy. "Since I'm an artist, it's okay that I can't hold down a job or get a man to love me for longer than it takes to walk a dog around the block."

"Neither of us left home to pursue artistic freedom, Syb." He smirks but sounds gloomy too. "I wish we could say we did—but we can't."

"But maybe we've both found refuge in artistic freedom."

"Or maybe it's just an excuse."

I swallow hard. "'Abscess' suits me, Rob. I want to write about tampons—I don't want to mince words. I don't want to be careful." I shake my head, closing my eyes. "I'm not hurting Jeff. Jeff thinks this is a funny column about a missing tampon."

Rob is quiet.

The waitress puts the check down.

"You write like a temp, Sybil."

I'm quick to respond. "You're a temp too."

Rob says nothing and pulls out his wallet.

"Let's just be struggling artistes, okay?" I take money from my purse. "We'll make *art.* Who cares if we temp?" I place a few bucks on the table. "We're *different.*" I take a swallow of my water and put the cup down in a wet spot.

Rob slides out of the booth. "Let's go."

I stand, and Rob helps me with my coat. "Should we bring something?" I ask. Glass Half Empty is playing at the Fedora at midnight, and miscellaneous artists and Glass Half Empty fans are holding a preshow party in a warehouse-turned-apartment near CBGB. "I've got some coffee beans we could give them. They're at my place—it'll only take a sec."

Rob twitches his nose. "Nah. I've seen what you've got. That Costa Rican Moonbeam Blend and Zimbabwe Mulberry shit." He pulls out a goofy Holden Caulfield hunting hat. "Let's not." He pushes me toward the door. "Let's just go."

We walk to the Bowery. On our way, we pass people protesting the onslaught of Starbucks Coffee. They're taking over the world, sprouting on every street corner, growing like fungus, seducing innocents just like Walgreens and soy milk have done already. Soon everyone will be drinking uniform cups of coffee and partaking of all kinds of national averages. The protesters scream, "Shut 'em down! Support local cafés!" It's like witnessing an alien landing. I sympathize, I really do. But, wow. How surreal to see disparate sorts band together in order to rid the world of all those inexcusable coffee beans in one big store.

Ho-hum, I think.

Having passed the Starbucks protest, we get to the Bowery building. A homeless man lies in the gutter by the door, looking ravaged: black ashy spots like mold on his face and hands, torn clothes the color of dirty dishwater, a smell like a sports-arena toilet. He may be dead. I stop in my tracks—everything a whir of photographic images: young yuppie couples outside Benji's, red vinyl booths in the Gay Purée, my Laverne-and-Shirley basement barred windows, the Starbucks demonstration, a dead man on the street. I stop and can't remember how to walk. Rob, a pace in front of me, turns like Lot's wife must have done before becoming salt. He stands still too; he reaches his hand out and whispers, "Sybil." I take my eyes off the dead man. I take his hand in mine, and we pass the dead man to ring the doorbell. "He's just drunk," Rob says.

Tailgating for rockers. Everyone's with the band.

Rob and I squeeze onto a couch next to the lead singer of Atrocious Deformity, a punk-rock group that Rob says is pretty good. They sing "Cat Got Your Tongue."

A literary publicist tells me about Salman Rushdie, whom she met for salads at the Boathouse Café in Central Park. Meanwhile, Rob talks to the manager of Milkbone about a major label. "I met him once," the publicist says of Rushdie, and I move my head to watch the words come out of her lips. "He does exclusive readings. Comes out of exile for a little book signing."

"What's he like?" I peek over my beer into her sparkly world.

"Kinda sexy—in a Vladimir Lenin way." The woman, tall and angular, puts a Triscuit with cheese into her mouth. I watch her chew. I think biblical thoughts; I think of the gnashing of teeth.

Like Alice falling through the hole and Dorothy whisked away by the tornado, I'm in. The mysterious, forbidden, sensual world of celebrity opens before me. I see book-signing parties at SPY Bar, readings at KGB. I look at Rob and see rock concerts at Irving Plaza and benefits for the Third World at Carnegie Hall. Artists all over, none of them struggling. Parties at Le Bar Bat, the Bitter End. Cabs, tipping, private cars. Blintzes at Kiev and Veselka—three a.m., weeknights.

Everywhere you look: artists with stories to tell, stories about being undiscovered, on the verge, latent, dormant, hopeful.

Suddenly I'm sick. An overpowering nausea washes over me. I'm physically shaking. I pull my body away from Rob, not wanting him to feel me tremble. I have the urge to call Jeff, who's in Nantucket with buddies/colleagues/associates, and I want to ask him how he's doing, if he's okay.

"Will you excuse me for a sec?" I say to the publicist, standing. "I'll be right back."

Rob looks concerned. "You okay?" He thinks I'm going to hurl. And I may.

"Yeah, I'll be right back." I search for the bathroom, walking through the party. There are no doors or walls in the warehouse-apartment, only gauzy cloth dividers hanging from high ceilings and pipe rafters. White bookshelves segment the vast emptiness into separate rooms. Very postmodern with this questioning of space and presence of housing doubt. I pass incomprehensible paintings and a coffee table with four TV sets, one on each corner, all tuned to different channels, all facing out, no sound from any of them. An ominous blue light from an unknown source illuminates the galactic backdrop. As I hunt for the toilet, the gauzy dividers dance in provocative routines and the shelves create a maze straight out of *The Shining*. I'm worried, anxious, nauseated. My head spins—like that of the girl in *The Exorcist*. I'm a nervous wreck, and I feel guilty too. I can't find the damn toilet. Traffic jam in my brain: I'm afraid of death—this place makes me afraid to die. There's a dead man on the threshold. I'm going to vomit.

Finally, the bathroom.

I have to wait by a strip of gauze in the threatening blue light for two supermodels to hurry up and pee. A breeze from somewhere makes the gauze fly up and cling to my legs. The shelves don't even have any books on them. My God, why are there no books on the shelves?

When it's my turn, I go inside, flip on a light, and lock the door. The bathroom is reassuringly normal with a light switch above an electrical outlet and pale pink porcelain fixtures. I lift the toilet seat with fingertips, run them under the faucet like a good clean freak, bend over, hold my hair, force a few fingers into my mouth, and gag till it works, till junk food has been expelled, till my stomach is as empty as this postmodern pad, till I'm like the stranger puking outside my brownstone, till I've forgotten my fear of death and the guilt surrounding my treatment of Jeff Simon with my acerbic dip into the art world. Afterward, standing before the quiet mirror, I splash cold water on my face, rinse my mouth, and spit. I look into the nonjudgmental mirror and take my leave.

When I return, Rob speaks to a stranger. He's talking to Focaccia, the lead singer of Dollar Movie. Also represented are Demi's Double D's, No Plans for Marriage, and the Sugar Plum Fairies. I see Dave Stomps in the distance, standing next to his wife. They sip from big cans of beer. Rob has his hands between his gold knees. I listen absently to his conversation with Focaccia, a handsome man in a weird, possibly horrifying, way—he's gothic, dark, purposely tragic. A little Steven Tyler, a little Bette Davis.

"Your manager's name is Paul McGuiness?" Rob asks. "Isn't that U2's manager?"

"They're not the same person." Focaccia grins. "Different guys, same name. Sometimes *our* Paul McGuiness fakes an Irish accent, though."

"Isn't that illegal?" Rob asks.

Focaccia lifts a chicken wing to his mouth. "To be Irish?" He sucks the wing and drops the bone into his plate. "Let me get beer." He walks away.

I turn to Rob with raised eyebrows. "Focaccia!" I repeat the guy's name.

Rob rests his chin in his hand. "Yeah, I've got a problem with that. You can't just name someone *Focaccia*." He scratches his chin.

"Does everyone here have a record deal, Rob?" I ask.

"No, but they all want one." We whisper to each other.

"What will become of them?" I mumble, thinking about Jeff at Sin-é when he asked me about having a plan. Do these people have plans? Don't they want one? Are they merely existing in the moment—this myopic, unreal, fantastical, faux-postmodern moment? Don't they know what's behind those gauze curtains? And now I'm thinking about the Wizard of Oz, and what's behind the curtain. . . .

Rob focuses on my face. I'm the girl who decries plans, claims artistic freedom. "They'll play cornfests, chili cook-offs, Groundhog Day celebrations. Some will have lifetime careers with little fame or fortune. Others will go back to school. A few will paint houses or lay carpet. One or two will write incredible songs, entire symphonies."

"What about you?" I whisper. "What are you going to do?"

"I don't know," he whispers back. "We're temps, Syb."

Focaccia returns. I feel Focaccia staring at me, sizing me up in a discomforting way. There's something pornographic about it. I consider resting my hand on Rob's thigh, but I don't. Focaccia hands me a card. I take it, noticing he's wearing eyeliner. I read: *Focaccia Green. Poet/Singer. Ten years of experience. In catering. Call 212/989-5200.*

And then I decide. I decide to use my artistic freedom, to forgo any obligation to truth. I wince at my own existence, my temporary freehold on life; I wince and accept the consequences of a temp ethic. Looking at Focaccia's card, I say, "This is your redemption." I'm pithy, glittery, not like me at all. "Without it, you're just a man wearing makeup."

"Funny girl." He addresses Rob. "You know you're with a funny girl?" Focaccia looks at me. "What d'you do?" His voice is full of sex the way Daisy's was full of money.

"You're at a party with a bunch of musicians who couldn't care less about their jobs. You're asking me what I *do*? Ask me something else—something intriguing."

Rob still has his hands between his knees. His face is red.

Focaccia says, "Who *are* you?"

Rob spins in my direction, apparently wanting to hear who I am.

"Sybil. Sybil Weatherfield." I lower my voice. I speak in soft, seductive cadences. I'm making myself sick.

"I've read your work." The lead singer of Dollar Movie also speaks in low tones. "You're psycho." He licks his lips, adding, "In a good way. I like psycho women." Focaccia tosses his head toward Rob. "Are you two together?"

Rob quickly answers in a slightly vicious pitch. "She can go home with you if that's what she wants."

"I go home alone." I put an elbow into Rob's side.

Without blinking, Focaccia continues, "Are you a—" He pauses before continuing, "*starfucker*?"

Well, you know you're in trouble then. Rob radiates heat beside me. Focaccia awaits clever banter. I say, "That's not how I'd put—"

Rob interjects. "Focaccia," he says, "she's my *friend*." He breathes heavily through flaring nostrils. "Come on. Can't you find someone else to—?"

Just then, the bassist for Demi's Double D's calls, "Focaccia, come here, man."

When we're alone, Rob stutters, "What the *hell* was that?"

There's this party around us, but we're squeezed together on a puke-green couch. Party noise is distant, and silhouettes of singers and people we know blur in hazy blue. "Rob." I turn to him on the couch and see him staring into my face. He's blazing from that strange fugue. I see the rage in his eyes, burrowing deeply in lines on his forehead. I repeat his name: "Rob." When I see his face, so intent, so fixed, so committed, my breathing slows and I want to see only him, hear only him, block out the surroundings of this gathering of artists. I look at Rob blinking in confusion, and I have a compulsion to do something curious on this strange night of mixed messages and possible infidelities. I reach up and touch his face. I put my hand on his cheek. I'm surprised to feel the slight sandpaper texture of warm skin under my palm. I didn't expect this. I don't know what I expected—maybe something less gender-specific. "It was," I shake my head side to side, "*nothing*." I feel so conscious of touching him. "It was absolutely *nothing*." Like one-night stands, like temp jobs. Nothing.

The party, the party for Glass Half Empty, whirls around us. I don't know what Rob's thinking. I think about kissing Rob Shachtley. I look into his heated face; I feel the temperature of his cheek.

"You flirted with him." A sharpness in his voice. Kissing is not on his mind.

"It was banter, badminton." I remove my hand from his cheek.

He takes his glasses off; he can't see a thing without them. "It qualified as bona-fide cheating. You crossed the line." He puts his glasses back on. "It was *filthy*."

"It was empty." I pause. "Rob, I was *playing*."

Dave Stomps steps up to the puke-green couch. "You two look like you're talking about serious stuff. Nietzsche? Proust? Aristide?"

Rob and I simultaneously turn to the drummer. A silver suit.

He looks like the Tin Woodsman. We're all about Oz tonight. Rob uncrosses gold legs. Silver and gold. Rob's disgusted. I smile at Dave. Dave, unwittingly, smiles at us. Rob looks stunned. "Are we gonna rock tonight, or what?" Dave asks.

Rob mutters, "We should probably go." He stands.

I reach my hands up to him. "Help me?"

He grabs my hands and pulls my body to a standing position, releases me, and wipes his hands on his gold lamé pants!

That night, I sip Sprite and wait for Glass Half Empty to play while I sit with the members of Atrocious Deformity. Rob's last song is "Norwegian Wood (This Bird Has Flown)." I watch him sing, embarrassed and hurt.

I have a heavy kind of sadness; there's difficulty in locating it. While he sings, I keep thinking about the ravaged guy in the gutter and the four TVs on the coffee table, the way they were turned on without sound. At the end of the set, I check my watch and briefly picture Rob walking out on a girl in the middle of the night. In my head, he always checks his watch before leaving. He waits till the girl's asleep. He pulls the covers off. He dresses soundlessly. Quietly, he steps through a silent house. When he reaches the door, he checks the time.

Then my mind shifts, and I see that dead man in the Bowery. It's a heavy kind of sadness.

SIXTEEN

Hildy in Maine

Thursday, April 20, 1995

Yesterday the Alfred P. Murrah Federal Building in Oklahoma City was bombed. One hundred and sixty-eight people are dead.

I'm left alone for hours and hours sometimes, just me and my lemon poppy-seed muffin. Assigned to an office near the mail room—out of the way—someone, somewhere, must have said, "Go. Get a temp!" No one refused; no one declared it unnecessary, a waste of money, extraneous. Instead someone called my agency, Temps Like That. And here I am: just like that.

Despite the fact that one hundred and sixty-eight people died yesterday, I'm not at all baffled to find myself discontent over the fact that I'm alive and extraneous. I learn very little from the death all around me.

As a body filling space, what I do is of no concern to anyone. And, suddenly, I don't want to do anything. So I guess it works out after all.

This is what I do.

I work long and hard at tearing a drinking hole into my plastic coffee lid. This takes so much effort that by the time I'm done, there are tiny beads of sweat along my hairline and I have chapped lips and no lipstick left because I've been running my tongue all around the outside of my mouth. Finally, when the coffee's lukewarm and the lid is simply disposed of due to massive crater-sized ruptures in its spill-proof surface, I slip a floppy disk into the computer. Today is the day I'll finally write my brother a proper letter. I'm gonna type it.

On the first morning I was here (I've been here for two weeks already), I ate seven doughnuts and threw up in the bathroom: powdered sugar, jelly-filled, honey-glazed, chocolate rolled in nuts, orange sprinkles, two devil's food. This job will last till the middle of May, for much of the spring. There should be additional free doughnuts.

I take minutes at their board meetings. When I distribute them, my boss, the vice president of programs and special events, reads what I've written and says, "Bravo."

Every morning, he asks me to turn on the light in his office so it's ready for him. Really so it looks like he's there when he isn't.

Last week, I made Madeline come with me to an evening reception because I had to write a blurb about it for the company newsletter. Board members, most of them well over sixty-five, floated in and out of dark conference rooms, sipping wine and eating vegetable sticks. A rumor persisted that the UN secretary-general was going to show. Holding a tiny plate of chilled shrimp, Madeline looked at all the strings of pearls and powder-blue dresses and piles of hair on the tops of heads resembling Wilma Flintstone's. With steady, weary eyes, she droned, "I've never seen so many corpses before in my entire life."

I didn't know whether I was *embarrassed* or *amused*.

This is what I do.

My boss calls me into his office. He's behind his oak desk; I'm in a soft leather chair. He weaves his fingers together on top of paperwork. I hold a yellow legal pad on my lap while examining his diplomas and the pictures of his wife and kids. His handkerchief matches his tie; both seem to be made of silk. "What did you find challenging about yesterday?" His expression is earnest but condescending. It's like I'm a little girl who's been summoned into the principal's office. I remember how I was taught to spell *principal* and *principle* in third grade. The princi*pal* was my *pal*. In front of me, the vice president of programs and special events uses careful diction and a simple vocabulary so I can understand.

My legs are crossed; a legal pad balances on my knee. "Do you want me to be honest?"

My boss, who admires my note-taking skills, nods his head. "Please."

I write for *New York Shock*. I don't want to mince words—I don't want to be careful. "I didn't find anything challenging," I say. "You need someone to accomplish tasks, and that's what I do."

My response surprises him. For a full minute, he doesn't say a thing. He stares at me in silence. Apparently I've rendered him speechless. And then, "You can go now."

I call Rob when I'm alone. Maybe he's not working. Maybe he's there.

He answers on the third ring. "Hello?"

"Rob Shachtley, Sybil Weatherfield. What are you doing? Tell me now." I hold the phone with one hand and a pen with the other, so if someone walks by, I'm okay.

"I was just debating whether I should clean my bathtub today or tomorrow. You?"

Does he hold a sponge? Is he wearing rubber gloves? Are his glasses steamed up? "I'm working." I twist the phone cord in my fingers. "Don't laugh."

A man in a suit passes my office, does a double-take, walks in, flips through Hildy's mail (I'm at Hildy's desk), and whistles.

"Hi," I say. "Hildy's in Maine."

"She needs a vacation." He smiles, leaving.

"Sorry," I say to Rob. "Stranger Danger. He's gone. What was I saying?"

"You're working."

"What are you wearing?" I ask.

"Gray sweatpants and a U Mass sweatshirt."

I try to picture him. He's definitely holding a sponge. "Are you standing or sitting?"

"I'm now sitting," he says.

"I've never seen you in sweats," I say.

"I make it a policy: *Never Be Seen in Sweats*."

"Why?" I study Hildy's family pictures. Two boys, a non-descript husband, a Long Island suburb.

"I wear cheap suits. That's why. I'd like for you, right now, to envision me in a suit, okay? Make it blue. Navy blue. That's what I like."

"I wish I could see you in sweatpants," I moan.

He doesn't say anything. I listen to him breathe. I sneak a sip of lukewarm coffee, getting luker. "You *can't*, Syb. It has very little to do with you," he finally says.

"Why, Rob?" I remember touching his cheek at the party.

"Just because. Think of me in a cheap suit. Okay?"

I change the subject because we're uncomfortable. "You know what temping requires of me?"

"What?"

"Guess."

"I can't."

"Absolutely nothing." I play with an empty creamer. "If I'm lucky, they'll call me back tomorrow." I sniffle. "What do you think of that?"

"Syb, are you about to freak out?"

"I'm waiting for Calgon to take me away." I hear him moving. "You're moving. I hear you." I sort Hildy's mail, separating advertisements into piles.

"I'm in the kitchen. I'm pouring myself water."

I envision him carrying his glass back to the couch, wearing his U Mass sweatshirt; he looks so normal, so like the boy next door. "You look like the boy next door, Rob." He doesn't respond. "Do you know why Jeff Simon likes me?"

"Why?"

"You have no clue?" I scrunch up my face. "No clue at all?"

"You're pretty? You're relatively smart?" He sips water.

Relatively? "He finds me *eccentric*. I'm like taking a walk on the wild side."

Rob laughs as if this were a sidesplitting joke. I have to pull the receiver away from my ear.

"It's not *that* funny." I frown at Hildy's photo.

He's still laughing. He can barely speak.

"I'm eccentric and fun, aren't I?" I picture myself dancing in a low-cut red dress in a club past ten p.m. I picture myself at a Ray's Pizza in the Village, grabbing a slice with friends who throw their heads back in wild laughter. I picture myself jogging, singing karaoke, drinking blue daiquiris. That sort of thing.

"Yeah." He makes a gulping sound. "You're fun."

Oh, no! I'm not fun! *I'm not a fun person!* Suddenly I'm speaking into the phone in a very loud voice. "I'm in a relationship that demands this crazy, oddball performance—and I *can't* do it, Rob. *I can't do it.*" I slam my hand on the desk.

A woman peeks into my office. "Everything okay?"

"Yeah," I answer. "Do you guys need toner?"

"You might want to talk to Debbie, the office manager. She'd know."

"I will." I smile agreeably.

The woman slips away.

"Sorry," I tell Rob.

"It's okay," he mutters. "Syb?"

"What?" I open the top drawer of Hildy's desk to look around.

"So, why are you with Jeff?"

I have to think for a second. I can't really remember. I know I had a reason, a pretty good one. Everyone wants to be with someone. Jeff's nice. Jeff's cute. Jeff's stable. Jeff's smart. He's like that favorite ex-boyfriend of mine. Yes, that's it. He's like my ex-boyfriend when my ex-boyfriend was being very quiet. Nice and quiet. That's Jeff. Except Jeff's a better dresser. "I don't know," I say to Rob. "Jeff makes me feel like an adult living in Manhattan."

"Oh."

I hold my breath for a second and then the air slowly slips from my lungs. "I'm so tired."

"Syb." He says my name and nothing else.

"I'm holding out for that grandeur stuff, and it doesn't even exist. In the meantime, I'm surviving off these pathetic little New York moments—stories I can tell people back home." I play with a rubber ball I find in Hildy's drawer. What does Hildy want with a rubber ball? "I'd like a story that I'm not going to tell. I'd like to live for something other than for writing about it later. I'm sick of temping." I stop. "And I wish to God you'd wear sweatpants in front of me."

Nothing on the other end.

"Rob?"

"I'm here."

My message button on the phone suddenly lights up. "I have to go. Message, if you can believe that."

"What are you doing for dinner?" he asks.

I look at the poor lemon poppy-seed muffin on my desk, desolate, wondering what it did wrong. "I'm broke and I bought a jumbo muffin this morning."

"I'll make you dinner. How about that?" He seems to perk up.

"Can you do it at my place? I don't want to go out tonight—unspoken phobias. Fear of Thursdays."

"That's fine. Six?"

We hang up. The message is about ordering toner. I guess I could do that.

After work, Rob arrives at my place. He's wearing gray sweats.

He heads straight into the kitchen, where he boils water and gets busy. I follow him and then pinch his butt: a spontaneous thing. He jumps. "I like your pants." I focus on the stove. "What are you making?" I lift the top off the pot.

"'The Single Person's Special.' You'll love it, despite any first impressions." He rinses a glass. "Only three ingredients required."

"Which three?" I turn around and stare at his pants. This makes him blush, but he bravely carries on.

"Pasta—in pleasant and appealing shapes. Canned corn—unsweetened. And tuna—preferably white, in spring water, dolphin-safe." Triumphantly, he rips into a box of pasta shells.

I try not to react flamboyantly. I take off my shoes. "What do you do with it all?"

Rob takes down my sole skillet from my sole shelf. "It's very simple. And cheap. *And* surprisingly tasty." He reaches for the can opener. "You prep the pasta and quickly heat the corn and tuna together in a skillet. Then you mix everything together." He begins to work on the cans. "Trust me, Syb. I know what you're thinking—it's good."

He turns his back to me and I stand there for a moment, watching him huddle over canned corn, the pot boiling next to him, the backs of his legs in sweats. "Go take it easy," he says. "It'll only be a few minutes. Get in there and dream up a book."

I walk into my room and set up two TV trays. I have two—one for me and one for company.

This is what I do.

Sitting on my bed, my knees pointy, my shoes off, I listen to Rob in the kitchen. He whistles a song. I can't make it out. I listen and grow quiet and think about what it's like to have someone in my microscopic kitchen, forgoing grilled swordfish, choosing tuna, frying instead of sautéing, whistling instead of playing violins, wearing sweatpants instead of suits. Then I just listen to him whistle; I close my eyes and lean back.

Six minutes later, he comes into the room carrying piping-hot plates. He's beaming. He puts them down. "Just a minute—" He dashes back into the kitchen. Barefoot. In sweats. He returns with a bottle of wine. "A little white wine with your fish?"

I smile up at him. "Yes, please."

He fills my glass and I pat the place next to me on the bed. "This is very lovely."

We sit side by side, TV trays next to each other, bending over our plates and sipping wine together, and I wonder what we're each in this for.

SEVENTEEN

ABSCESS
STARDUST

SYBIL WEATHERFIELD FOR *NEW YORK SHOCK*

From Friday, May 12, 1995

I follow a band and I hate beautiful women.

I may actually have a celebrity fetish. It began when my mom allowed me to audition for a local production of *The King and I* when I was six. In pairs, little actors and actresses approached a piano, lingered over sheet music, and belted out "Getting to Know You." I stood there paralyzed when the little Shirley Temple next to me rolled her eyes and sang at the top of her way-too-strong lungs. The whole thing was humiliating; all I could do was mouth the words. Afterward my mom and I went out for Chinese to ease my heartbreak. I choked on a mint and upchucked on the table.

Neither food nor fame has meant the same since.

In New York, I get to see stars: Richard Chamberlain just walking around Times Square, Brooke Shields also just walking around but this time on the Upper East Side, Edward James

Olmos at a play, Naomi Campbell in a canary-yellow pantsuit on Fifth, Isaac Mizrahi sipping coffee in the Village, Ethan Hawke at the Chelsea post office (twice!). One of my friends accidentally tripped Woody Allen in Central Park. She got to apologize profusely.

The best, though, was John Malkovich at Dean and Deluca. I thought it was my big break. Through him, I imagined, I'd enter the art world, dabbling in beauty.

I stared. Surely, he'd look over and his eyes, falling first on the carapace of my soul, would penetrate deeply—finding the kernel of truth about who I am buried within my bones, revealed in my skin's outward glow. Then, noting the creative energy haloing my body and finding something about me simply riveting, he'd approach. We'd discuss my potential to sculpt and write plays. By the end of the day, artistic paths would be forged, cleared by the machete of entrepreneurship and the names of the right people. I'd go home and paint in watercolor all night. In the morning, Robert De Niro and Tina Turner would call, wanting to collaborate (separately). I'd take up ballet.

Though it was a lot to ask of Malkovich, I fully planned on thanking him with every Oscar nomination.

But Malkovich never looked up. He ignored me completely. So I follow a band.

If you attend enough shows, memorize the lyrics to enough songs, sing along whenever possible, and cozy up to the lead singer and whomever plays guitar, then you make a pact with the fans, with your friends, with the band. You promise to *anticipate,* to *hope,* to *trust* that something grand is just around the corner. With that covenant, you vow never to deny another the pleasure of believing that a future is possessed, that a future is possible.

As for beautiful women, well, who needs them? Aren't they downers? Skinny hussies.

Recently I heard about a movie agent who needed an admin assistant. Friend of a friend of a friend. The agent wanted to meet at the Old English Pub on Broadway at 9:30 p.m. on a weeknight to get to know me.

Can you say *big break*?

I took a cab since any expense was an investment.

He'd make things happen. In six months' time, I'd be living above the poverty line, working on a novel, and liking beautiful women. The next thing you'd know, an avant-garde man with extreme personal integrity would ask me to marry him if only we spent a year in Provence first. Barbara Walters would *eat it up.*

You know what else? Health insurance. That's right. Regular checkups. Maybe even dental.

Meaty lasses, red arms, Guinness beer, and fish and chips met me as I entered the pub. Then a Kelsey Grammer look-alike called out my name: "Sybil!"

Two Academy Award winners were with him. First was a woman, a set designer, who had gray braids swinging across saggy breasts covered by a hippie madras blouse. A bead necklace hung over the breasts apologetically. "We're sorry," said the beads. Second was a guy, a cameraman, with a handkerchief sticking out of his pocket, drinking something in a tumbler. He reminded me of Mr. Howell from *Gilligan's Island.* I liked him immediately.

"They're leaving soon," said Kelsey. "If they don't, I'll kick their asses."

I smiled shyly and sat down.

The woman was telling them about the time she ended up racing Sidney Poitier from Philly to New York City, from the Liberty Bell to the Lincoln Center. I guess they happened to be on the same freeway. "Our windows were open, the wind was blowing, and I was *flying.*" She beamed proudly. "It was better than sex."

"I had a similar experience with Juliette Binoche and a speedboat," Kelsey triumphantly declared.

"We should go." Handkerchief nudged Beads, careful to avoid breasts.

Suddenly I was alone with Kelsey. In the distance, someone sang, "For He's a Jolly Good Fellow." We were in a tavern, stuck in a Canterbury Tale—the Prioress had come undone.

"I gotta eat." He waved his hands in the air. The barmaid/waitress came over. "Fried clams." Kelsey rose. "Will you excuse me a minute? I gotta make a call." He sped away like a cartoon character. I looked around, wanting to slap someone's back, wanting to eat bangers and mash.

The fried clams arrived when he did. He was positively bouncing off walls, eating in an unsanitary, manic way that could've shut the place down. His hands were greasy, his mouth wet. Watching him made me think of the Monday Night Movie on bulimia in which the starving debutante heads into the kitchen while her guests and perfect boyfriend are in the living room sipping aperitifs so she can make a sweep of the dinner remains and chomp on a turkey leg (it's *always* a turkey leg). He was eating in such a frenzied, gross way that I wondered if a straitjacket might be a good idea. Or a tranquilizer. Or a stun gun.

This guy *had* to be on coke.

"Sorry," he said. "Haven't eaten all day." He knocked back his whiskey sour. "So tell me about yourself."

I could tell I was still going to hate beautiful women. This was *not* my big break.

"Let me guess." He wiped his greasy mouth with the back of his hand. "You're from a broken home, you've lived with a guy, you've been on antidepressants, and you smoke pot occasionally."

All I said was "My parents are still together."

"I'm a socialist and a manic-depressive," he admitted.

"That's nice."

"I need a person to handle all aspects of my business—someone with an *artist's sensibility.*" He studied my face and spoke as if he were delivering secrets. "You have that, I can tell." He took a swig of his alcoholic beverage. "Excuse me one more time." He was off and running, as if this were Pamplona and the bulls were chasing him.

We finally left around eleven. He whispered, "This is what you've been waiting for your entire life." At the cab, he kissed my cheek. "Call me in the morning."

I didn't. You know why? Quite simply, he didn't make me want to paint in watercolor or take up ballet. He was no Malkovich; Tina Turner would *never* want to collaborate with me.

And you know what else? Dental isn't good enough. I want more.

I returned to my old prospects, juggling time cards and floppy disks, managing files and story ideas.

That Friday, I dressed in something slinky, wearing glitter on my shoulders and gloss on my lips. Even if the lead singer can't see a thing with the bright lights in his eyes, the tender expression on his face makes me believe he knows who I am, makes me hope that one day, one Great Gatsby green-light day, I'll reach out, stardust falling from fingertips, and touch the moon. Beauty, majesty, a veritable promised land will be there. One day, when the music is right, we'll make it big, together.

So I follow a band.

EIGHTEEN

ANTIBIOTICS 4

FROM *NEW YORK SHOCK*

From Friday, May 19, 1995

It's a well-known fact that Sybil Weatherfield does quite a bit more than *follow* a band. Ask her whom she's seeing.

—Kat, Brooklyn

Sybil and I went to the third grade together in Southern California. She always had one foot in the entertainment industry. She played an elf named "Thinker" in the Christmas pageant, she wrote and illustrated several holiday stories made of construction paper, and she lied to everyone saying that her father cowrote many of the songs on the soundtrack to *A Star Is Born* with Barbra Streisand and Kris Kristofferson. I'm the guy with the *Dukes of Hazzard* lunch box. Now, an accountant on Wall Street.

—Dan, Lower Manhattan

Listen to David Bowie's "Fame." Resist the Dark Side, Sybil. Celebrity will suck you dry, sister.

—Liz, SoHo

Sybil feels the need to reply:

Dan, is that you?

NINETEEN

CLUTCH

Friday, May 26, 1995

Jeff and I see *Miss Saigon* on Broadway and have drinks at Anarchy Café on Third. The whole time, I hold a dark blue clutch purse that matches my cocktail dress, and I feel *ravishing* because of the clutch purse, the beautiful man, the big musical, and the many drinks.

We can't get through the door fast enough. Stumbling over one another, his hands on my neck and shoulders, *shh*'s on our lips, we fall into my basement apartment. I put a finger to my mouth, demanding silence, forgetting Tom's in Greece.

Jeff, stunning, drunk, laughing, undresses. He loosens his collar, removes his tie. I drop the dark blue clutch purse and take off my earrings. Holding my wrists, he pulls me over. He grins and backs us toward the couch. Strips of light from the street slip through the heavy curtains, delicately illuminating the room.

"The couch?" That's what I say, and we keep moving backward till he pulls me down, till I lose sight of his grin and just feel his hands dancing over zippers, through my hair, till I forget things like my name and why we should even be quiet, why we can't make noise.

And it's Jeff Simon and me on the couch, Jeff Simon with me, on me, in me. Can't get away from Jeff Simon. Not even trying.

From beginning to end, this is *bodily*, a bodily deed. In the beginning, our eyes meet as our bodies work. Soon, absorbed in rhythms, his eyes lose meaning, and I can tell he no longer sees me. His eyes glaze over and he's looking without seeing.

What an amazing thing to realize!

I want to turn away, but I don't. Instead I stare into the absence of his eyes, thinking this is no out-of-body experience, thinking this is so body-bound. What would we have if we did not have these body parts working together like this?

It is the releasing of a clenched fist.

Almost immediately afterward, we attend to the logistics of disengagement, to the arrangement of distinct limbs. This is what we have, this working together toward the unclenching of a fist. After, it is all we can do to separate as quickly as possible.

In the morning, when he's gone, while I'm still naked, I reach for the dark blue clutch purse and hold it against my white stomach, just to see the sharp contrast of colors. The ravishing feeling goes away so soon.

TWENTY

Like Animals Forgetting

Saturday, May 27, 1995

Christopher Reeve, a.k.a. Superman, is paralyzed from the neck down.

The thing about really tragic events, the thing that *sufferers* of really tragic events, learn—pretty quickly—is that, though others empathize and are genuinely affected by the sufferer's suffering, their lives go on. When all is said and done, you have to know that other lives continue, despite irreparable change to your own.

Deep in the night, snug as a bug, sweaty from too many blankets, I get a call.

"Is this Sybil Weatherfield?"

I pull myself together, sitting upright, tossing off sheets, hoping this isn't a hospital. "Yes, I'm Sybil Weatherfield."

"Rob Shachtley named you when we asked if there was someone we should call."

Like film noir, my eyes widen and my lips part. Kate Hepburn in a Garfield nightshirt. "Who is this? What's wrong with Rob?"

"He's okay. I mean, he's not dead. Or dying." A fifteen-year-old girl speaks on the other end.

"Where is he?" I'm already looking for my keys and watch.

"He passed out, here at Ramone's. Somebody's gotta pick him up."

I look at my digital clock: 3:07 in the morning. "He passed out?"

"He's fine. He threw up, and now he's sleeping on the couch backstage."

Yuck. "I'll be there as soon as possible." I slip on sweatpants. "Do me a favor?"

"Yeah?"

"If he wakes, keep him there."

"Do you know where Ramone's is?"

"I do." She already envisions me as uncool. "He's okay?"

"Yeah, he's fine. He just needs someplace to go."

I'm a girl in New York City, so middle-of-the-night retrieval is a big deal. I have to take a cab too, since murder is likely in the subway and no direct routes exist anyway.

Linty and unfashionable, I open my front door and hesitantly sneak up the cement stairs leading to the street. I hate this part. I picture a hand over my mouth, a shove backward. I act like that won't happen, but I know it will. The stores are closed, bars and barricades lowered, and it's pretty damn quiet for Manhattan. No taxis in sight, so I walk with a stiff upper lip to Seventh, where, hopefully, there's life. After five excruciatingly long minutes in the dead of night, I catch a cab and head to the Bowery, to Ramone's, a punk-rock venue in a seedy part of town. Since I listened to mostly British melancholic suicidals as a teen, as opposed to those into self-mutilation and Satan, I know I'm going to be a tad "displaced" by the surroundings.

I expect Ramone's to be closed, but there's an after-hours show featuring Bruised Monkey. I'm forced to pay cover, so rescuing Rob takes up my entire entertainment allowance for the week. I'd better start having fun *now*.

Inside, punk rock greets me. The music bounces off the ceiling, rolls around the floor, and runs up to you like it's going to suck the meat right off your bones. Wiping my hands on my sweatpants, I stray down Ramone's graffiti gauntlet, a cavity of entropic writing on the wall. Like in a funhouse, I can't walk straight; the walls or floors seem to be moving. It's dark, and objects blur in warped silhouette. It's a funeral for someone no one knows in post-apocalyptic times. Though somber, no one cares about the dead. We're the only ones remaining on a war-ravaged planet. We may as well wear leather.

Dear God, this place compels me to call on the name of my missing God, *let Mad Max be around here somewhere.*

Approaching the back, I see a stage. Bruised Monkey plays. Judging from their appearance, the apocalypse was nuclear. Their hair is gone from either chemo or holocaust; their clothes look like dogs are after them and they've only narrowly escaped. They literally scream, which leaves me disillusioned, and the kids in the audience sway as if Bob Marley were grooving. *But he isn't.*

My eyes move in slow motion from Bruised Monkey and the alien kids in the audience to the left side of the stage, where a three- or four-year-old child and his alleged guardians watch B.M. The parental figures hover over the child and teach him how to do the Satan's Salute hand gesture, which mimics devil horns. I haven't seen it since my brother dragged me to a Mötley Crüe concert a long, long time ago in a land far, far away. Even back then, the Duranie in me was mortified.

I look at Bruised Monkey. If someone's screaming, shouldn't we *do* something?

I have to go. The poor child. I move through the crowd. I prepare to lift heads off wet, beery surfaces, demanding, "Find Rob Shachtley for me. Now."

I head backstage; no one stops me. A girl, seventeen, maybe eighteen, blond, pigtails, black leather vest, approaches. "Sybil?'

"You called about Rob?"

She eyes me from head to toe. *You're no Patti Smith*, she seems to say.

And, kiddo, you're no Mel Gibson.

She tosses her head over her shoulder. "Come this way."

I follow the blond girl deeper, deeper, deeper into the punk-rock funhouse. When it's too late to run, she points to a ripped yellow couch. Rob Shachtley, out cold.

He's curled up in an uncomfortable-looking fetal position. I sit in the "C" his body makes and touch his damp forehead.

"I didn't mean to do anything," the girl says. "I really didn't."

I look Rob over, unconsciously counting fingers and toes. "What happened?"

She tightens her pigtails. "I'm really sorry."

"I'm sure it's not your fault. What happened?"

The punk people backstage look at me as if I were somebody's mother. I kinda want to yell, *Get!*

"We were just messing around, and I guess he drank too much."

Not a picture I like.

I flash her a compassionate, tell-me-more look.

"He started to cry." She buries her hands in her vest pockets. "I didn't mean to upset him." Her skinny elbows stick out. She's a kid.

"It wasn't you." I smooth the hair on his forehead. "I'm glad you called."

"He's all right, isn't he?"

I nod my head. "He's drunk, that's all."

"You'll take care of him?" She stands in front of me, pixieish, pigtails on a punk.

I'm taking mine and getting out. "Yeah. Thank you."

She turns around timidly, like she's not sure it's the right thing to do, and walks off toward Bruised Monkey. Nice punk girl.

Rob stirs. I watch him rouse. I wonder about the throw-up, but he looks pretty clean. He opens his eyes, staring at me without recognition. "You're a pretty girl."

"Thank you," I answer.

"I like your silk blouse."

"I like your plaid pants."

Rob reaches out to touch my nightshirt, which isn't silk but rather cotton. "I bought them for you," he says of his pants. He brushes his fingers over my breast. I reach for his hand and hold it away from my body. He shoots me a coy smile. "Will you go home with me tonight?"

I give *him* a coy smile. Releasing his hand, I pretend to punch him in the nose. "No. You're coming home with *me*."

"If you insist." He reaches up and touches the side of my face.

I give him a wink. "I insist."

"I must have died and gone to heaven."

"Sorta."

It's not easy schlepping a man who weighs maybe fifty more pounds than you through Ramone's. The combination of impaired man and powder-blue sweatpants is cause for concern among the punk rockers. Punks look, but they don't get up. Rob is like a ton of bricks, a sack of potatoes, a bundle of clichés. I get him out the door, and immediately it's desolate and quiet again. The door shuts behind us, and it's like we've been cast away, spit out, and launched into another world. This hour, streets barren and bleak, me with sleep in my eyes, Rob drunk and heavy—it's a mise-en-scène for every darkly tinted futuristic film I've ever seen.

We're alone.

With him leaning on me and my legs spread to bear the weight, I try to hail a gloomy taxi daring to pick up the living from this dead but once-urban landscape. A lone light on a slowly moving cab declares, "On Duty." The taxi stops, and I bend over to look inside. The driver peeks through an open window. "Get in, lady."

I open the door, push Rob inside, and scoot onto the seat next to him. I give the cabby my address. If he wants to come over later to torment me, he can. Up to him.

Outside my basement apartment, I struggle with the keys and Rob falls against my landlords' front door, perched like a scarecrow. When I open it, he stumbles in like Jeff and I did last night, but he trips over the cord to my fan, which results in this trot-like dance step of four or five strides. Regaining his composure, he waits for my direction. I lock the door and point to the couch where Jeff and I had sex yesterday, and he plops down. We're fine and it's 4:30 a.m.

"We're sleeping now." I begin pulling the cheap knickknacks off my Woolworth's trunk/coffee table to open it for blankets. "You know what?" Hands on my hips. "You've gotta get up for a sec so I can make your bed."

He stands. "Whoa." He teeters, having some difficulty with balance.

"Do you have puke on you?" Always charming. I never forsake my charm. He doesn't know what to do with himself. He looks here; he looks there. Finally he sits on the floor. After I make a bed, I turn to him. "Do you want me to help you wash up? Brush your teeth? Clean up a little?" My voice sounds slightly schoolteacherish.

I'm into cleanliness, and I'm sure this is a major stumbling block in my journey to becoming a great writer. What kind of artist am I if I won't let the rock star with puke on him touch my things?

We struggle and plod toward my bathroom, knocking cornflakes sweetened with fruit juice off my portable plastic shelves. I sponge him off with a towel, clean his glasses, remove his shoes, put toothpaste on his finger and show him what to do. This isn't sexy. I have to tell him to urinate too. I close the door behind me and hope for the best. I figure I'd better not risk malaise. Everything seems to work out fine.

We return to my couch. "Keep your pants on," I insist. "It gets cold."

Then he empties his pockets. Out comes a wallet, a key chain, and a pair of purple panties. He holds them up for me to see.

It's like he's showing me a dead lizard or a glow-in-the-dark bug. I peer into his gleeful eyes, mortified. "Where'd you get those?" I ask.

"I don't know." He displays the purple panties, giggling. Satin and lace. Possibly punk-rock panties. "Take 'em."

"I don't want them." This distresses me like the alien punk kids, like the child learning Satan's Salute. "How come you have purple panties in your pocket, Rob?"

He leans into the cushions, holding his treasure, now balled up in his fist. "I must have," he pauses, "*collected* them." He grins fiendishly. Then he adds, "Maybe for my rock 'n' roll scrapbook, Syb."

Which we've never mentioned. But this isn't memorabilia.

"Well, put them away," I say.

He looks at the underwear in his palm. "I guess I don't really want them."

"Then I'm throwing them out." My hands are back on my hips.

He holds them out. I reach over, grabbing elastic with index finger and thumb as if holding a rat by its tail. I slip into the kitchen, lift the plastic garbage lid, and trash them. Then I wash my hands, of course.

When I return, he's stretched out on the couch, the sheet covering him. I dim the lights, walk over, and sit on the trunk.

"You're a nice girl." He smiles like children do when you're tucking them in. "Let me touch your silk blouse."

"I'm not in the mood, Rob." I kneel and remove his glasses, still upset about those lousy panties. "What happened at Ramone's?"

He collapses onto his back. "I can't remember." He closes his eyes.

"Did you drink a lot?"

"Yes."

"What did you drink?"

"Scotch."

"That's shit." I get up to walk to my bed.

"Sit with me." He reaches a hand out. "Don't leave yet." He searches for my wrist, finds it, and takes my pulse.

I sit on the floor next to the couch. I close my eyes and put my head back. He closes his eyes too, and I think he'll fall asleep in ten minutes. But I hear him talking softly, so I lift my head. "I'm Rob," he says, introducing himself.

"I know who you are," I whisper back.

"I know who you are too." His eyes fix on mine.

"I don't think you do."

He brings a hand up to my face. "Tell me your name."

"I thought you knew."

"I do. Just tell me." He watches my lips, waiting for my pronouncement.

"You say it." I lean close to him. "*You* say my name."

He pauses, staring. Then he speaks: "Cynthia." He takes a deep breath. "It's Cynthia."

Rob's dead wife.

He closes his eyes. The moment he said her name, he knew it wasn't true.

I didn't expect this. "Rob—"

"Say, *It's Cynthia. My name is Cynthia,*" he begs.

"I'm not—"

"*Please*." He raises a hand to his temples. "Say it. Just say—"

"Rob, I can't."

For a moment, there's silence. Then he starts sobbing. He's sobbing, and I sit on the floor helplessly, feeling cruelty in my sinews. I put my arms around him, first one and then the other, and I hold him tightly. "I'm sorry, Rob. I'm sorry. It's only me." In my grasp, his body quakes. There's a rhythm to his sorrow: we rock gently.

For twenty minutes, he weeps. Then we sleep. Me on the floor, Rob on the couch, my arms entangled with his torso, his tears streaked on his cheeks, a pain in the small of my back, dust in my nostrils, a chill underneath the door.

At 6:30 in the morning, I try to rise. He shifts when I remove my limbs. His eyes open, and I can tell he knows it's me. I sit down again, my back to the couch. Rob grasps his pillow. After several moments, he speaks quietly.

"Cynthia died of a brain tumor." He traces the shape of my skull. "The fucking brain." The 1, 2, 3, or 9 train shakes my walls.

"What do you do now?" I whisper.

Rob stares up. "I do what I have to. Whatever it takes to sustain my losses."

"Are you always *only* sustaining your losses?" I touch his hair. "Is that what you were doing at Ramone's? *Sustaining your losses*?"

Rob blinks. "Yes. That's what I'm *always* doing."

So then we sleep. When I get up for my bed, there are no protestations. If there is vomit on him, it's vomit on me. A rose is a rose is a rose. Vomit is vomit is vomit.

We sleep till eleven, and when we wake, I drink a Bloody Mary and Rob has a pot of coffee. We don't mention a thing. We take a walk along the Hudson, wearing dark glasses. We're like animals after they've killed—not remembering the killing. We're gentle, tentative. We move shyly, and when we bump against one another, we are kind and apologetic.

We try and try to stop remembering, but we're not really like that. Not really like animals forgetting.

TWENTY-ONE

Spilled Beans

Saturday, June 10, 1995

Rob knocks. I open my front door and pull him inside. I see him standing there, red pants on, an "I Love New York" paper cup in hand, sunglasses shielding eyes, and I grab his arm, tugging him forcefully. "Get in here."

"Where's the big guy?" Rob saunters inside sluggishly, looks around sleepily, and blows on his hot coffee. He acts like ten a.m. on a Saturday is five a.m. on a holiday weekend. He puts his sunglasses on top of his head. "I've still got sleep in my eyes." He rubs his face. "What's *sleep* anyway?" he asks. "That whole *Sandman* thing is disturbing, don't you think? I mean, who the hell thought *that* up?" He watches me, then repeats his first question: "The big guy: where is he?"

"He went to get coffee. He'll be back soon." I begin to pace.

"Does he *really* have to come?" We're going to Long Island for the day.

I point a finger in his direction. "Stop."

For a second, Rob drinks and watches me. I pace a little. I look behind doors, peek around curtains. Okay, so I'm a bit frenetic. "What's going on, Syb?" Rob asks.

I halt. "Nothing, Rob." I look straight at him, keeping still. "*Nothing's wrong.*"

Last night, after French food at Caffe Lure in the West Village and exotic drinks somewhere in SoHo, we came back to my place. Jeff, a man who lives and dies by his ability to cross things off a great big ubiquitous to-do list, takes me for what I am: a fill-in, a temporary assistant, there when someone else is on vacation. Afterward he crosses me off the list. But last night, for a moment, I think I felt him shudder in repulsion. Or maybe sorrow.

After solving for *x*, we rolled away from the center of my single bed, having originally approached one another from opposite places. Last night, it hit me hard: we defied all descriptions of love-making; we were concrete and void of abstraction. Taskmasters. This was sex; there was no room for love.

In that same awful moment, I felt Jeff Simon fold his pillow over like a stuffed pizza slice, and I heard him sigh. I didn't roll over to him, but I felt something steely, chilly, divisive between us. My despondency didn't just perplex him; it hurt him. I was capable of *hurting* Jeff Simon. And there was something in me, something so frosty; I didn't want to roll over to him.

Today, ten a.m., he said, "I'll get us coffee." He was trying to keep his cool.

Rob puts his "I Love New York" paper cup down on my trunk. He wipes his hands on his pants, runs his fingers through his hair, and adjusts the glasses on his nose.

I watch him intently. He tries to avoid my eyes, apparently feeling them on him. "Rob," I say suddenly, "why do you sing me songs?"

His face reddens. He stammers, stutters—even sweats! "I can't believe you're asking me this now, right now, when your goddamned boyfriend is coming back any second—"

"What do you want from me?" I stand in front of the trunk.

"Sybil. Sybil Weatherfield." He stares at me. "If I thought for one second—that's all I need, *one* second—that either of us could actually escape our detachment, our despondency: your post-twenties cynicism and my postmortem skepticism—I'd be there. In a heartbeat—"

"You don't think we could?" All of a sudden, my eyes tear up.

He's quiet, thinking. He shakes his head. "I don't know." There's a knock on the door: confident, manly, Jeffish. "But I do know one thing."

"What?" I walk to the door.

"I'm afraid." His voice is quiet. "Our despondency really, *really* frightens me."

My hand is on the doorknob.

Another knock.

"You should open it," he says, looking at the knob.

I open the door. Jeff stands there holding two coffees. A New York backdrop behind him. Sunshine all around. Jeff walks over the threshold. "Half-and-half for you, black for me. Freshly ground beans." He looks at Rob. "Hey there, Rob. Ready for Long Island Day?"

Rob claps his hands. "Ready!"

TWENTY-TWO

RAPUNZEL

Still Saturday, June 10, 1995

Madeline has a car, an old VW.

She has this car, which she parks two blocks away from her Brooklyn brownstone. She never moves it unless it's really important—otherwise she'll lose her parking spot. Meanwhile, the ancient car sighs its thick black nasal drip onto the broken pavement.

We love her car.

She says, "It's important to me that, at all times, I have one."

She'll drive us to Long Island. The outing, this field trip, is her idea. Every once in a while, Madeline insists on something like going to the suburbs or a chain restaurant, something to make us "get in touch with the heartland." She says, "It's the same with *Planet of the Apes* movies. You should always watch one around the holidays."

We take the A train to Brooklyn. Jeff and I hold hands on the subway, on the streets. He took mine. What's a girl to do? Arriving, we walk to Madeline's apartment along hot sidewalks. I watch Rob stroll ahead of us. I see tension in his stride (imperceptible). Rob's red pants will scare the Islanders. But I stare at those pants; oh, I *stare* at that man. He is neither sexy nor well-coiffed; he is not Jeff Simon. He is not graceful; he is not sleek. He is clumsy and clownish.

I think I love him.

What does that mean?

Madeline's apartment is in an old brownstone in a mostly African American neighborhood. It's noticeably quieter than Manhattan, and it makes me want to be Spike Lee. Leaves on sidewalks, cracks in cement stairs, rusty bikes against trees: every once in a while, a kid on a bicycle with training wheels looks at us like we're invaders from outer space.

I squeeze Jeff's hand reassuringly as we climb the old stairs of a ramshackle brownstone. Rob rings the bell. There's no response, so he rings again.

From up above, a head pops out an open window. "Okay, *okay*, you crazy kids! I'm coming!" Madeline yells.

Rob puts both hands to his mouth and shouts, "Rapunzel, Rapunzel, let down your hair!"

She hangs out the window. "I don't think so!" She drops a sock on the stoop and Rob picks it up.

She's not entirely ready to go, which is no great surprise. Both Jeff and Rob wander around and touch her things. Hand-painted furniture and exposed fixtures are here and there. Her walls are multicolored: lime green, lavender, yellow. There are photographs everywhere, picture frames with popcorn kernels, seashells, and bottle caps glued to them. She has bowls spun and decorated on pottery wheels from pottery classes taken in San Francisco. There's an empty papier-mâché piñata shaped like a shark on top of the refrigerator.

"Eat my California rolls!" she calls from the bathroom. "I made them this morning!"

"But we're going for lunch at Happy's!" I shout. Happy's is a good way to start Long Island Day. That's the plan.

"Yeah, well, it's almost eleven. You have to eat breakfast first." She peeks out, holding a tube of mascara.

Rob enters the kitchen, and I pretend to examine the piñata. Jeff flips through Madeline's cassettes. "Where are the California rolls?" Rob asks, standing as far away from me as possible. I point to the counter. He walks over and picks one up. He puts the California roll into his mouth and I glare at him. We say nothing, but now we stare at each other as he eats. I watch him chew, moving it around inside his mouth. He tears up suddenly, fully. He swallows and reaches up to grasp his throat. He's about to cry.

"Maddy!" he screams after he's swallowed, still staring at me. "What's in these rolls?"

Just then she comes traipsing into the kitchen, shuffling in on wooden floors, wearing clunky clogs. Her hair is wet and hanging down. "Wasabi, Robby!" She turns to me as I stare at Rob. "Okay, guys. Let's go."

TWENTY-THREE

ABSCESS BE HAPPY

SYBIL WEATHERFIELD FOR *NEW YORK SHOCK*

From Friday, June 16, 1995

Every year, Sheila's family goes to Milwaukee for a square-dancing convention. "Maybe it's a polka festival—I can't remember," my friend Sue explained. Sheila lives in Archie and Edith's house in Queens, she's never eaten Thai, and she's seen every Tony Award–winning musical since 1981. "Each month, one of her cousins gets married to the boy next door—*excuse me,* the *goy* next door—and Sheila's a bridesmaid."

Plus, Sheila loves—I mean, *adores*—Happy's ice cream.

Sue and Sheila work together, and lately my friend has been enamored by Sheila's down-home charms. "She makes me long for home, for the days of lunch boxes, stirrup pants, and the dawn of MTV."

"Yeah?" I say.

"She makes me crave *normalcy.* Didn't we once have normal lives outside the concrete jungle?"

More and more, my friend has been saying how we've got to get out of New York City while we still can. To complement her lamentations, she goes on and on about Sheila. Sheila this; Sheila that.

Don't be *dense,* true friend. Don't be *naive.* You think we can make it outside the city? You believe that? Watch us curl up and die. Watch us sink into ourselves and become eccentric *introverts.* Don't count on *acceptance.* Don't you dare count on *normalcy.*

We made a special trip to Happy's, since it would be a good opportunity to test our suburban survival skills. Apparently, elsewhere in America, Denny's, Coco's, Happy's, Village Inn, Stuckey's, Big Boy, and the like positively *thrive.* Two men from Manhattan joined us: one from uptown, one from downtown. Someday the uptown man may get a job transfer. Someday the downtown man may get a job.

I've been on this road before. Once I went to the Mall of America in Minnesota. A business trip, if you can believe that. The strollers, frozen yogurt-eaters, and hand-holding couples scared the hell out of me, but I liked the rental car quite a bit. In the final analysis, I couldn't wait to get back to my local beggars and anonymous neighbors.

Happy's smelled like day-old grease. Our waitress looked like a dirty Alice from *The Brady Bunch.* A high school kid mopped the floor. As we carefully hopscotched across the wet tile, I whispered to Sue, "Remember, Sheila suggested lunch so we can eat ice cream afterward."

Sidling up to a booth, Sue sneered. "Screw lunch. I want breakfast."

Alice, Peds on feet, approached. "What can I get you folks?"

The four of us city slickers studied our laminated menus. Speaking in a singsong voice, Sue said, "I'd like the French toast with crispy bacon, please."

Alice didn't move. The wrinkles around her mouth began to tremble. "I'm sorry. We don't serve breakfast after eleven."

We all looked at our watches: 11:17 on a Saturday morning.

Sue looked at Alice as if she were crazy. Alice quaked. Sue's eyes were like the pig's in *The Amityville Horror:* red, beady. "You don't serve breakfast after eleven?" It sounded like, *Are you fucking nuts?*

I tensed up. So did Uptown and Downtown.

Alice smiled sweetly. "I'm sorry, ma'am. Is there something else I can get you?"

Silence followed.

"I'll need a minute." Sue ducked behind her menu.

"I'll be right back." Alice shuffled off in her Peds.

When Alice was gone, Sue's mouth dropped open. "Can you believe *this*? Can you believe they don't serve breakfast after eleven? I was *so* ready for French toast! You have no idea—no *fucking* idea!" She dropped her menu on the table. "Who ever heard of not serving breakfast after eleven at a shit diner?"

"Order something else, Sue," Downtown broke in.

"I don't want anything else! I want breakfast."

Mental-institution material, right here, folks. Sue slapped both hands down. "This is why I can't leave New York City. This is why!" She looked at us wildly. "In New York City, you can get breakfast anytime. There are no *designated* breakfast hours! If you want breakfast at eight p.m., so be it. Three-thirty in the afternoon, that's fine." She flipped her hair over her shoulder. "Do you realize that the *rest* of America *only* eats breakfast *before* eleven?"

"We're actually technically still in New York City—this is Queens," said Uptown.

Downtown, more comfortable with idiosyncrasy than Uptown, put a hand on top of Sue's. "That's right, Sue. That's why we live in New York City. So we can get breakfast anytime we want."

"Damn right," she responded.

Uptown pointed to the corner of his menu. "Get a cup of soup."

Everyone shot him a look of disgust.

"I *really* wanted breakfast," Sue whined.

I reached across the table to touch her arm. "I know, honey. But if Sheila were with us right now, she'd be having lunch."

Sadness spread across her face, clouding her eyes. "I'll never be able to leave." I watched the grief drift over her forehead. I studied the anguish unfurling across her brow. Sue could never leave New York City. She loved her French toast too much.

Alice cautiously returned. "Have you had time to think it over?"

Sue stared up at Alice. In an itsy-bitsy, sugary-sweet voice, Sue said, "Can you make an exception just this once and prep an order of French toast and crispy bacon?

I didn't think she'd go this far. Under the table, Downtown pinched my thigh. Uptown stared in disbelief.

"I'm sorry, ma'am. We can't do that." Alice, stiff-legged and poised to write on her paper pad, probably desperately hoped that this weird, witchy woman would just order a damn turkey club.

Sue, completely fraught now, clenched her teeth and closed her eyes. "*Surely* you have white bread and eggs. Pretend you're making a B.L.T., but mess up."

Downtown flipped. "For God's sake, get a goddamn Reuben sandwich!"

Sue, red-faced and teary-eyed, said, "Could you just tell me one thing?"

Alice cautiously stepped back. "What?"

"*Why* can't I have breakfast after eleven?"

Alice stared at her head-on. "Happy's policy."

Sue exhaled deeply. "Get me a cup of soup."

Yes, I'll tell you. I've lied. When people ask me why I stay, why I choose to live in mayhem, isolation, extravagance, and disease, I lie. I mutter something about art, diversity, the naked truth. That's my usual one: *truth.* On and on I go about the *rawness* of the streets—the hard, cold facts. I say that's what I need. I need to be surrounded by reality, engulfed in it, nearly swallowed by its gritty, truth-telling jaws. That's when I feel honest. That's when I feel like I could sincerely love the world. That's when.

But it's a lie. The truth is this: I like French toast after eleven. I like it so much that I'll never leave New York City. Give me that, above everything else.

TWENTY-FOUR

LONG ISLAND DAY

Still Saturday, June 10, 1995

In East Hampton, Madeline parks the car. "Come on, everybody!" She yanks up the emergency brake. "Put on your khakis; we're going to the Hamptons!"

Outside the beloved VW, East Egg greets us. Rob immediately says, "Keep an eye out for Jay Gatsby, folks."

Madeline, locking her car, dryly responds, "He's dead, Rob. Don't bother."

In the Hamptons, the rich and famous fix their boats, train for marathons, and memorize commercial jingles under the canopies or eaves of beachfront property. Movie directors with personal assistants who are hired to lick the Publishers Clearing House sweepstakes' red Corvette sticker and place it on the right entry form yell, "Fax me the script changes!" from helicopter landing pads. Couples have sex standing up in the dressing rooms of expensive and exclusive boutiques. Duck, crumpets, golfing, and cappuccino beat out Irish pubs, want ads, and Folgers in terms of both number and popularity. Most people seem to be on the healthy side of middle age. I notice a preponderance of dashing older men with young, beautiful women. Sometimes it's the other way around!

Rob takes off his sunglasses, stepping ahead of us. "Wow," he mumbles.

Jeff puts his sunglasses on.

"Wow," Rob repeats.

I move next to Jeff. He looks like a tennis pro. I reach for his hand, feeling sorry about my despondency.

"What do we do now, Snuffy?" Madeline asks.

Jeff gets authoritative. "First, let's grab lattes."

"Wow." Rob turns around and his eyes go straight to my hand holding Jeff's.

"I need a cigarette." Madeline fidgets with her bag, quivering like a drug addict. She pulls out a cig, sticks it in her mouth, and struggles with the matches. It's painful to watch. It's like seeing the elderly struggle to open childproof aspirin bottles. After it's lit and she's sucking, she says under her breath, "I'll never be able to leave New York. It's so *fucking* obvious." She angrily shakes out her match. Rob makes a big production of fanning away smoke. His forearms flail and he induces a cough. Madeline continues, "The roasted red peppers scare me. And there are just too many scones around here." She blows gray rings into the sky. "These people are so removed from reality, it isn't even funny."

Jeff's smile slips away, slides right off his face. "Madeline," he begins, "they're only here on the weekends." He shakes his head. "This isn't their *reality*."

All of us are quiet, reprimanded by Jeff Simon.

We're arrogant SOBs. We think we're so cool for rejecting fake tans and croissants. We think we're so terribly chic and smart and one step ahead because we wear mismatched clothes and think in one-liners. I look at Jeff, holding my hand gently, and I'm embarrassed to have him see our mockery.

Madeline's still bitter about the French toast. "They wish it *were*, though."

We walk around East Hampton. We drink iced mochas, snack on almond biscotti in long white bags that we hold like flower bouquets, glide into kitsch galleries to peruse what's hot and what's not in the art world, and wander into stores selling gourmet kitchen gadgets.

In a boutique filled with quilted pot holders and fruit juicers, I ponder an egg holder shaped like a speckled hen. I study it, turning it over, counting how many eggs it can hold. I'd like to have one, to be honest, but it's a purchase I can't really justify. Especially since I never buy eggs. But wouldn't it be nice to have a speckled chicken egg holder inside the fridge, holding a dozen farm-fresh eggs? Brown ones? If I had it, maybe I'd start making omelets. Or soufflés. French toast—definitely French toast.

Rob sneaks up behind me. He scares me, and I nearly toss the speckled hen into the air. "If it were you, Sybil, it can't just be a despondent sexual relationship."

I stand there, a chicken in my hands.

He looks around the gourmet kitchen store suspiciously.

I suck in air. I stare at Rob, rock star, widower, friend. Then I put the hen back on the shelf, lifting my eyes to the gadgets beyond. Jeff's on the other side, near picnic gear. Rob and I stand side by side, no longer looking at each other but now ardently examining cloth placemats covered in thickly painted, garish strawberries.

He grabs the placemat I'm holding so I'm forced to look up at him. I turn, glowing fiercely. We each hold the end of a garish strawberry placemat. "I haven't figured it out," he whispers. "Why do you think I'm in Long Island today? You think I like hanging out with your boyfriend?" He lets go of his end of the placemat.

"Oh, there you are!" Madeline, from the seafood accessories row across the store, shouts, "I'm getting this lobster fork." She holds one up. "For the next time I'm in Maine!"

Rob reaches for my elbow. "C'mon. There's someone over there who wants to hold your hand."

I'm still clinging to the placemat. I look frazzled, and so Jeff, approaching with his hands in his pockets, stops whistling and asks, "Is everything okay?"

I look down at the strawberry placemats. "Yeah. I just want to get these."

By now, Madeline has joined us. In some kind of weird and respectful silence, everyone watches me gather four strawberry placemats. Madeline dares to ask the question: "Those, Sybil?"

"I like them," I say softly.

Madeline fakes a laugh. "I thought you had more taste than that."

"But I don't," I respond. "I really don't."

After I buy four ugly placemats, we walk onto the street. This time, we sip vanilla lattes and nibble on chocolate biscotti. Madeline lights another cigarette. She tips the ashes off the end of her smoke as we wander. "Do these people even know what's going on in the world? Do you think they know about NATO? The Balkans?"

Jeff flinches. "They know *exactly* what's going on, Madeline."

"I'm sorry," she says. "This feels like Disneyland for the intellectually deprived and monetarily endowed." She hesitates. "Maybe it's me."

Jeff, arm around my shoulder, pulls me close, stiffening. I watch Madeline quietly reel from sensory overload. Rob seems to straddle feelings of embarrassment over having said too much and resentment about Jeff's rigid arm on my unresponsive body. I cling to my bag of placemats.

On the way home, I stare out the car window. We pass Sears and the Olive Garden. We stop and take pictures by a field of red, yellow, orange, and pink flowers. We buy summer squash on the side of the road. Back in the car, the guys doze. Madeline and I sit in front. She tells me, "It's so much easier to keep a lid on things back home, isn't it?"

When we arrive, New York City seems strange, foreign. In an hour or so, the strangeness wears off. Then it's as if we've never left.

TWENTY-FIVE

ANTIBIOTICS 5

FROM *NEW YORK SHOCK*

From Friday, June 23, 1995

French Toast with Orange Zest and Blueberry Grand Marnier Sauce:

For Toast:

Beat 3 eggs with 1/2 cup milk. Add cinnamon and 1/2 tsp orange zest.

Slice a baguette into 1–2-inch-thick slices. Arrange slices in a deep baking pan, pour egg mixture over bread, and refrigerate for 30–60 min until bread is thoroughly soaked but not soggy. (If egg mixture is not enough to cover all bread, mix another few eggs with milk, etc., as above).

For Sauce:

Place 2 cups fresh or frozen blueberries into saucepan. Add 1/2 cup sugar, 1 tbsp water, and 1 tbsp orange zest. Bring to boil for few minutes (until sugar is dissolved and blueberries let out juice). Remove from heat and stir in 2–4 tbsp Grand Marnier. Keep warm.

Heat large skillet with a small amount butter or vegetable oil. Cook slices of egg-soaked bread over medium-high heat until golden brown, then turn and cook on the other side. Serve immediately with warm blueberry sauce.

Goes well with mimosas.

—Siobhan, Upper West Side

Downtown is Sybil Weatherfield's boyfriend Rob Shachtley, the lead singer of Glass Half Empty.

—Neil, the Bronx

Sybil feels the need to reply: ***Siobhan, sounds great, but what the hell is orange zest?***

TWENTY-SIX

PANTS DOWN

Wednesday, June 28, 1995

I'm absorbed in the daily news. First, Hugh Grant, who's so cute, British, and gentlemanly, got caught with prostitute Divine Brown in a car yesterday, which sort of changes the whole gentlemanly thing, though he's still cute and British. Second, "Antibiotics" in *Shock* is filled with "Downtown" identifications—word is Downtown is actually my boyfriend, Rob Shachtley, lead singer of Glass Half Empty. There's even a photograph of us coming out of Taylor's Bakery on Hudson one Saturday morning. We're holding two cups of coffee and a bag, which (I know) contains a decadent cheesecake brownie we'd eat on a curb while my laundry tossed in the same Laundromat we'd met in months earlier. I wonder what Jeff thinks when he sees it. Rob simply says, "Hey, they know my band."

But Hugh Grant, a dapper man with a drop-dead gorgeous girlfriend, was in a car with a whore—and that's certainly more questionable than my link to one Rob Shachtley. Nothing illegal going on there. Though the brownie far exceeded my daily caloric allowance and later resulted in serious hurling.

Madeline wants me to join her for lunch in the Rights International back office. Since I'm between temp jobs (Fred is telling people I'm working on a cultural analysis of the Chelsea Hotel), I go. On Madeline's desk are piles of reports on Guatemala. "I've been pilfering from the supply closet," she explains. "Look through them—maybe you'll want to write a column on Latin America. Refugees, human rights. You know."

"There's no time for altruism, Madeline. I write self-absorbed pieces about me living in New York—they're about how *I'm* doing, what *I'm* thinking, what *I* want." Pathetic and true.

"Well, what did you have in mind for your next piece?" she asks.

"Something on supermodels," I admit, instantly ashamed.

"How's Jeff?"

The phone rings. One of Madeline's jobs is to screen calls from nuts. She has lengthy conversations with individuals who believe that cavity fillings are bugged, that microchips have been planted in buttocks, and that turnips and bananas in the produce section at the local grocer's emit telepathic waves to the brain. A surprising number of commonalities exist between stories. They all complain about microchips. They've all got *issues* with lettuce. Perhaps there's something to this bugged-butt thing, after all.

A half-eaten McDonald's hamburger sits on her desk next to a stolen salt shaker. Fortune-cookie fortunes decorate her computer monitor along with a picture of Lenny Kravitz. Pressing the speakerphone button, she signals for me to be quiet.

"Rights International," she dryly intones. "How may I help you?"

“I’m being tortured by the government.” Nut.

We look at one another knowingly. “How’s the government torturing you?” she asks professionally.

“I live on Long Island.”

“Is that how they’re torturing you?” She unwraps a big yellow-and-red-striped straw and shoves it into a chocolate milkshake. “Are you exiled on Long Island?”

The guy speaks quickly, as if he were in a hurry, as if he were on the run. “No. They’re reading my mind.”

“How?” Madeline violently stirs her shake with the straw.

“They’ve planted a chip in my brain.”

We raise our eyebrows simultaneously, though Madeline doesn’t look up from thrashing her ice cream around. “When did it happen?” Her voice is cool, and she nods her head in understanding. She puts her mouth on the end of the straw and sucks up some shake.

“During the war.”

She quickly swallows. “Which war?”

“The one with England.”

She pauses, wiping condensation off the cup. “I see. . . .”

The guy must detect doubt in her voice. “You don’t *see*, ma’am. They’re reading my thoughts. I’m getting messages from the Dalai Lama, ma’am. They’re reading my masturbatory thoughts. Do you understand?” He’s getting belligerent, and I’m contemplating the use of the adjective *masturbatory*. “I can’t be alone anymore. It isn’t safe to go outside, and it isn’t safe to stay inside. I’m prisoner in my own—”

She stops him. Madeline Blue’s done it before; she’ll do it again.

She licks her finger and dips it into the salt crystals left on her hamburger wrapper. "Sir, sir—I have to stop you." She breathes calmly. "Rights International works on behalf of those whose political rights are being violated. Your case, though serious, doesn't sound like it falls within our mandate." She picks up her milkshake and jiggles her straw around to unsettle ice cream at its bottom. "Perhaps I can suggest some other resources for you."

"Bitch." The guy hangs up.

We sit there in silence for a while. She finishes her shake and works on her food. Stuffing a soggy fry into her mouth, she looks closely at me. "Sybil, do you care about the homeless anymore?"

I turn away, staring at a poster of Aung San Suu Kyi, her fist raised in the air. It's just one among many—there's a collage of human rights stars plastered on the back of the door, MLK in Washington by the window, Desmond Tutu in church above the computer, Mother Teresa feeding the hungry near the exit. I reach out and touch Madeline's knee. "When I remember."

She smiles absently, distantly. "Too bad about Hugh Grant, huh?" And then she stacks human rights documents into neat piles.

This is what I do: on my way out, I go into the bathroom and throw up a Quarter Pounder with cheese.

In the afternoon, I head over to Dave and Lynn Stomps's place, where Dave and Rob are practicing. Dave lives in my neighborhood, and his wife and daughter aren't home, so I'll work on his computer. When I get there, Rob isn't around.

I put my stuff on the floor and turn on the computer. "Where is he?" I ask Dave.

He puts a finger to his lips. "He's in the bedroom. It's Cynthia's birthday. He always calls her parents on her birthday."

It feels like it did when I was in third grade and some guy, a twin, an evil twin, punched me in the stomach for no apparent reason. "Oh," I manage, looking at the computer screen, not seeing a thing except random messages. Microsoft Word, virus scan, checking drives, doing a memory test. He's calling Cynthia's parents because it's her birthday. His dead wife's birthday.

"So, I saw 'Antibiotics,' Syb." Dave's voice hits me like a rubber band shooting the back of my head. "I guess you guys are *the* hot item."

Not if he's calling his dead wife's family. "Yep." I stare at the terminal.

Dave gets up from the drum set he keeps in the living room, much to his wife's chagrin, and heads into the kitchen. I look toward the bedroom. "How long has he been in there?"

Dave looks at his watch. "I don't know. Fifteen, twenty minutes."

"That's a long time." I stand.

This is what I do: I head toward the bedroom. Peeking in, straight out of a horror movie, I manage a feeble "Rob?"

He's sitting on the bed, his shoulders hunched, his head lowered, the phone on the hook. He doesn't look up. "I'll be right out."

I begin to pull the door shut. "Okay."

But no. I don't. I can't. I won't. I push it open again. "Are you all right?"

His voice is a murmur, barely audible. "Yeah, I'm fine."

"May I come in?"

He looks up, his eyes red. He beckons me over with his hand. "Shut the door."

Very quietly, I enter. I sit next to him on the bed. I put my hand on his leg. We say nothing. So I turn, I turn toward him to hold him, to bring the other arm around, to pull him down, to still the grief, and he's in my arms so I'm lover and mother, and I hold him there in the unlit, wordless afternoon of the dead woman's birthday.

TWENTY-SEVEN

ABSCESS

LOVE SLAVE

SYBIL WEATHERFIELD FOR *NEW YORK SHOCK*

From Friday, July 14, 1995

I can write the pants off any man.

I thought the powers of seduction were in the tips of my fingers and could be manifested on any good word processor. Only a year ago, thinking myself a temptress, I plotted to win over a junior exec at a summer temp job through witty e-mail. E-mail was fairly new, so I figured my dry wit and prickly good humor would come off as avant-garde, risqué. Unfortunately, he only replied with variations of "yes" and "no."

ME: The coffee pot on your desk looks like hell. Is it a prop used to set a mood, create an aura, suggest you read really good books, indicate you listen to fabulous music, and proclaim to the world that you drink black coffee just like you would in a French café, a Seattle coffeehouse, or somewhere deep in Greenwich Village; or do you just need to wash the pot and change the filter?

HIM: Wash pot/chng fltr.

After a month of my charms, he switched to the Fulton office. Okay, so I guess I was wrong about this pants-off business.

This is what I know: love is a battlefield, love is blindness, and love is a stranger.

But: Love Me Do.

If love is a stranger, what kind of stranger are we talking about? Is he tall, dark, and handsome? Or is he a perv in a trench coat?

A guy once said to me something about being his love slave. I rolled my eyes, clucked like a hurt hen, scrunched up my face in an unflattering way, and said, "You're kidding, right?" *Slave?* That suggests all kinds of things we women fought against for decades.

But here's the truth: *I wanna be a love slave.* It's a paradox: smart women are rewarded in school and work but penalized in love.

"Guys don't make passes at girls who wear glasses." Tell me about it. Why do you think I pull the delicate-skin-around-my-eyes-I've-been-warned-about down and stick tiny plastic shower-cap-shaped objects over my eyeballs? Why do you think I do that? Because it's fun?

"Lovers aren't responsible for intellectual stimulation; you can get it elsewhere."

"She's too smart for her own good."

I'm not making this stuff up! You know you've heard it! I'm not even a feminist! I love men and bras!

I know what some of my male readers are thinking: *She's bitter. She needs to get laid.*

Truth is, underneath this edgy, dare-I-say dazzling intelligence lurks a desire, rampant, scorching, *hot,* to be a love slave.

I say, *Slay Me, Love. Make Me Yours.*

But what are we talking about exactly when we say *love slave*? What does that involve? Is this going to offend my feminist friends?

I launched an effort to comprehend what is meant by *love slave.* I consulted traditional orthodoxy, poetry from different eras in different languages, a slew of Meg Ryan films. Nothing.

I had a heart-to-heart with this couple I know who has an arranged marriage. One faxes an application ("Application to Marry") to their cult leader (a short, balding, happily married man), and he matches applicants according to height, weight, and spiritual proclivity.

The cult couple tried to set me straight over pizza. They explained how they consummated their marriage in a three-day ritual. Instruction books were handed out at the wedding ceremony. While I micromanaged the pepperoni and mushroom on my slice, I checked them out—fascinated both by a sex life dictated by formal procedure (edible underwear is out, then?) and a semiofficial pact via fax. They had conspiratorial looks of goodwill on their faces as they explained who gets to be on top and when. I stopped chewing as they spelled it out.

Just looking at them made me sweat. Surely the poor woman cried herself to sleep every night. Surely her alien husband would die for one night alone with, say, Christy Turlington. I wanted to ask, *What do you know about love?*

Close to my Village abode lurks an enigmatic structure. A photograph of the silent film comedian Ben Turpin is visible through its window; in it, he's cross-eyed. This mysterious edifice is the First National Church of the Exquisite Panic, Inc., and Ben Turpin is their prophet or patron saint. I've spent my Village years creeping by in wonderment. Maybe they knew about love slaves. Enlightenment, at last. Religion is often a good place to look for understanding.

I grabbed a friend and headed to church. Outside Exquisite Panic's gates, I told my friend about the cult couple. "Can you believe it? Arranged marriages? By fax!"

My friend thought about it. "It's *perfect.*"

Huh? My jaw dropped. Not what I was expecting.

She continued, "Imagine loving someone you're *given* to love rather than someone you've *chosen* to love."

Just the way I stopped eating pizza when the cult couple explained their sex life, I stopped at the gates of Panic. I held my breath and tried to envision love as a decision rather than as a force that sweeps you off your feet, blows you over, and makes you agree to dress up in an Uncle Sam costume (this only happened *once*).

My friend folded her arms across her chest. Exhaling deeply, she said, "Sybil, this isn't a church. It has to do with Dadaism. Art."

This cult has art shows? "You knew about this?" I shouted indignantly.

An exquisite panic washed over me. *The* exquisite panic: Not only was I messed up about love, but I couldn't even tell the difference between art and a cult. Where, oh where, could I find out what is meant by the words *love slave*? That was *all* I wanted. I was sick and tired of getting good grades, of being brainy on the job, of showing people examples of my work.

I want to know what love is. If you love somebody, set them free? Tainted love, the look of love? Shock the monkey? What's love got to do with it?

The exquisite panic!

Sweating profusely from both the cult couple and Exquisite Panic, I abandoned one friend and headed over to the house of another. "I'm having a little problem," she admitted when I got there. "I can see directly into the apartment of the people across the street from me," she began. "With the blinds open and the curtains drawn, they have *really* kinky sex." She put her hands on her hips. "What do I do to make them stop?"

I drew in a deep breath. "Rate them. Hold up placards as if this were the Olympics and they were fucking gymnasts. No pun intended. Use negative integers." I paused. "Pretend it's the 1968 Chicago Democratic Convention. Put up a sign that says, *The whole world is NOT watching*. See what happens."

"You know," she 'fessed up, "the crazy part is that, even though I don't want to, I can't help but watch."

Is *she* a love slave? How about the cult couple with their decisiveness?

I'm thinking about star-crossed lovers. Are they love slaves? Or must love be able to survive the uncrossing of stars?

Yikes.

The next time someone says to me, “Be my love slave,” I want an exegesis of the verbiage. I’m begging someone to say it, mean it, explain it.

Panic is out of the question since I can barely draw a cube and I lack artistic finesse.

As for the marriage cult, I *am* rather good with applications. I even keep a file that includes several blank Peace Corps apps as well as a few requests for official college transcripts. But I e-mail; I don’t fax. I have way too many pairs of edible underwear, and I refuse to let them get stale. However, I’m struck by this picture of love—this arrangement, this accord, this *treatise* on commitment.

But I still want to know about love slaves. And I think I’d like very much to be one.

TWENTY-EIGHT

ANTIBIOTICS 6

FROM *NEW YORK SHOCK*

From Friday, July 21, 1995

Do cell phones make radar love obsolete?

—Shark, the Bronx

Get over yourself.

—Scott, Chelsea

Sybil, orange zest is the orange part of the fruit's peel, the outermost part.

—Siobhan, Upper West Side

Sybil feels the need to reply: ***Thanks for clearing that up, Siobhan. I think I'll stick to instant oatmeal.***

TWENTY-NINE

Secret Agent

Friday, July 21, 1995

Refer to yourself in the second person. It's like talking about someone you don't know.

Rob calls to invite you to a show at the Fedora. You have to meet *Shock* people at Secret Agent in SoHo later that night, but you'll go to the Fedora first. "Okay," he says. "Good."

At the Fedora, walk down the carpeted steps and stop by the skinny platinum blond with the VIP list. Wait till she sees you clad in the black velvet cocktail dress you bought on sale. Smile when she nods you along since your name is *always* on the list. This is the biggest perk of your entire life: you're with the band. Repeat it whenever you feel down: you're with the band, you're with the band, *you're* with the band.

Though it's dark and another indie rock group plays, saunter to the front. Find an empty table, a little wet from the bottoms of glasses, and sit alone. Know there's something about a woman—especially one in black velvet—sitting by herself at a table in a dimly lit bar. Cross one leg over the other, put your tiny purse on the table, and look for a waitress. Then order white wine.

You can't fit a single thing into that purse. One key, a driver's license, ten bucks.

These are the things you have: you're with the band and you can sit alone in a bar wearing black velvet. And the ten bucks.

When the other band finishes, he comes to you. He sits down without kissing your cheek like he usually does. Find this disturbing. Does he refrain from the casual kiss because he's afraid you'll take it the wrong way, or does he refrain because it *does* mean something?

You're more like the *New York Shock* Sybil than you care to admit. *Get over yourself*, Scott in Chelsea said.

"You look great," he says. He checks you out, looking at your legs. "Silk tights?"

"Tights?" Be confused. It's summer! You're thirty!

He points to your crossed legs.

Say, "My nylons?"

"Yeah."

Tell him, "Tights are thicker."

"Oh." Rob pushes his glasses up along the bridge of his nose. "Are they silk?"

Touch your legs, aware of the fact that you're hoping his eyes follow your hand. What's going on? What are you doing? Is this a feeble attempt at *seduction*? "They're not silk."

When you look into his eyes, he's already somewhere else, though. He puts his elbows on the tiny table, locks his ankles behind the legs of his chair, and looks around. "What's the occasion?" he asks. "Why are you dressed up?"

"Secret Agent. A book party."

"I gotta go." He puts his hand on yours, and the physical contact is like any other time. "You wanna meet tomorrow? Coffee? See what's playing at the Angelika?"

"Yeah." Look down, look away. He gets up and leaves. Admit to yourself you were hoping for something. But there's nothing.

Remember, then, you're wearing black velvet.

Oh, yeah.

Sit there, lonely. Wait for Glass Half Empty. That name: *Glass Half Empty*.

Be honest with yourself: this is *not* the kind of music you'd normally listen to—it never was. Originally you did it for Madeline, for a weekend plan. Then for Rob: out of fidelity, friendship. Glass Half Empty's songs are like nothing you listen to on your own time, and yet, be honest again, you're so entangled in these pop-rock sad-happy melodies, you wouldn't know what to do without them. You can hum the tunes, sing the words right along with the singer, almost—not quite—feel the agony of the man lamenting the dead girl. You drink in this music like painters devour museums: possessively, tenderly, with long-standing commitment. You listen because you *love* it, and, though it *wasn't* you, now it is.

Feel a little starstruck because Rob has such a good voice and Dave's so cute. Look around and see how others look dazed, lustful, and generally impressed. Rob's like an artist. He *is* an artist! Be overcome by the way he moves onstage with comfort, ease, confidence, and rock-star sex appeal.

Admit it: you find him *sexy*. Even in that green suit. *Especially* in that green suit. Just admit it. Make yourself repeat it the way you repeat *You're with the band*. He's sexy. He's sexy. *He's* sexy.

Blush. Turn red. Say a little prayer that you're not also sweating because sweat can't be good for velvet.

Okay, admit other things. It's dark. No one can see the hue of your skin.

Say to yourself, *I love Robert Shachtley*. Use his full name.

Rob shimmies up to the standing mike. "'A Little Help from My Friends.'"

Then he sings to you. You know it; he knows it. This Bud's for you.

But. Feel perturbed. Try not to be, but it happens anyway. Go over the songs he's sung you. "Norwegian Wood" comes to mind particularly. He may as well be singing "Yellow Submarine" right now. You're not ungrateful. You're not. In fact, you love the Beatles. But "A Little Help from My Friends"?

Friends?

Fold your arms over your chest, your velvety black breasts. Hah! You want to laugh at yourself in this silly dress! There's something so wasted about your body, your thoughts, your life.

The music ends. Go. Get thee to SoHo. New neighborhood, new vibe. Cobblestone streets, art galleries. Money, money, money.

Enter Secret Agent. Again, your name is at the door. Another cause for celebration. Walk in off the street, the door closes behind you and you're in another world like the time you entered Ramone's. Once inside, you feel sealed in, as if you were in a spaceship traveling through outer space. The *outer* is very outer.

Secret Agent is thick and gothic. Feel the pretense of make-believe, the sex in the air, the suspension of disbelief. It's dark and you can barely see. People hover in groups of two or three silhouettes. The colors are bloody: reds and heavy blacks. Velvet parlor couches stand alone, empty beside atmospheric black cats. There's seriously a black cat lounging on an antique couch, his long sleek tail whipping against the cushions. Dramatic chandeliers throw beams on Mapplethorpe flower arrangements, erotic like everything else, in black vases on stark marble tables. Look around and feel out of place even though you were that woman who could sit alone in the dimly lit bar only a couple of minutes ago. What happened?

Peer through darkness into the back of Secret Agent. A long table stretches out underneath an oil painting you can't quite make out. Barely see the shapes of seven well-dressed men sitting beneath it. They're all smoking cigars and throwing their heads back in laughter. It's like a mafia movie. You've always wanted to be in the mob, or at least have an Italian mobster lover. It strikes you as odd that there are no women with them.

The artifice of the whole place *gets* you, fills you with repulsion, a longing for those pop-rock sad-happy melodies that don't require any suspension of disbelief. You know that whatever those men in their Versace suits are laughing at, it isn't that funny and half of them wish there were a woman around.

But you're also sick with desire. You're seduced by the make-believe and the suggestion that other people, all these other people, have something in their lives that you don't. Something icy cool, poignant, and deep. Something that makes them *fit.* A *grandeur* of sorts.

But who are they? And why don't you recognize any of them?

"Yoo-hoo, Sybil." A *Shock* intern, eighteen or nineteen, approaches. She's trying to become a model. She showed you her portfolio once. Pretty girl. You're glad to see that flip of golden hair, her silver eyelids, those pink frosted lips, her shiny unbuttoned blouse. "You look beautiful!" She reaches out to grab your hand.

Grip her arm and whisper in her ear, "Grace, who *are* these people?"

The intern smiles broadly, sparkly; you can see *Vogue* written all over her face. "They're Bella's friends. She's got lots of friends."

Bella is the author.

Follow Grace. Everyone seems to know her, and when they talk, they rub each other's backs. Have more white wine. At the bar, hear someone say, "There's male-model backlash from the opening of Supermodel Café. The male models are opening up a sports bar and grill. They're calling it Jackets and Vests."

Someone else says, "Why don't they call it Jock Strap Patisserie? Be different. We've got enough sports bars. What we need is a manly bakery. Cakes with muscle."

Laugh.

"You're laughing," says a voice from the left.

Turn your head to see who is eavesdropping on you eavesdropping. How postmodern.

Whoever he is, he looks how you want New York to look in a man. Mid-thirties, gray temples, a dozen silver loops climbing up the slope of his ear, blue jeans, combat boots that tell you he's done some scary dancing at scary clubs to scary industrial music. Plus, he has the face of a pretty boy, a hardened criminal, Cary Grant, Patrick Swayze. Despite signs of aging, there's nothing passé about him.

Say, "That was more of a chuckle." Look at him, read things into his combat boots and silver clash of earrings like rebellion, nonconformity, and other things that usually make you go *blah blah blah*. Feel like he might be better for you to follow around than the intern.

"Who do you know here?" he asks.

Get the distinct impression he's trying to pick you up. "I know Bella. I know a lot of people. I just see very few of them right now." You've never been a big fan of the pickup scene. The thing you like least about it is its *obviousness*. To participate, it seems like you have to come out and acknowledge that you're one desperate individual and you'll do *anything*—even try your luck at a hit-and-miss game with strangers—not to spend one more wretched moment alone. So when you see this Apollo before you, you're simultaneously disgusted that he's resorting to such an act of desperation and majorly attracted to him. Say, "I don't think I know you."

"I did the painting on the cover of Bella's book."

Another artist.

Sometime after midnight, gothic ambience all around, demand: "Tell me your name. Maybe I've heard of you."

"You haven't." He leans against the bar. The two of you are statues, fine-limbed, languid, like orchids in a thin vase.

Huh. So this is how it goes.

"I'm Michael Miéve." He offers you his hand.

"I'm Sybil Weatherfield." Both of you have silly names. Give him your hand too. "I work with Bella. Do you know where everyone is?"

"Playing pool upstairs."

"There are pool tables upstairs?"

"There are." He moves closer.

"It ruins something. I'd rather imagine that everyone is just hanging around in languorous repose, talking about their trips to Milan." Put a hand on his wrist. "I don't want to know one can shoot pool upstairs. What does that do for the place?"

He looks at your hand on his wrist. He doesn't pull away, so you don't remove it. "To clean, you know they've gotta turn on all the lights," he says.

Say, "Let's go sit by that tomcat." Pull him toward a red couch. Sit, looking moony and provocative through a skillful management of gestures.

The tomcat jumps off the sofa. Can't fool him.

Talk for an hour, and finally see several people from *Shock*. Mostly talk to Michael Miéve, who name-drops. He doesn't say, *Naomi Campbell* or *Matthew Perry*; rather, he says, *Nietzsche, Kandinsky, Einstein.*

He's a little arrogant, but—then again—so are you. So approve. Approve wholeheartedly. It's an arrogance you can appreciate. Okay, some people might be a little miffed by his use of words like *ineffable* or his lengthy monologue on Leni Riefenstahl and then *superstructure*. (Notice the fascist strain, but dismiss it as silly and unlikely.) He's so beautiful. He's so smart. He's an artiste. Endorse him. Give him a thumbs-up. Want to be his friend.

Sit there, lost in Secret Agent's oppressive sensuality, an erotic farce. This guy doesn't know you're unlikable. He doesn't know you'd rather be at home wearing old sweatpants, a concert t-shirt with a robe over that, watching *The Nanny.* He doesn't know you can eat an entire chocolate cheesecake in one sitting or that you call Madeline every day or that you're not a very good writer but you have nothing else to fall back on. Nor does he know you have a boyfriend and another man you love altogether.

He doesn't know these things.

Tune in to what he's saying: deconstructionism, postmodernism. *Blah blah blah.*

But go with it.

Don't ask why.

Just go with it.

Get involved in a conversation on modern art. "I have an easier time grasping Mantegna over Pollock," you say. You don't know what to do with large canvases marked by single, unexplainable black splashes. Suspect he's that kind of artist.

Know you can't approach Michael Miéve's canvases. Know you don't even want to.

"I live in the Bowery," he says. "Would you like to go home with me?"

Tonight is a night for making decisions. Stand up and smooth down the black velvet dress. Admire Michael's lack of disdain for the Secret Agent artifice. Think about Long Island Day and how ugly the contempt was. Though Secret Agent is gothic, these are your own Dark Ages. Consider this move, this infidelity, the violation of the math equation you've got going with Jeff Simon. Would this be unfaithful to Jeff? Or to Rob? Think of it as a well-written essay: a stunning introduction that gets your readers' attention, a body that develops your thesis, and a conclusion—get out and do it neatly, quickly, without mess. But make a point. Never forget your point.

Your point is this: you are not made for loving.

You do not love.

Look again at Michael Miéve. Know what it's really like to be sick with desire. You stand before him; he waits for an answer. You count his earrings. Seven. You wonder where the tomcat sleeps. Where he eats. On whom you'd be cheating.

You don't need to go through with it to get the point. "I don't think so, Michael. But thank you for asking." Stunned or not, he says nothing. You just turn and leave.

The second-person point of view dissipates, leaving you with dirty hands. Slink back into "I" with all its ugly subjectivity problems.

THIRTY

Black Velvet Dress

Saturday, July 22, 1995

So, of course, I go to Rob's at 2:30 in the morning. The streets have that desolate Manhattan look: an occasional homeless person, garbage blowing though there's no wind, heavily barred storefronts with Lotto ticket signs lit up in windows, an uncanny dead sound like the hum of a flatline in a hospital.

I take a cab.

I ring the bell and wait. Then he responds. "Yeah?" He's half asleep.

"It's me," I say, hoping that's enough.

There's a moment of nothing. A long pause. I look up and down the street. All of the Indian restaurants are closed. I'm a little nervous to be out here by myself. He finally buzzes me in. Climbing the narrow staircase with the royal-blue paint, I see him standing in the entryway watching me clamber toward him. I stop at the threshold so we're face-to-face.

He looks at me, gaping at my dress and not saying anything. He wears Scooby-Doo boxers, his glasses are crooked, and his feet are bare.

He steps aside to let me pass. "Come in."

I'm self-conscious, even though he's practically naked. I push hair behind my ears. "I'm sorry, Rob. Go back to sleep. We'll talk later."

He looks me up and down. "Are you injured?"

My arms hang at my side. I hesitate. "No."

And so I tell him what happened, and then he goes to bed.

In the morning, he makes coffee, gives me some old clothes, and hands me an A&P bag for my dress. I slip on my heels, which don't go with the outfit. "Are you showing me the door?"

He grabs his keys off the kitchen counter. "No, I'll walk you home." He puts on his sunglasses and walks to the door. "Let's go."

"You're looking very retro today, Mr. Shachtley," I tell him. "Sunglasses, sideburns, orange pants."

"I'm *always* retro, Sybilizer. Get your baggy ass down those steps, and don't forget your minute purse."

As we head down the stairs, me ahead of him, we meet Mr. and Mrs. Gupta. I'm *obviously* wearing Rob's clothes, and they *obviously* see it. They say, "Hi," smiling sincerely at Rob. From behind, Rob puts his hands on my shoulders as we move to let them pass. I'm grateful for this. He claims me, in a way. When we walk down, I hear the clunk-clunk of Rob's shoes on the stairs echoing behind.

On the sidewalk, he closes the door and shoves his keys deep into a pocket. We stand there. Rob digs into the other, pulling out random change. He counts, digs again, and flashes two bucks.

In front of Bombay Café, I watch. People shove past him, knocking his shoulders. But he's immune, a New York boy, used to the tussle of bodies on the street, each going about his or her own business. He pays no attention, focused on the money in his hand. I watch him sift through nickels and dimes, his sunglasses tinted yellow and no doubt prescription, his orange pants on because if he's not wearing a suit he's wearing thrift store clothes that bring to mind words like *groovy* and names like *Jimi Hendrix.* I stand there in plum pants and a Peter Frampton t-shirt, watching.

He catches me staring. "I have to buy paper towels on the way home," he explains. He puts the money back into his pocket. "Okay." He opens up his arm to me. Then we walk side by side down Sixth, beyond the Indian restaurants, Peter Frampton tee fluttering in the muggy breeze, Rob's tinted glasses reflecting sunshine.

I have the urge to reach for his hand and hold it as we walk from the East Village to the West. I'd like to hold his hand, clasp it tightly, swing it gently, my fingers intertwined with his.

THIRTY-ONE

ABSCESS

BLEEDING-HEART LIBERAL, OR HOW TO SHED YOUR IDEALS, OR THE TRUE MEANING OF THROWING YOUR AFFECTIONS TO THE WIND

SYBIL WEATHERFIELD FOR *NEW YORK SHOCK*

From Friday, July 28, 1995

My love is a waste of your time.

Picture us standing outside a movie theater on the Upper West Side—a bunch of girls, women really, with college degrees from good schools who have dead-end jobs bordering on volunteerism and meaningful platonic friendships with men who think VD will never happen to them. Picture us with our colored hair. Notice older guys looking at us; we don't care. If you saw our résumés, you'd be impressed. We speak several languages. We've worked in hospitals and taught Sunday school. Most of us have slept with a foreign guy, at least once.

We stand in a cluster, having just seen a Parker Posey film. Newspapers tucked under arms, attaché cases purchased by visiting moms, bananas for later.

That's when he makes his approach. Mind you, we're not talking about a brooding megalomaniac traffic-stopping male entity who can conjugate *to think* in seven different languages. No, we're talking about a short man who's wearing too many clothes for a hot, not-really-sultry summer evening. He also smells like a rat died in his pants (surely these shelters have showers), but not before defecating in his mouth.

"Spare change?" he says.

And the truth of the matter is this: I have *nothing* to spare.

We're New York girls; we know about these things. When we first came here, we had illusions about feeding the world—silly notions stemming from Live Aid, Band-Aid, and that election in which we all voted for Dukakis. In order to avoid despair, we made contingency plans that involved giving a dollar a day to the man on the street. That got pretty expensive, so we gave the bum at our subway stop five bucks when we received a raise at work. Then we saw him drinking bourbon. Fuck that. We're New York girls; we know about these things.

This nomad/wreck-of-a-man won't leave us alone. He holds an "I Love New York" paper cup and jangles it around. "Twenty cents," he says. Then, in a bout of frustration, he pleads, "I'm *only* asking for *twenty* cents."

I stand with my friends; the hour is late. We gotta go. We work tomorrow. We have breakfast plans in the morning. When we say good-bye, we press our cheeks together and blow kisses to the wind.

On the train, I think about the bum, about how I went from being a woman who used to hold candlelight vigils for miscellaneous peaceniks to being a brandisher of stock reports and beauty tips. Once subject to broken hearts, now heartless.

And it's only a matter of time before I remember a woman I once temped for. A thin wall separated us, and sometimes I'd hear the phone slam down and she'd yell, "Shit! Shit! Shit!" (always in threes). She had carpal tunnel syndrome, her skin was extremely dry, and her computer software was outdated. She wore muumuus and, like me, drank a lot of coffee.

I admit it now: I didn't like her one bit. She scared me with that *shit, shit, shit* business. She made me fear employment and middle age and being a single, straight woman who drank cold coffee.

On my last day there, after a three-month stint, she took me for lunch. Over Thai, I told her about my second cousin in the Peace Corps in Peru. "She got pregnant, never told the father, and came home," I said. "Now she has an Inca baby." My entire family loves that Inca kid.

My boss looked at me distrustfully, as if I were lying. Her cynicism ruined my appetite. With every bite of Pad Thai, I felt like a liar, and damn it, I *wasn't* lying!

Now, riding the train, post–Parker Posey, I feel shackled to that cynicism. Am I a cynic too? Does ignoring the bum mean cynicism?

While we ate, my boss told me her story, sharing intimacies

even though she thought me a liar. "My ex-husband and I were finishing up our dissertations in East Africa," she began. "We were cultural anthropologists in the sixties." Her eyes became glassy as she recalled an early marriage. "The only other nonindigenous people were two missionaries and a relief worker who was rumored to be CIA. There was a lot we couldn't talk about. We avoided religion and Vietnam," she laughed, having finished her Thai coffee.

When she spoke, I envisioned days under a hot African sun, hours atop cracked earth, eons among the windblown greens. Her hands must have been blistered, her heart full. Swahili, pottery shards, farming, repression. Every day was a storm; every day people recovered in its wake. No matter what happened, they sang. No matter what happened, they cradled children. Day in and day out, they harvested crops, simmered food, loved migrant workers, nursed the hungry, and clamored for shared bars of soap.

"We were both anthropologists," she told me, "but I was supposed to get dinner on the cardboard box, clean the sheets on the cot, mend the mosquito nets, and recharge the batteries." Her voice soured, and her story ended in a failed marriage. "I relied on the African women. If I fell backward, they'd catch me. That's how strong they were."

She returned to America in the midst of the sexual revolution. *I Love Lucy* was over. She got a divorce, put on a muumuu, and started saying "shit" in triplicate.

Now, train-borne, I wonder if she's me. She put Africa behind her. I've put Live Aid, Band-Aid, and candlelight vigils behind me. She has carpal tunnel syndrome; I have both an inferiority *and* a superiority complex.

The train arrives at my stop. On the street, I think about my friends, the way we kiss the air over each other's shoulders.

Those kisses take flight. They float upward and out. The higher they soar, the thinner they become. Floating up, up, up. Finally, moving toward the heavens, those kisses dissipate like a fine vapor, unable to sustain any substance. A mist of disaffected kisses. Gone in moments.

What made those African women so strong, so able to uphold the American housewife abandoned in the bush? What made us turn from our college-girl idealism? Why did we reject our hopes for world peace? Once we gladly took on tree-hugger jobs. Once we befriended depressed men with disastrous libidos. Surely there was something there, some smidgen of hope. Unlike the African women, though, we lacked the strength, the endurance, the ability to recover from cycles of storms. Why have we become so cynical, so capable of disaffected kisses? What made us ferment like bad wine?

That my love is a waste of anyone's time stings me to the core.

THIRTY-TWO

ANTIBIOTICS 7

FROM *NEW YORK SHOCK*

From Friday, August 4, 1995

Has your boyfriend read this?

—Beth, West Village

THIRTY-THREE

NURSERY RHYMES

Wednesday, August 9, 1995

It's August 1995 and I've been seeing Jeff for nearly a year. It's time to break up with him.

We're supposed to meet at the Fondue Fête in Midtown. Before I go, I sit on my couch, which is loaded with perverse memories, to read "Antibiotics." I want to binge. Then purge. I turn to "Antibiotics."

Has your boyfriend read this?

—Beth, West Village

I wonder which boyfriend she's talking about.

I drop *Shock* and go meet Jeff. When I enter the Fondue Fête, I see him sitting at a booth in the back, framed in faux–Swiss Alps charm. The whole place looks like a cuckoo clock. Little powder-blue birds, waitresses dressed in Mother Goose milkmaid costumes with fondue pots instead of milk buckets, painted backdrops of snow-covered mountain peaks and deep Disney valleys. It's a mythic Switzerland, amusement-park-cum-Old-Mother-Hubbard.

"I'm sorry I'm late," I say, dropping into the seat across from him.

He looks like the soap star he could have been. A strong, clean-shaven jaw. Brown hair. He looks at his watch. "You're not late," a subdued—do I detect *shaken*?—voice offers assurance. "I just got here." He lowers his wrist, and yes, he's shaken. He's somber and muted like his beige pants and taupe shirt. Jeff Simon is a lovely-looking man, which is something I'll never forget. "Leave it to you to pick a place like this," he says, reaching across the table to help me pull my arm out of a summer jacket sleeve.

"What's this?" I grab a cocktail napkin. It features a recipe for a Harvey Wallbanger. "What do you have?" I reach for his napkin, trying to avoid eye contact. I'm *really* nervous. And Jeff looks so nice, like such a nice guy.

He picks up his cocktail napkin and studies it. "Pink Lady."

I snatch it from him and put both in my purse. "I'm giving them to Madeline. Ask for a stack. Tell 'em I drool." I attempt a smile.

Next I lift the fondue fork: a thin wand with tiny tines at the end. I point it at him. "What do you want?" I open my menu and use the fork to guide my vision. We should have dinner first, and I'll tell him it's over during chocolate fondue. We can be friends. He'll take it like a gentleman, water off a duck's back, possibly indifferent. Though he has a heart to break, I'm not the woman for the job. "I'm buying," I say.

Jeff doesn't open his menu. "You decide. I'll buy."

I point the fondue fork at him again. "What's wrong?" He's upset about something.

He folds his arms over his chest. “Let’s figure out what we’re ordering and then we’ll talk.”

“Is everything okay?” I lower my fork.

“Yeah, I just want to talk.” He reaches over to my menu and taps it. “Figure out what we’re eating. It’s your night.”

My night. I sink my eyes into the menu.

A milkmaid strolls over. “What can I get you two to drink?”

“Sybil?” Jeff waits for me to choose. “What would you like?”

“We’d love more cocktail napkins.” I prop my elbows on the table. “How many recipes are there?”

The milkmaid’s eyes lift to the ceiling of our alpine chalet. “Let’s see, there are grasshoppers, gimlets—”

I interrupt her. “Gimlets?” I look at Jeff. “You want a gimlet, Jeff?”

“Two gimlets.” He nods at the milkmaid, holding up two fingers in a peace sign.

“I’ll bring more napkins also,” she says cheerily.

“I’m not sure I’ve ever had a gimlet,” I say when she’s gone.

We order Swiss-cheese fondue, a meat-and-shellfish entrée, and a chocolate dessert. While we wait for the cheese, Jeff and I literally stare at each other with bizarre smiles that make us look constipated. We cross our arms on top of the table. Between us, a cauldron of white wine slowly heats.

From somewhere nearby, I hear a discussion about a T.G.I. Friday’s restaurant in Tulsa. One table over, two hairy guys who look like they would know a little something about letter bombs discuss the nature of political revolution (bloody) and the psychology of sex (ugly). I sneak a glance. They talk rapidly and dip chunks of sourdough bread into hot cheese as if this were a regular ritual before they head to Brooklyn for the weekly Marxist reading group meeting. I envy them their comfort level in each other's presence.

With arms still folded on top of the table, I peer down at the wine list. "Did you notice the dot over the *i* is a green olive with a toothpick stuck through the pimento?"

Jeff looks. "Nice."

"What did you want to talk to me about?" My mouth is dry, cottony.

The milkmaid arrives with our cheese. She dumps shredded Swiss into bubbling wine and adds garlic, lemon, black pepper, and nutmeg. She puts down little dishes of bread chunks, vegetables, and apple. "Dip and twist," she says. "Dip and twist."

She leaves, and I stab an apple and plunge it into Swiss. "Dip and twist," I say. Then I fix my eyes on Jeff. I point my fork in his direction and order, "Dip and twist."

He makes no move.

"Why aren't you dipping and twisting, buddy?" I scrunch up my eyes.

He pokes a broccoli stalk with his fork and slides it into the pot. "Would you rather a serious talk now or later?" He lifts his fork, twirling it, then blowing.

I had planned for a serious talk over dessert, but I can see it's really *not* my night. "Talk to me now."

"I'll tell you why I'm with you, Sybil." It's recited. He's rehearsed.

I dip and twist.

He continues, "I'm a pretty conservative guy."

Dip and twist.

"When we first met, I think we wanted the same things." He sips the gimlet.

He's breaking up with me. Dip and twist.

He plunges a mushroom into cheese. "We weren't looking for love. We'd both admit that?" He tries to catch my eye. We've never said this aloud. "We'd admit that?"

I nod slowly, suddenly knowing it's a terrible thing to toss up love like a bunch of pick-up sticks.

After he swallows the mushroom, he says, "I'm not sure if I believed we'd eventually fall in love or if I thought of our relationship as some kind of comfortable short-term thing in which I'd take care of my individual concerns until I was ready to think about someone else—I don't know."

I put down my fondue fork.

"But I guess I knew that eventually it had to change into *something*." He reaches for my fork. He pokes its tines into a chunk of sourdough bread. He hands it back to me. He whispers, "Dip and twist." I drop it into the cauldron. "But it *hasn't*."

For a while, we eat without speaking, our jaws working, our lips closed, our eyes sad. When there's nothing left, the milkmaid arrives with more food. A pot of boiling broth steams between us, and we have lobster tails, shrimp, filet mignon, marinated chicken chunks, and a thousand different colorful sauces ready for dipping. We get new fondue forks, and while my eyes stay focused on Jeff, the milkmaid says, "Use your fondue forks to cook everything, but always eat from your dinner forks. Cooking time is about one and a half to two minutes."

As she leaves, Jeff says, "Thank you."

"Thank you," I echo.

"Sybil." Jeff reaches guardedly around the scorching pot and touches my arm. "Sometimes you make me want to go on Route 66. You make me want to eat grilled cheese sandwiches in diners. You make me want to visit Graceland. You can do that to a man. . . ." His voice trails off. His hand is on my arm and he slowly pulls away. "It isn't what I thought it would be, though." He touches his lips with his napkin. "This isn't a comfortable short-term thing in which I take care of my individual concerns until I'm ready to think about someone else."

I immerse a shrimp. Funny how my first response is resistance. I came here to break up with him, and I have this urge to convince him to stay and love me forever.

We eat fondue.

"What is it, then?" I manage to say.

With great care, he forms his sentences. "You present this very romantic picture, Sybil. This Jack Kerouac vision where we go to poetry readings and kooky art shows. You know band members, and all your friends complain about being disenfranchised," he pauses and continues, "but they're all decidedly middle, maybe even upper middle, class—"

"Just middle," I interrupt.

"Do you want me to stop? Am I going too far?"

I pull out a piece of cooked chicken. "No." I feel myself turning red. "I'm just dipping and twisting." I cut the chicken. "Go ahead—"

"I don't think you have to dip and twist anymore."

"Oh." I plunge poultry into peanut sauce. "But I like to."

He continues, "Don't get me wrong. I'm sure that part of the appeal for me was the fact that you really approach the bohemian thing from a very safe vantage point. I doubt I would have wanted it differently—"

I stop eating and watch him closely.

"So you're not *alternative* and you're not a yuppie. You're very white, very heterosexual, and very educated. You're neither here nor there." He watches me watching him, squirming from the indictment. "You're *nowhere*."

Vicious, after all.

Jeff puts a piece of steak onto his plate. "Though I may have wanted an interim period with you, I'm not sure I wanted a woman in a constant interim period herself. I don't think," he hesitates, "I really wanted a temp."

I look down at the table, hurt, embarrassed, *ashamed*.

"I'm sorry," he dips the steak into teriyaki, "but I read 'Abscess.' We're not in love." He eats the steak and we're silent. "And you'll tell the whole world we mean nothing to each other." He shakes his head. "When we part tonight, there's no love lost."

My eyes fill with tears.

"Love was never an option." He reaches across the table and touches my cheek. "Sybil, I always get the feeling that I *could* have loved you," he swallows and adds, "but I don't."

After the entrée, the milkmaid brings melted chocolate with slices of bananas, strawberries, pineapple, and hunks of cheesecake and brownies. "Put a marshmallow on your fondue fork," she instructs. We stab marshmallows and she does something to send a flame into the air. Fire rises in blue and orange, and we flambé our marshmallows till they're a toasty hue. Now we avoid touching each other's forks; our association has changed. It was more brutal than I expected.

"Jeff?" I dip a strawberry into the chocolate pool.

"Huh?"

"Why now? Why did you decide to break it off now?"

Jeff stops manipulating fruit on his fork. He drops his head. "I guess, after this long, I'd expect *someone* to love *someone*."

We're quiet, absorbed in chocolate, in dipping and twisting, sometimes drizzling.

When the bill is paid, he rises. "Ready?"

"Yeah."

I follow him through the Fondue Fête, walking behind him, stepping in his steps, aware that we don't touch, won't touch. When we get outside, we face each other on the sidewalk. "Let me escort you home," he says. Manhattan whirs around us, dark night with flashes of yellow and red, air like warm breath, people with shopping bags hitting their legs.

I step back. "No, that's okay. I'm fine. It's fine."

"It's not a problem." He wrinkles his forehead. "I know you're fine."

"No, really."

We stand in front of each other. We think of things to say. "Do you have anything at my place?" he asks.

I try to remember, try to think, know I have never left anything at his place. "No." I shake my head. "Do you have anything at mine?"

"I don't think so." A soft breeze makes the awning flap overhead. "Are you sure I can't accompany you home?" he asks, shoving his hands in his pockets.

"No. Thank you, Jeff." I start walking backward. "Look. I'm already gone."

He blows me a kiss. I pretend to catch it, turn my back, and walk toward the subway station. I cry. I'm not sure why, but I weep the whole way home.

THIRTY-FOUR

Lump

Wednesday, August 16, 1995

What happens next happens very quickly.

On Monday, I was writing "Abscess" via laptop computer on my bed. The fan blew my papers off the pillow and I awkwardly bent over to get them. I had to fold my body over like a hideaway bed or a fat taco. At that cumbersome angle, I felt it. In my chest, my breast: a *lump*.

At first, I thought I was imagining it. I mean, what did I know about lumps?

So I spent the rest of the day casually touching it, trying to make up alternative scenarios while standing naked in front of the bathroom mirror unable to see a damn thing. Whatever I did, the activity always ended with my fingers kneading what could only be that which would kill me. And I was scared. I was resigned. I'd die of cancer. You knew it was gonna happen.

Today, a Wednesday, I look at the books on the shelf while wearing a paper dress and reclining on a metal table in a doctor's office. They have titles like *Surviving Cancer* and *The Breast Book*. *Great*, I think. My arms extend down the length of my body; my dress crunches with every move.

Suddenly, I'm aware of my breasts, which—for all my self-absorption—I've never really considered. They're fairly normal, and this is nice since there are so many things about me that defy normalcy. I'm grateful for my standard breasts. Neither large nor small, neither saggy nor perky, they're simply there. They look good in clothes. I don't want to lose them.

The doctor comes in to examine me. I lie back on the table, exposed, looking up at the ceiling. Then I figure I'll watch him. He doesn't actually fix his eyes on my breast, which is something he must have learned in med school: *Whatever you do, do not look directly at the breast.* He finds the lump with his fingers, pit-pats around it like a dog smelling the ground, feels elsewhere, and returns to the scene of the crime. I try but fail to read signs of doom. Trained stoicism in his countenance leads me to rely on his fingertips dancing around the lump planted heavily on my left, supposedly standard, breast. *I've seen it all before*, say his tapping fingers. I look away because I'm a dead woman.

"Let's try a needle aspiration," he says. A long, thin needle that'll only pinch appears in his hands. "If liquid comes out, it's fine." He jabs me, I feel the small pinch, and no liquid comes out. He closes the paper dress over my breast. "Okay, we'll do some lab work."

Distraught, I go to the Fedora in search of Rob Shachtley on a Wednesday night.

There's a new girl, same platinum-blond hair, manning the reservations list. I walk toward her, lean over her podium, and search for my name among the VIPs. Ten people are listed and it gives me great pleasure—or, it *would* give me great pleasure if I weren't dying—to point to "S. Weatherfield" among the names. Still with the band. She smiles broadly and says, "Go right in."

"Thank you." I walk off, humming, "That's the way, uh-huh, uh-huh, I like it." But my heart isn't in it.

It's dark. Adjusting slowly to shadowy chic light, I see it's already busy at 9:30 p.m. PJ Harvey, my soul sister, wails on the sound system. The tables are noisy with falsetto girl laughter and cramped with the working stiff crowd, all of them skinny and glamorous. I bet not a single one of them is dying. Plus, I'm the only person in denim. I'm dying *and* I'm wearing denim. I find an abandoned table off to the side and sit.

It's Dave Stomps, not Rob, who joins me. "May I buy you a drink?" He pulls the chair in under him. He's wearing a maroon suit.

"I gave up alcohol a few hours ago."

"Huh." Dave squints. "Club soda?"

"That's fine."

We sit together, a bit stiffly. We're not used to being alone, especially in. bars. He orders our drinks and taps his feet on the floor. "So, I heard you broke up with Jeff."

"Yeah." I shake my head. "No. He broke up with me."

I mop up little wet spots around my club soda with the cocktail napkin. "We live in the same neighborhood, Dave. You're like a block away. Aren't you supposed to invite people over since you're married? I thought married people are supposed to invite single people for dinner, and single people are supposed to bring over soda. Isn't that how it works?" I tilt my head and appear confused.

"We would." He hunts for an excuse. "But we wouldn't know where to put you. It's a one-bedroom. A lousy one-bedroom. You've seen it—I don't know where you'd sit."

"You guys should move." I sip my drink, looking at the sophisticated people and keying in to Liz Phair over the speakers. "Go cheaper and sacrifice the trendy neighborhood."

Dave grows rigid. "Our lease is up at the end of the year. We'll see."

People ask for our extra chair and we practically fall all over the place to give it away. Then it's just our seats, our bodies, our drinks on wet cocktail napkins.

"Get a two-bedroom in Midtown," I say. "Chelsea's probably not any cheaper."

Dave sits up straight. He looks into his tawny brew and then gazes up. "We're thinking of going back to Rhode Island, Sybil."

For a moment, I just sit. Then I speak. "You mean, you're thinking of leaving?"

"Yeah." His mouth stays open, suspended.

I'm stunned. "You can't do that. You've got a life here. Things are *happening*. You can't just *leave* and go back to *Providence*. What would you do in *Providence*?"

Dave leans in. "I have a wife and child. We live in a one-bedroom. My daughter sleeps in the living room. My wife works eight to three every day, and I cater when I'm not out being a rock star in a small, unknown band. This isn't what I want."

I feel frantic. I feel the lump growing. I hear PJ Harvey again, and all the sophisticates are rising up in dark silhouettes to do a "Danse Macabre" performance. "But Dave . . ." I'm bewildered. "What about the *band*?"

Dave licks beer foam off his lips. "I have to do what's best for my family, Sybil."

"What about the band? What about Rob? What'll Rob do?"

His mouth twitches. "He'll go solo."

I fold my arms across my diseased breasts. "*Solo*!" I repeat. "Rob can't go *solo*! He goes solo on everything. You can't leave. You're the cute one! What'll happen to him? What'll happen to Rob?"

"Sybil." He reaches across the table to grab my face. "I love the guy. I've been there for him. I was there when he needed someone to pick him up off the ground. I lived *his* dream. I'd do anything for him. But this, Sybil. I can't mess up my family—"

"But you're about to make it—" I whine. "You guys are about to make it."

"We're *one* New York band among a million." He looks away. "I have a family."

I try not to hear. "Other people do it. *Other* people make it."

"You're a smart girl, Sybil, but for a smart girl, you don't know shit about marriage."

We say nothing. Then I stutter, "Does Rob know?"

Dave flattens his lapels. "Yeah. We've discussed it."

"He's never mentioned it." I rip the corners off a soggy napkin.

When he leaves, he smoothes his crazy maroon jacket, leans over, and kisses me on the forehead. And there I sit, dying in denim, knowing Glass Half Empty is on borrowed time and Rob will be lost. Around me, the Fedora spins, glowing like a state fair. Laughter and voices slur, ice cubes hit each other in tingly crashes, dresses creep up thighs. The instruments onstage are bare, stark, dormant, waiting to be played, and my breath comes out in slow, rhythmic bursts of loneliness.

And that's when I see him. Rob moves through tables, weaving past well-wishers, stopping occasionally, leaning over to whisper in ears, smiling, chatting, meandering among pretty marionettes obscured by dim light, and I see—it's the very first thing I see—he's not alone.

A girl walks in front of him, holding his hand loosely behind her back. When he stops, they unlock fingers. She smiles serenely, patiently waiting. I watch him with the girl. I stare hard. She has that look I was never able to master, the look that eluded me, mocked me, said, *Dream on*. She's skinny and tall, maybe taller than Rob, and she's wearing a black tank top with spaghetti straps and no bra. Why do girls like her never wear a bra? Her hair is short and choppy, and I've always wanted short and choppy hair.

Then Rob sees me. I don't know how he happens to find me in the dark, hiding behind shadows like Nosferatu, but Rob sees me and whispers something no doubt reassuring into the girl's fragile ear. She understands and goes away.

"Sybil." He stands before me and speaks with formality.

"Rob." I pull out a chair. "Sit for a minute?"

He plops down. "Only for a minute." He looks around conspiratorially and whispers, "I've kinda got something going."

"Yeah, I saw." I go for flippancy, what I do best. "Who is she?"

"Her name's Robin."

I expected something like Fawn or Brandy. "She's pretty." I put my hand on his arm. "Rob, I've gotta talk to you."

"Now? Tonight?"

"Yeah, tonight. I'm sorry." I flash an earnest, heartfelt look. "It's *really* important."

He rubs his eye with his finger, searching for refusals, and that's when I see it: he isn't wearing his wedding ring. "Can't it wait till tomorrow?"

"Where's your wedding band?" I reach for his hand, turning it over in mine.

"I took it off." He looks at his hand in mine.

I touch his ring finger. "Why?"

"You're supposed to be happy. This is supposed to be a step in the right direction. Where's your praise?" He frowns. "My mental health is at stake."

I pull my hand away. "No," I say disingenuously. "It's *great.*" I pause. "I *really* do need to talk to you, though." We have a mini-face-off and he knows I want to get rid of the girl and I'm messed up about the ring. "Not here," I add.

He sighs. Then he digs into his pocket and pulls out his keys. He throws them on the table. "Here," he says briskly. "I'll meet you at my apartment after the show."

"I'm sorry," I say. "Really." Neither of us believes me.

Glass Half Empty plays, and Rob is infused with an antagonism that makes their pop-rock sad-happy melodies sound raw. He does new things with guitar riffs that make Dave Stomps sweat big wet beads onto his snazzy maroon suit.

When it comes time for the Beatles, Rob tears into "Day Tripper." When they finish their set, I snatch up the keys and make my way out, aware that I'll never move with the grace of a girl with choppy hair.

THIRTY-FIVE

METASTASIZE

Still Wednesday, August 16, 1995

I enter Rob's apartment, maybe twenty minutes ahead of him. It's midnight, but the East Village is lit up like a video arcade; the Guptas clean a glow-in-the-dark Bombay Café below. Inside the apartment, I drop my purse, shove my shoes next to the scrapbook, and open his fridge because I'm sick in the head. Mayo, Muenster, apple juice. On the counter: Cap'n Crunch and four fruit roll-ups, one half eaten.

I sit down and touch the lump. I try not to think about it. I look at my watch, a fake Rolex I bought on Madison Ave. out of a briefcase belonging to a guy wearing a trench coat. I stand and walk to the window overlooking Sixth. Peering through curtains, I yawn falsely—stretching my mouth in appropriate shapes—and touch the lump again. The street is empty, and only a few people walk by. Again I go for the lump. It won't go away. No matter what I do. It won't leave.

I let the curtains drop, knowing I'm going to die. I wander

around the room's margins, absorbing its edicts. All these books, all these tapes and CDs. A guitar I've never seen. Even Rob has *things*. Even Rob builds up possessions.

I study pictures on the wall. A wedding picture—Rob looking like a teenager. Very Flock of Seagulls, very Thompson Twins. One of a girl wearing a bandanna around her neck at a hot-dog-and-beans cookout. I look closely at Cynthia, since I rarely do. She's a girl, practically a child. Strawberry-blond hair, full pink lips, stereotypical almond-shaped eyes, soft freckles, skinny in the way adolescents are skinny—like she still needs to fill out and grow up. She's not that pretty; she's ordinary but attractive. She's a sweet-looking girl, but Cynthia Shachtley is neither stunning nor beautiful. She's heartbreaking and lovely. I can understand this, this transformation of commonplace sweetness into transcendent beauty. But then, poring over her ordinary features, I feel a little angry. I wonder why he does this, why he lets himself indulge in misery, why he doesn't say, *Enough is enough*.

Maybe cynicism is easier. Hope is hard. Hope is demanding; it requires vision.

I gaze sadly, remorsefully into this picture Rob keeps of the dead woman. She smiles hugely the way college girls in love do, and there's something perfect about the dead; she's a regular Marilyn Monroe, an ordinary James Dean.

I continue wandering, and there are more pictures of Cynthia. Snapshots of Rob and Dave in the early days, sweaty faces, loud suits. Photos of Providence, some of Manhattan, a couple of Dave's kid, a few random friends, including me. Thumbtacked to a bulletin board above his desk, a grinning girl on the steps of the Met, knees together, sunglasses covering eyes. I'm not that pretty either.

I turn to his bedroom, walk inside, and avoid touching his things. There are open drawers with clothes sticking out, a book on the pillow, deodorant and dental floss on the dresser, a torn envelope on the floor. I look at the book. I bend down to see the envelope. I gawk at more photos, and she's posted, again and again, till I don't know how he lives like this, surrounded by her, and the urge to purge fills me with every discovery of a new photo bearing her fairy-dust image.

The doorbell rings six times, and I know it's him. I jump and run to open up.

He whisks past me. "This *better* be good."

Immediately I feel melodramatic and guilty. He knows about cancer. He knows all about it. I should slink away like a dying animal. Why bring him down? Why do this? How wretched. How selfish.

"I had a good thing going there." Rob races around, not looking at me. He takes off his coat, leaves on the tie. "What's so important that it couldn't wait till tomorrow?" He wrinkles his nose.

I pat the cushion next to me. "Sit down for a sec. We won't move a bone in our bodies."

Maybe he hears something in my voice. He freezes, obediently walks over, sits, and doesn't move. I take his hand, sans wedding ring, in mine. I interlace our fingers like he did with the girl in spaghetti straps. We hold hands like lovers, not moving, not speaking. Then I say, "I found a lump in my breast, and they don't know what it is." I say it matter-of-factly, like I'm disinterestedly reading newspaper headlines announcing famine on a global scale.

Rob is a madman, up on his feet, flying. He wants details. He speeds through thoughts, showering his monologue with words like *carcinoma, lymph nodes, metastasis, fibrocystic*. He's a specialist; he's *Cancer Man*. Bringing his hands to his head and pacing, he turns to me. "When's the biopsy? We'll look into chemo. You caught it early." He rushes to the window, to the kitchen, looks frantically at me—another dying woman with whom he's involved. "We'll move in together." He dashes over, eyes darting. "That's what we'll do. You don't have to worry." He blinks rapidly. "We'll get another apartment, a bigger one. I'll make some calls tomorrow."

I stand up, floored. "Whoa, Rob, slow down." I reach for his left hand again, pulling him over. "Just sit with me."

He's jumpy, frantic. "We need to move in together. You need to have someone. The Guptas own another building. They'll give me a deal. We need to take care of—"

"Rob—" I hold his hand tightly.

"Sybil, I know how it is. We've got to make sure we're prepared—"

I release his hand to reach for his chin. "Rob, Rob, listen to me—"

"I don't want this to take us by surprise—"

"Rob, listen to me. I'm not your wife—" I pause with his face in my hand. "And this isn't going to be another cancer story. This *isn't* a cancer story." It's not a cancer story, and it's not a bulimia story. It's something else.

He's quiet. I hear him breathing. I hear myself breathing.

"I shouldn't have told you like this, Rob." This is not a cancer story, and our relationship won't hinge on it; our bodies will not be driven by it. "I just didn't want to be alone with the news."

We settle into our places on the couch, maneuvering pillows and removing shoes. "Rob?" I say when we've been quiet for a while.

"Hmm?"

"Did you take care of Cynthia at the end? I mean, did her mom move in, or was she at a hospital?" Did he sit with her while she died, hold her hand while pain made claims on her body parts, walk her to the bathroom if she were able, clean her vomit, clean her skin, feed her, talk to her, watch her die? Did he do these things?

Rob's eyes are closed. "I took care of her." He hesitates. "That's what we wanted."

I pull a blanket around me. "Was it very bad?" I pause. "At the end?"

Rob still doesn't open his eyes. "Yes, it was very bad."

"Did she know you? Did she know who you were?"

He lifts his lids and stares at me. "No." He stops and starts again. "She didn't know who I was."

"You never mention that. You never talk about the fact that she didn't know who you were. That must have been very painful. The most painful thing of all."

Rob speaks a little sternly. "Why should I talk about that? Why should I remember her other than how I do?"

We're quiet for several minutes. "Rob?"

"Huh?" he mumbles.

"I kinda want to ask you something—*invasive*."

"Ask."

"What keeps you from going on with your life? Why are you still mourning?"

Rob massages his temples. "It's very complicated, Syb. People always want to know why I keep her stuff, why I don't take her pictures down, why I act like every relationship is necessarily fleeting—it's complicated." He says nothing for a few minutes. Then: "The truth is, I *do* hold on to my misery; I admit it. I can love her by never getting *over* her."

"That's too sad." I roll over and look at the back of the couch. "If I die, you don't mourn. You let the dead bury the dead. Cynthia would want the same. She would. She'd be so happy you took off that ring."

THIRTY-SIX

ABSCESS
OH, JIMMY, I HATE YOUR DEATH

SYBIL WEATHERFIELD *FOR NEW YORK SHOCK*

From Friday, August 25, 1995

John Belushi

January 24, 1949–March 5, 1982

Rest in Peace

Kurt Cobain

February 20, 1967–April 5, 1994

Rest in Peace

James Dean

February 8, 1931–September 30, 1955

Rest in Peace

Marvin Gaye

April 2, 1939–April 1, 1984

Rest in Peace

Jimi Hendrix

November 27, 1942–September 18, 1970

Rest in Peace

Rock Hudson

November 17, 1925–October 2, 1985

Rest in Peace

Janis Joplin

January 19, 1943–October 4, 1970

Rest in Peace

John F. Kennedy
May 29, 1917–November 22, 1963
Rest in Peace

Robert F. Kennedy
November 20, 1925–June 6, 1968
Rest in Peace

Martin Luther King, Jr.
January 15, 1929–April 4, 1968
Rest in Peace

John Lennon
October 9, 1940–December 8, 1980
Rest in Peace

Marilyn Monroe
June 1, 1926–August 5, 1962
Rest in Peace

Jim Morrison
December 8, 1943–July 3, 1971
Rest in Peace

River Phoenix
August 23, 1970–October 31, 1993
Rest in Peace

Elvis Presley
January 8, 1935–August 16, 1977
Rest in Peace

Gilda Radner
June 28, 1946–May 20, 1989
Rest in Peace

Those I failed to mention:
Rest in Peace

THIRTY-SEVEN

IDENTITY CRISIS

Saturday, August 26, 1995

When I first met Madeline, I felt relief. Here, at last, was a woman I could talk to. She walked with jerky knees; she wore wraparound skirts; she chain-smoked; she carried a leather bag filled with coffee-stained papers belonging to ESL students. On subways, she read Toni Morrison and Ernest Hemingway. Every day, she passed a halfway house on her way to work. Outside, she saw the same old man with gooey Van Gogh-painted hair and Brezhnev eyebrows made of black shoe polish. She affectionately dubbed him "Shellac Head," and she told me the daily installments of their sidewalk exchange as if they were episodes of a radio show: part *Mean Streets*, part *My Favorite Martian.* Madeline had stories; Madeline had lessons. She taught me to wear brown lipstick for big events. Before Tom left for Greece, when she discovered he set his alarm clock to wake him with the orchestral version of Pat Benatar's "Hit Me with Your Best Shot," she whispered into my ear, "He's *so* Hootie and the Blowfish." She once lived in Santa Fe with a heroin addict/artist. She once seduced a minister's son who lived next door to her parents.

Much can be said of Madeline.

I share my lump news with her, and we go to a bar. She says, "Let's eat fatty foods and drink heavily." But we only order two beers. "So Windows 95 was just released," she says. "Imagine that!"

I raise my eyebrows. "Is it okay that we're just sitting here? Shouldn't we be downloading or adding RAM?"

We're an unlikely pair. Madeline is willowy, breezy, deadpan, and she makes men wonder; they look her over, hear her smart comments, and want to know who she is. I am stressed out, high-strung, tightly wound. I've worn *101 Dalmatians* boxers and green socks to the gym. I've fallen on wet tile in grocery stores. Madeline once told me, "You're so uncool, you're cool." Sometimes men like to talk to me. *Wonder*, though, isn't something I inspire.

We're the only women in the place. Everyone looks like a construction worker, which can be an attractive thing. Once I dated one in San Diego. My brother would chase me into my room when I came home, saying, "Ask him if he'd know Jane Eyre if she bit him on the ass. Just *ask* him."

Madeline taps her nails on the table. "I'm sure it's nothing, but when you go to the hospital, wear brown lipstick anyway."

A stocky, burly, hard-bodied, tan man approaches our booth. "Mind if I join you?"

I don't make room. I watch Madeline slide over, and this is one of the things I like best about her: she steps outside herself and speaks whatever language is being spoken to her. I see this man and my body tenses. I want him to go away. Madeline sees him and she makes room for him to sit. I envy this. She delves into the lives of others; she *experiences* them.

"I'm Joe," says the guy.

And I'm quiet, locked in my own identity.

"I'm Madeline, and this is my friend Sybil." Madeline is polite but casual. Self-possessed.

He checks us out. It's a slow process that I find degrading. Actually, it fills me with longing—longing for Rob. I want Rob to wonder if I'm wearing tights; I want him to push his glasses up the bridge of his nose.

"Are you ladies," he pauses and then continues, "*working girls*?" He lowers his chin and peers up at us, his eyes twinkling like those of a porn star.

He's asking if we're whores!

"I teach," Madeline says, nodding kindly—deadpan, like she's saying, *Uh-huh*.

"And I write. How about you?" I'm trying to be okay with alternative lifestyles.

"I'm presently looking." He says *presently* like it's a big word. "I used to strip."

"What's that like?" Madeline asks.

"You make good money," he says.

"Did you like it?" I'm participatory, open-minded. Forget the fact that he's a stripper who thought we were whores in a bar.

"Yeah, but once when I was stripping for a bunch of *hot* women, I got an—"

"We get the picture," Madeline interjects.

I'm sucked right back into my Sybil Weatherfield–self. The moment Joe the Stripper gets to the edge of acceptable conversation in my world, I cut across the border to head home. I glare at Madeline, letting her know I don't want to spend another precious moment—especially since I'm dying—with this guy. If we leave now, we can make it back to my place for *20/20*.

Madeline says to Joe, "Well, you should be leaving now. Nice meeting you."

When he's gone, I say, "Gross."

Madeline curls her lips. "You know, Rob gets erections too."

I turn red. "But you and I don't discuss them."

"You're *so* repressed." She rolls her eyes.

"I guess I don't care." I roll mine.

"I have to tell you something." She starts peeling the label off her beer bottle.

"What? Guatemala's out, Sri Lanka's in?" I sneak a peek down my shirt, which I do often now. "You wish we ordered wings?"

"No," she whispers.

"Okay, what?"

She holds her beer bottle by its neck. "When I was shopping for my sister's kid on the thirteenth, I ran into Jeff at FAO Schwarz. We went for a drink." She pauses, searching my face for comprehension. "Since then, we've seen each other five times."

I look at her. Her hands shake. She's a nervous wreck.

"I'm sorry." Her voice cracks.

She continues peeling the label, and we say nothing. Maybe three whole minutes pass. Then I reach out to cover her hands on the bottle with mine, forcing her to stop peeling. The bar is noisy, and we're quiet. Joe plays darts in the distance. Madeline trembles before me. "What was Jeff doing at FAO Schwarz?" I ask softly.

Her voice still splinters. "His boss's son had a birthday party." She shrugs and tries to smile. "He wanted to get the kid Parcheesi."

I nod my head. "Oh." I look around. "That's a fun game," I whisper.

She looks up shyly. "Do you want me to stop seeing him? Do you hate me?"

I make a sandwich of our hands. "Do you *like* him? Do you *like* Jeff Simon?"

Madeline twitches her nose. "You know," she looks surprised, "I do." She smiles hesitantly, timidly. "I like him a lot."

I pull my hands away. "And he likes you?"

She rips the label into strips. "Yeah, I think he does."

I let it sink in, slowly, like an IV drip. "What about you leaving in October?"

"He'll visit at Christmas." She sweeps the paper strips into a pile. "He's enrolled in a Spanish class—it starts next week." She reddens; she's excited. "Sybil, are you upset?"

Am I upset? I picture them; I picture Jeff at the Fondue Fête. I picture them running into each other at FAO Schwarz on a hot August day. Where did they have that drink? Did they go to the Plaza across the street at Jeff's suggestion, or did they drink cans of Coke, outside by the fountain, at Madeline's insistence? What?

"Nothing was going on when you guys were together—" she rushes to say.

"No, Madeline, I'm not upset. I'm just," I suck my front teeth, "a little *surprised*."

"I know, I know." Her voice is strained. "I'm surprised too—"

"What is it about him that you like?" I kinda want to know.

She takes a label strip and ties it in a knot. "You know how we bitch about people selling out? How we point fingers at Corporate America in disgust? Remember that time we went to Long Island and freaked out?"

"Yeah." I scrunch up my eyes.

"Well, Jeff doesn't allow me to be so one-dimensional, so simplistic. He's not a sellout, nor is he indifferent or disgusting. We must be wrong," she takes a breath and continues, "with our pessimism. We're not in touch with irony; we're just full of mockery. We always lament the presence of nice guys as if being one were a disease. That's so insane—we're like rebels without a cause; it's *dumb*."

I gaze into my beer. "Well." I pause. "You're serious?"

She waves a hand in front of her face. "It's too soon to say." She mumbles something inaudible. "Possibly."

"Oh." I smile.

Back at my apartment, after she leaves, I sit on my bed, stunned. Jeff Simon and Madeline Blue are dating. At first it was covert. Now it's not. *My* Jeff Simon, the financial analyst. He'll make demands on Madeline. He'll want her to change her neighborhood, move to a loft. She'll have to learn table manners, small talk, how to purify water and steam vegetables. He'll ask her to brush up on her golf game, her horseback riding. She'll be forced to wear clothes from Bloomingdale's. They'll sport matching designer watches. Madeline will need to join a country club.

Unless they love each other. And then I don't know what'll happen.

I always wanted Jeff to have an *edge*, a dark side. Minimally, he needed a tattoo or a pierced ear. He was so *nice*, so fresh, like ripe fruit. He hadn't been hurt badly.

On my bed, I slouch. I wouldn't even know if he had been hurt badly.

THIRTY-EIGHT

CUT IT OUT

Monday, August 28, 1995

I'm at St. Vincent's Hospital, and the lump is the size of a pecan. I've heard lumps discussed in terms of peas and golf balls, but never pecans. Madeline takes me in for the procedure; Rob will pick me up. The hospital is within walking distance, but I need an escort just in case I pass out or puke in the gutter, like others in the gutter I've seen before.

In the waiting room, I wear another paper dress and sit next to Madeline. We say nothing. We merely stare blankly into our surroundings. A male resident comes over and introduces himself. "I'll be assisting in your surgery."

When he leaves, Madeline squints and watches him go. I watch her watching him. "He's disturbingly attractive," she says, putting her coffee cup on the table between us. "Sybil?" Her ironed hair hangs in front of her. I search her face with its witchy grace, the pale skin, the languid posture, the long tresses, thick lashes, painted lips, sultry, ugly, wanted, unwanted. I experience the captivity of her eyes; she is captivating without beauty. Both of us have wanted to be beautiful.

"What?" I say.

She reaches for my hand. "Whatever happens, I'll be here." Her eyes fill with tears. "It'll be okay." She is captivating because everything she says seems genuine, heartfelt, entirely true. She'll be there for me, no matter what. It may be a lie, but *she* believes it's not. I know she isn't lying to me.

"I know, Madeline."

"I want you to know I'll stay," she says.

"I want you to go to Guatemala."

"I won't," she whines. We look into each other's eyes. She squeezes my hand, but I am far from her. It's then that I know that this pecan lump is not going to kill me. It's a roadblock, not even a test of character—just something over which I must watch my step. Madeline holds my hand. She needs to go to Guatemala. I love her; I do. Our hold on each other, however, is light. I need her today; I do not need her tomorrow. And I don't think she ever needed me. I admit this to myself with remorse. Madeline allowed me to sharpen my eccentricities; she liberated my quirks. With her, I became funny. But I gave her nothing. My dearest Madeline. *I gave you nothing. Like others, nothing.*

Why is it that I have given so many people nothing?

Hospital noises surround us; medical workers, busy and harried, rush by with metal tools in cold, clean hands. They approach illness and death with routine, and who can blame them? The smell of antiseptic rushes into our nostrils. The smell of old people fills the room. "The two of us have been positively *pillaged* by nostalgia," I say. "Everything between us, everything that's ever been between us, is a mutual past—shared memories of pop culture, a series of firsts." I surprise myself by tearing up—suddenly I realize that, though I'm not dying, I *am* saying good-bye. "First dates, first kisses. Our futures don't have anything to do with seventies cartoons or dorm life in the eighties." I wipe my eyes with the back of my hand. "Regardless of what happens, I want you to get out of here and make a future for yourself."

She looks at me, a little baffled. Then stoic. She pulls Kleenex from her purse. "So what, exactly, are you planning on doing if it's serious?" Her eyes are hard, her nose red.

"Rob. I'll stay and die with Rob."

"Kind of you." She wipes her nose. She stares at me. "I'm not leaving. You better think of a new strategy." She searches her purse, looking for more tissue. "Damn. I ran out."

"Here." I rip off some of my paper dress. "Use this."

She dabs her eyes. "When the lump turns out to be nothing and I leave for Guatemala, I'll miss you very much. Your friendship has meant a lot to me."

"Same here," I say.

A nurse comes in and takes me away. Madeline goes to work at Rights International. In the operating room, I'm drugged. I fall into a dreamy sleep that reminds me of Big Bird settling into his nest with a contented *brrr* sound. I guess that's when they uncover my breast and stick a knife into my heart.

I wake in Recovery, in love with the world. I want to tell the nurse I love her; I love everyone. I've found myself. I'm going to med school. I'll become a doctor. Maybe it's the drugs talking.

They move me via wheelchair into a room with a bunch of old, sick people, and there's Rob, whom I also love, sitting on a cherry-red recliner. "Hey," he says, rising to his feet. He kisses me on the cheek. "You're just in time. *The Price Is Right* is on." He helps me out of the wheelchair and into another cherry-red recliner. We're awkward; there's so much *body* in our way as we try to settle into two chairs.

During the Showcase Showdown, a nurse gives me toast and apple juice. "Would you like some?" I ask Rob. He shakes his head. He takes off his glasses and rubs his eyes; he's stressed.

After a while, I lean over and whisper, "I have a Barbie Doll breast."

"What do you mean?" he whispers back.

"They've bandaged me with a flesh-colored bandage so it looks like there's no nipple—just like Barbie."

Rob gets bleary-eyed—what's the word?—his eyes are *rheumy*. "I dig dolls," he says.

"I'm glad you're here."

Then we sit. A doctor comes in while we're fiercely concentrating on the final round of a match worth a trip to Jamaica. He stands in front of me, and Rob and I look up expectantly. "The lump appears to be benign," he tells us. "We'll do lab work, of course."

I turn to Rob when the doctor leaves. "See, I told you this wasn't a cancer story."

Twenty minutes later, we walk back to my place. Rob unlocks the door and I wobble unsteadily in, crawl into bed—drugged still—and fall into a deep sleep.

I wake three hours later. "I'll make you oatmeal," he says. "I'll put in a banana." He just woke too. He'd been asleep on the couch.

Rob sings while he cooks. He sings "Bennie and the Jets," including the piano parts. When the song's over, I sit up and he places a bowl before me on the card table.

"Thank you, Rob."

He sits on the couch, his socked feet tapping. "How's the breast?"

"Fine."

He watches me eat. "How's the oatmeal?"

"Very good." I take another spoonful. "Delicious. Do you want some?"

"No. I ate your apple. You had *one*." He walks over and sits by my side. "I brought you something to look at."

"What?"

He removes an object from a plastic bag on the floor: the rock 'n' roll scrapbook. "My book." He's reserved, bashful. "I figured you might want to look at it."

My eyes must flash; my skin must glow. "Oh, thank you."

Then we look at Rob's rock 'n' roll scrapbook for most of Monday evening, our legs dangling off the edge of my bed. My head spins from meds, nostalgia, rock 'n' roll history.

"So I took off my wedding ring," he says, out of the blue.

I'm red, red, red.

"By wearing the ring, I guess, I wanted to make of myself a living scrapbook of sorts."

"But you took it off." It's a statement and a question. "You took it off."

He opens and closes his mouth, like a guppy. I fill the silence.

"It's a small gesture, but I'm gonna stop bingeing and purging, okay? I'll stop." I pat his knee. "You're going cold turkey—I'll go cold turkey."

And then we watch TV.

The lump, which seemed so present, already seems very absent. There's supposed to be a scar when the Barbie bandage is removed. The breast appears to have lost no shape, as though my body has just folded up around the excavation, filling in the space and behaving as if nothing were taken away.

THIRTY-NINE

ANTIBIOTICS 8

FROM *NEW YORK SHOCK*

From Friday, September 1, 1995

"DEATH, BE NOT PROUD" BY JOHN DONNE (1633)

Death, be not proud, though
some have called thee
Mighty and dreadful, for
thou are not so;
For those whom thou think'st
thou does overthrow
Die not, poor Death, nor yet
canst thou kill me.
From rest and sleep, which
but thy pictures be,
Much pleasure; then from
thee much more must flow,
And soonest our best men
with thee do go,
Rest of their bones, and soul's
delivery.
Thou art slave to fate,
chance, kings, and
desperate men,
And dost with poison, war,
and sickness dwell,
And poppy or charms can
make us sleep as well
And better than thy stroke;
why swell'st thou then?
One short sleep past, we
wake eternally

And death shall be no more;

Death, thou shalt die.

—Sent in by Tracey,
Staten Island

Harry Chapin

December 7, 1942–July 16, 1981

Rest in Peace

—Syd, Greenwich Village

Just a bunch of dead celebrities.

—Barb, the Bronx

Mohandas K. Gandhi

October 2, 1869–January 30, 1948

Rest in Peace

—Phil, Upper West Side

FORTY

YOU'SE A MONKEY

Sunday, September 17, 1995

A couple weeks later, Barbie nearly gone, Madeline packing, Rob and I in that in-between place—a purgatory for lovers/friends, secular/sacred, committed/agnostic, where I've spent most of my life. He doesn't wear a ring but feels married anyway. I don't binge and purge but feel like a glutton in search of a treadmill or toilet bowl nonetheless. We're in; we're out.

And then we're walking the streets of Manhattan after dark. What are we doing? Why are we here? He finished a show, where he was rock star. We talk to others till they sneak off to other quarters. And then, like always, it is the two of us. So we search for an open diner, like any good New Yorker would.

Watercolor light, a guitar over his shoulder. He's on the road: a hippie, a beatnik. Marlon Brando, Jack Nicholson, a guy who carries around musical instruments. We're weary; our shoulders bump frequently. We're zombies, we have to greet the sun, touch morning dew—can we find morning dew?—listen for jackhammers and mockingbirds.

A diner, open twenty-four hours, winks ahead in pink neon. "There." Rob points like it's the Emerald City at the end of the Yellow Brick Road. "A big greasy breakfast?"

"Coffee, wheat toast." These are the moments that stretch slowly before dawn. *Rosy*, like in Homer. Rosy fingers made of clouds. I look like Ray Charles, except strung out. I look like a strung-out Ray Charles in the rosy dawn.

Rob deliberately knocks my arm as we amble toward this fantastic diner. "How's the breast? We should rest."

"It's fine. Thanks, Dr. Seuss."

No one's inside, not even the veritable and ubiquitous freaks. The waitress takes us to the back of the restaurant. In a hidden-away booth, she puts down two laminated menus and walks away. Rob and I look at each other. He looks exhausted. His clothes are wrinkly and disheveled; he needs a shave. He holds open his arm. "Scoot in on my side." He checks the time. "It's almost someone's birthday, and I'd like to sit next to a pretty girl."

"Whose?" I slide in, though I don't look so pretty. He glides in after me.

"I don't know, but you can be sure it's someone's." Our eyes roam over spread menus. My hands are between my legs, sandwiched between jeans. We examine the blue-plate specials. I've gone from strung-out Ray Charles to shy girl in *American Graffiti*. Now it's the fifties. We're in a diner. On a date. I'm next to a boy.

"I'm only having coffee." I shut my menu decisively. "And toast."

"Me too." He shuts his.

Mirrors, Pepsi-Cola signs, and a few retro logos hang decorously on pink pastel walls. *Happy Days* sans Richie, Al, and the Fonz. I really want—oh, how I want it!—a malt and fries.

The waitress interrupts. Rob orders two coffees and two orders of toast. "Have I ever told you about B.G.?"

"B.G.?" I cock my head as the waitress disappears.

"Bad Grammar?"

I shake my head. "I don't think so." I take a deep breath. "Pronoun problems?"

Rob licks his spoon and sticks it on his nose. It falls off. "I can do these tricks, Syb. These tricks with my toes."

I lower my eyelids, half-mast. "What kind of tricks?"

"Basically, I can break bones with my toes." He shoves his leg into the aisle.

"That doesn't sound like a *trick*. That sounds mean and nasty."

"Some girls *like* when I grab on to them with my toes and hold on for dear life." He beams. "Say we've just had awesome sex, maybe we'll be joking around in bed and I'll seize on to her shin with these steel toes, and—" He watches my reaction, which is a combination of horror and amazement that this goes on in America. He quickly adds, "This usually cracks the girl up." He stops when the waitress puts down the coffees. "Then we roughhouse and," he pauses, watching my face, "have more sex." He builds a coffee-creamer tower.

I turn away; I turn into the empty abyss of the twenty-four-hour diner. It's plain; it's simple. I don't want anecdotes about

Rob's sexual escapades. I'm done with them. I'm not amused. "Oh." I pause. "I guess I've never encountered toes like that."

"So this one time," he leans close and whispers, "I grabbed on and the girl squealed—"

"Squealed?" I ask, squinting, curious despite my caginess.

"*Squealed*, Syb." He nods. "She squealed, *You'se a monkey*!"

I repeat after him. "*You'se a monkey*?"

"You'se a monkey." He nods in disbelief. "So I called her B.G. Bad Grammar."

"Maybe she was joking, Rob. Maybe she was only playing around."

He shakes his head. "No, she wasn't. She was serious. That's how she spoke."

We're silent. I'm bothered. I don't like the picture in my head. Rob sees me fidgeting, trying to dislodge the vision. I can't look at him. I look into my coffee cup, thinking, *The horror, the horror.* He apparently feels it's necessary to keep talking. "So I couldn't sleep with her anymore; I was rendered impotent." He sips his coffee. "That was B.G." He laughs to himself.

"Then what happened?" I ask.

"Never saw her again, except for once. She made me go rollerblading in Central Park—"

"You don't know how to do that—"

"Yeah, I know. She wanted to race—me on rollerblades, her on foot."

"Yeah?" *This* is a vision.

He holds his breath for a second. "She won." He bows his head. "I never saw her again."

There's a long, uncomfortable silence in which I envision Rob and the girl naked except for helmets and wrist guards.

I reach for his chin, looking him in the eye. "Why would you tell me this?" I move against him in the booth. "I have to use the restroom." I need air; I need to recover from Rob's inconsequential confession to a random sexual liaison. The randomness of it. The miscellany. The perversity of bad grammar. Whatever happened to love? Making love? Two people together, not put out by sentence structure or races in the park? I need to breathe; my head is swimming. The coffee is shooting through my veins, leaving me wired while exhausted.

He moves out of the booth for me, and I practically run away.

When I return, he's quiet. We stare into our cups. Finally, after time enough to pray or take a catnap, he says, "Syb, I told you because . . . um . . . I want to provide you with a way out."

I stare at him, a little disgusted. "You're trying to scare me away?" He's his own temp. Punching his own timecard. "If you'd like me to be scared, I'll be scared." I scoot away from him in the seat. "The Midwest may be calling—really. The Windy City, something rural even."

He puts his hand on top of mine, and we look into the empty and stark restaurant, hands touching the tabletop, our eyes off in the distance.

I speak softly. "I guess I want something permanent. Something to measure my days with beyond how many Gristedes and D'Agostinos there are in the Village."

He scrutinizes my face, traveling over fine lines and dark circles. "You can't measure your days by me, with me."

I pause, consider. I hold back for a second. Then: "Why not?"

He's very quiet. Then he smiles. "You think I'll still be here for you tomorrow?"

I failed to abide by the requirements of my own temp ethic; I failed to eliminate *tomorrow*. "I think you will, Rob."

I reach for his chin. I could kiss him on the cheek, which is what we're both anticipating. This is what I intend in the four-second wave of planning in my head. But I turn his face toward me and our eyes meet so that what happens next is understood. There is time to think, time to resist. We kiss. And when the godless kiss, the hellfires bubble over. We're talking a *volcano*; we're besieged by this kiss.

It only ends when the waitress, who probably thinks we're cheap and creepy, puts a green slip of paper on the table and says, "Pay when you're ready."

Naturally, we're beet-red and speechless. Rob manages a weak "Thanks."

I'm a total idiot because I say, "*You'se* a monkey, Rob."

He pulls out his wallet, flustered. He doesn't look at me. He wipes his lips with the back of his hand.

I'm trembling. He slides out of the booth. He offers me his hand. "I'm glad that happened—but, Sybil, you can't count on me. You just can't."

FORTY-ONE

VEGAN NO MORE

Still Sunday, September 17, 1995

Though I haven't slept, there's Madeline wanting to talk at a café. We meet after I shower, and after Rob has apparently rejected me.

When Madeline arrives at Roasters Anonymous, she's wound up like the Tasmanian Devil. She may start whirling and run into a wall. The college kids next to us talk to each other loudly about personal things, leaving their books unattended on tables. They look like they have all the time in the world. They think their secrets are safe. Their stuff isn't going to be stolen. Tomorrow is a guarantee. College life will go on and on. Madeline is the opposite. Her eyes dart to and fro because *everyone* wants to steal from her. She doesn't look upon her time lovingly—tomorrow will change everything, for the worse. These kids. That girl. Only a decade separating them. "Do you remember what it's like to *feel* like they *feel*, Sybil?" She turns toward a boy and girl holding hands and practically breathing into each other's mouths. "The *pleasure* of that privatized moment, that singular moment. God, do you *remember*?" She's somewhere I don't have access to. "You loved some boy so fiercely, so purely, so completely. And it was always hot outside, and you were always in a cool sweat, and everything you did was so single-minded, so black and white. You remember that? You wore short shorts and your legs looked *great*." She nudges my shoulder. "You and I, Sybil, we were nineteen-year-old heartbreakers. Morose girls who seemed both deep and smart—a lethal combo for collegiate femme fatales. You remember?" She laughs. "And you always had your contacts in." I smile, and she continues, "We'd listen to the Smiths and get A's on every test—" Madeline stares at the two kids. "We were less practiced but more devoted. We loved the guys so much—none of this ambiguity *crap*. There were *virgins* too, Sybil." She takes a quick breath. "Some were *virgins*. Everything was so *nice*." She turns to me, and I see she's crying. "Clumsy, privatized love." The tears keep falling. "*Selfish*," she hisses. "That's such a *goddamn* selfish love." And then, without announcement, she's up and gone, headed onto the street, her leather bag full of papers slapping her hip.

I catch up and slip my arm around hers, but she pulls away to light a cigarette. The lighter won't catch despite her maniacal flicking. She searches her purse for a match and finally lights up. She exhales smoke and pulls out a pair of sunglasses. "I'm leaving soon, Sybil." She puffs on her cigarette. "I'm accepting that my life didn't go as planned." She smokes her cigarette like it's a hit. "I didn't move from a singular, privatized love to a marriage. I'm not having a baby. I'm not buying a house." She lowers the sunglasses onto her face. "Rather, I'm leaving the country." She turns to me with wild eyes. "Maybe I'm like Rob. I want my dead wife." She fakes a laugh.

Madeline leads the way; I don't know where we're going. "I went to the Jersey Shore with people from work last week." After extinguishing her cigarette against a brick wall, she puts her hands on her hips. "Do you know what someone said to me?"

"What?"

She searches for Kleenex in her purse, trembling like a junkie. "A guy said I was *cynical.*" She sneers. "He told me I was a *cynical* woman."

And so cynical Madeline Blue, shaking like a junkie, hoping for a singular moment, stops suddenly under the arch in Washington Square Park for a lovely, filmic moment. Around her, laughing NYU students dash by in minimal clothing; they are wholly selfish but completely sincere.

Two girls stand nearby. One girl cries violently, hot tears leaving black mascara ribbons on her cheeks. She cries to her friend, "*You* have parents. Tell me, what do *I* have? What do *I* have?" It's all inexcusably about them. When you find yourself the center of the world, it's only natural to be unhappy.

Tell me, cries the girl, what do *I* have? *What do I have?*

"I gotta get home. I just wanted to see you before the logistics of leaving really get going." Madeline's eyes are wet. She pulls out a subway token. "So much has changed. I used to be a vegan. Now I smoke and eat hamburgers." Her eyes glisten, and she whispers, "What happened to us that we should be so full of yearning?"

I watch her walk away.

FORTY-TWO

ABSCESS

THE PANCAKE PIECE, OR NEW YORK EMBARRASSES ME

SYBIL WEATHERFIELD FOR *NEW YORK SHOCK*

From Friday, September 22, 1995

At the Pancake Piazza on Lexington, one has the option of ordering silver-dollar pancakes, standard pigs in a blanket, a variety of French crepes, Belgian waffles, buckwheat and buttermilk batters with a miscellany of fruit and chocolate and nuts, or even potato latkes.

Then there is the Epic Proportion Pancake Plate, which carries with it no caveat.

In truth, the pancakes on the Epic Proportion Pancake Plate are the size of manholes—too big for the Jolly Green Giant, just right for Goliath. They're jokes for pancakes: decadent, opulent, *improper*. Tasty. They come in the same varieties as the others, only bigger.

Generally speaking, whenever I coerce people into ordering them, there's laughter, a deluge of hot maple, a slathering of real butter, and a doggy bag for when the fun is over. Sure, there may be guilt, forced elimination, and bouts of self-hatred, but the pancakes are well worth it.

I always say, "I'll never do it again." I do it about four or five times a year.

A story from last summer. A *true* story.

Second cousin Maggie arrives, fresh from Middle America, and I figure we'll go nuts. We'll be outrageous! We'll break world records! We'll eat flapjacks of shocking, scandalous, indecent proportions! I mean, she's never been to the Big Apple! It's her first time! She's gotta have some fun!

Maggie wants to see a *Saturday Night Live* taping, pose for pictures with Sirajul and Mujibar from *Late Show with David Letterman,* go to the Hard Rock Café, and maybe find a few squirrels in Central Park. The Met would be nice too.

Maggie, arriving at JFK, takes the shuttle to Grand Central. I haven't seen her since our cousin's wedding in Ohio a year ago. On the subway, she straddles her suitcase protectively and whispers, "Should I keep my money in my sock?"

I make excuses for the sound of the train vibrating through my walls. "My rent is only six hundred and fifty. All my friends pay much, *much* more."

Leaning against the kitchen counter and strategically placing my hand over the century-old water stains that make the place historic, I tell her, "Just down the road, Dylan Thomas drank himself to death. There's *a lot* of history around here."

When Maggie showers, I stand outside the curtain, ready—at a moment's notice—to turn the dial from hot to cold. The water makes swift temperature changes at the most inopportune times. "This is something new. I'm sure my landlords will get right on it."

I read Maggie's thoughts: *Is Sybil aware that all of her friends have recently bought new Saturns? Should I tell her our student loans are paid for?*

Maggie wants Ray's Pizza, having heard so much about it. It's a good thing any old one will do.

We walk around Greenwich Village. Pretty scary stuff. All those freaks.

She wants to see the Statue of Liberty. I flat-out refuse. "The lines are too long. Have I shown you the Church of the Exquisite Panic? Incorporated?"

Three solid days of burgers at Planet Hollywood, cheesecake at Carnegie Deli, hot pretzels on the street. Since she tends not to substitute food for love, these aren't quite the experiences I had hoped they'd be.
Rather, we're just spending a lot of money on too many calories, taking half-hearted advantage of photo opportunities.

"You walk too fast," she complains.

"But I always have somewhere to go," I explain.

And there's this point, this moment in time, when we sit at a table at Dean and Deluca by Rockefeller, sipping mochas and taking a breather. It's raining and we have standby tickets for *Saturday Night Live*. We're uneasy. She wants to see the show; I need Maggie to love New York. She has to love it. I sip my coffee and look out at *The Today*

Show Window on the World. The AP rattles off headlines. I read them, one after the other, a tickertape of doom, a garland of truly epic proportions, streamers of another kind. And the latest news is that people are dead around the world. They just keep dying. I turn to Maggie, moving slowly as if the air were thick, and I wonder—I really do—if I'll survive the night, if I'll make it through. I want to ask her, "But do you *love* New York?"

On the very last day, we go to the Pancake Piazza. Having considered the options, Maggie closes her menu. "I'm getting blueberry silver-dollar pancakes with syrup on the side."

"Did you just say *blueberry*?" I cock my head. "*Silver-dollar*?"

Maggie, who doesn't even drink coffee, spoons an ice cube out of her water glass and drops it into a side dish. "Yes. Blueberry. Five silver dollars."

Oh. My. God. I lower my menu onto my chest, in which I experience uneven palpitations. I plead. I beg. "Maggie, this is what they're known for. Big pancakes. *Huge* pancakes. Pancakes without a God! Why do you think we came here?" *Do it, Maggie! Be outrageous! Be a sport!*

"I can't eat all that," she says.

Understand, my life is on the line. "You don't do it because you're going to eat them, Maggie. You do it just to *do it.*" She stares at me; I stare at her. "You take them home with you. You roll them up into little pancake balls and play catch with the neighbor's dog. You keep them in the fridge till you have company and then you bring them out as a conversation piece. You don't *eat* them."

She folds her arms over her chest. "What do *you* do with them?" she asks.

"Well," I hem and haw, clearing my throat, "I eat them." Then I quickly add, "Over the course of several days."

And so Maggie has blueberry silver-dollar pancakes with syrup on the side. The sadness, the disillusionment, the stark reality hit me like the sensation of standing on a street corner waiting for a lover who's not going to make it, never was going to, didn't even plan on it.

When she leaves, I eat her leftover blueberry pancakes. I'm like an Israelite wandering in the wilderness, begging for meat. I eat pancakes till they come out my nostrils. I wish things with Maggie had been different. Maybe if I lived some other place—a place that didn't take on a life of its own. A place on which I could impose myself instead of the other way around. I wouldn't need to explain why I live in a basement or why I risk getting scorched in the shower.

I want to tell her things. Eat pancakes, Maggie. They're a deal—just like my rent. Break out of the pizza-or-Chinese chains that bind you. That's what we do here. We walk fast and eat a lot. I want you to eat those Epic Proportion apple and cranberry pancakes, and when you're done, you'll eat some of my banana and coconut ones too. I want you to eat and eat until you're so damn bloated you'll need a good long walk to work it off because then, by God, you'll appreciate my life.

And over and over, the question pierces my head like a migraine: *But do you love New York? Maggie, do you?*

FORTY-THREE

A New York Moment

Sunday, September 24, 1995

Madeline strikes a pose before me in the back garden of Yaffa Café on St. Mark's around nine p.m. on a Sunday night. The garden is crowded with hip East Villagers snacking on pseudo-healthy, pseudo-vegetarian cuisine with a Middle Eastern tinge. Tabbouleh. A smattering of white meat. Like Ramone's and Secret Agent, it's a different world from that of the streets. Though we're surrounded by East Village grime, decay, plight, filthy alleys, and nearby crack houses, Yaffa's back garden is a pretty gazebo with a deck floor, chrome tables and chairs, and a big mural of a woman with an Icarus tattoo I've seen on Led Zeppelin stuff that cool people seem to know about. Yaffa is generally described in cool-people terms. I'm a pretender, along for the ride.

"Guess what I saw at Tompkins Square Park yesterday," I say. Tompkins is the East Village version of the West Village's Washington Square—a park, a square, in the Village, filled with weirdos and their friends, occupied by assorted passersby and their dogs.

"What?" Madeline delicately picks at her tofu quiche. "You know you shouldn't walk there alone after dark."

"Funny you should say that. It was dusk, and," I hunker down as if I were telling a ghost story, "a dazed-looking girl was wandering around aimlessly, holding—I kid you not—a gushing head wound. Blood coming out. All over the place."

Madeline plays with a Greek olive in her mouth and sighs. She shakes her head. "So David Lynch."

I shrug. "I was leaving Life Café on Avenue B, just minding my own business—"

Madeline's eyes flash. "What did you eat at Life?" We love food. We're morbid, nostalgic, sentimental girls who love food. "Why were you there?"

"Vegan nachos, a soy cappuccino, and caramel-walnut pie with vanilla ice cream on top. I met Lynn Stomps—she was taking a baby break." I check Madeline out. "You remind me of Bette Davis tonight, smoking, looking like a black-and-white photograph." This is chic-speak—changing subjects without warning. I peer up at the brownstones overlooking Yaffa. "I bet old people with rent-controlled apartments sit in those windows and watch us. How come I can't find a rent-controlled apartment?" I slam my hand down on the chrome table, making my basmati rice tremble.

We're having a get-together at Yaffa Café in honor of Madeline's departure for Guatemala in a little over a week. Rob is expected, and I haven't seen him since the kiss and blow-off. Jeff is coming too.

So Rob. I think of him constantly; I may have mono from misery and exhaustion. As we wait, my excitement grows. It's like waiting for Elvis.

He walks onto the deck with his hands in his cheap suit pockets, and he's whistling, feigning normalcy. His eyes float over the crowd, and his song goes silent. We see him before he sees us; I can't keep my eyes off him. I want to rise, greet him. Rob, right there, searching quietly. When he finds us in the crowd, his expression changes. I notice it; I do. The surprise in seeing me: we are glad to see each other. We didn't expect relief.

He kisses me on the cheek; he kisses Madeline on the top of the head. He pulls up a chrome chair. "Hi, ladies." His voice is cautious, guarded.

We smile. "Jeff will be a little late." Madeline pushes garnish to the side of her plate. "We ordered and ate—we were starved."

My arms are folded on top of the table. "How've you been?" I ask, nodding my head.

He nods too. "Fine. And you?"

Madeline clucks her tongue against the roof of her mouth. "You guys have to hurry this part up. I haven't explained the situation to Jeff. And it's only a week since your, um, exchange." She looks around for an ashtray. "So be quick about the sheepish crap."

Rob blows air from his lips, funneling them so it sends his hair fluttering across his forehead. I turn to Madeline and say, "This is one of the oddest situations I've ever been in."

Madeline puffs on a cigarette. "Knowing we've slept with the same guy?"

I color. "Well, yeah, that." I had something else in mind.

"Think of the bright side," she says.

"What's that?" I squint.

"I've never slept with Rob."

"Neither have I." I spin around to Rob, who's red and miserable. He clears his throat and touches the knot in his tie. I rush to speak. "When I first started dating Jeff, Madeline lit a cigarette, blew smoke from her lips, and said,'I'm not super fond of him, but you look thinner'—that's what she said," I laugh nervously. Rob laughs nervously too.

Madeline reaches over and rubs Rob's forearm. "Are you cold, honey? We can go inside."

It's chilly this September evening. "No, I'm fine." Rob smiles. "Random thought: Remember that one-eyed crack addict in Washington Square Park I told you about? His shirt said P-I-P? Did I tell you that P-I-P was in quotation marks?" He uses a spoon to make marks by the side of his head. "Like this. 'P-I-P.'"

I mouth the letters: "P-I-P"

Madeline says, "Boy, that is random."

And then Jeff arrives. I didn't see him coming. He walks to our table, puts his hands on Madeline's shoulders, and greets us each in turn with a bounce of the head and our names: "Rob. Sybil." Tables turned, musical chairs in full swing, dance partners switched. I try to control my face, but I'm sure I have a twitch or a spasm.

Jeff grins warmly, sits down, and covers Madeline's hand with his. Nutty. I'm weirded out, pained, sipping a warm drink. This was a bad idea. Whose idea was this?

Rob leans forward and speaks. "Guess what I saw this morning."

"What?" I say, hopeful.

Madeline says, "A one-eyed crack addict named 'Pip'?"

Rob snickers. "Nope."

"What, Rob?" I touch his arm for no reason, just wanting to touch him. I linger longer than I have to, my thumb rising and falling over the fabric of his coat.

He begins his you'se-a-monkey story. "This cop slowed down on Sixth to watch a man walking his dog—one of those giant poodles. The cop slowed down when the dog squatted to crap. The cop, of course, wanted to catch the man not picking up the shit. Then he could fine the guy. So you had the cop watching the man watching Muffy, the giant poodle, take a crap."

All of us pause dramatically—picturing the policeman, the dog owner, and Muffy on Sixth.

"What happened?" Madeline asks. "Did Muffy freeze up? Did Muffy still shit?"

"Muffy shit, the man picked it up, and the cop drove away." Rob leans back in satisfaction. He reaches for my water glass. "Is it shit or shat?"

"Is there a moral to this story?" Jeff puts his arm around Madeline.

"I'm still working on *effect* and *affect*," I tell Rob. "I don't know about *shit* or *shat*."

He lifts his palm to my cheek. "Oh, Sybil." It sounds like a breath.

Jeff clears his throat, and Madeline rips open a sugar packet.

Rob moves his hand to the back of my neck. "No. No moral." He rubs my neck. "Not this time around."

"There's always a moral," I say.

Madeline—smarmy and subterranean—senses unease and hidden communiqués. "It's just a New York thing—a New York moment: lovely even in its grotesquery." She grabs a menu. "Who wants dessert?"

After we order carrot cake and chocolate éclairs, Madeline, bare-shouldered and Bette Davis, speaks. "I feel like the city is a character in my life, my own Lenny and Squiggy." This is a lovely Manhattan scene: a crisp autumn night, a café, an urban garden. I may have come here for scenes such as this. "Suddenly the door flies open, and no matter what you're doing or thinking, you know you live in Manhattan." Rob and I slant into each other; Jeff beams at Madeline, who's in her element: soliloquizing in a cool-people place. She's always been one of the cool people. "This is the only spot in the nation where so much of our conversation revolves around talking about where we live." She lifts the hair over her neck and drops it. "People don't talk like this in Iowa." She's decisive. "Those quirky little New York moments are not enough to sustain my interest anymore." Then she smiles triumphantly. "*I'm getting out.*"

Rob removes his glasses. "It's no different anywhere else, Madeline."

Madeline Blue is prepared for resistance. "No matter how long you've lived here or how many places you've visited, it's never enough. That's the essential problem of New York: it's never enough. You're still going to be an outsider."

Rob puts his glasses back on to watch Madeline, Jeff taps his dress shoes like a nervous wreck on the gazebo floor, and I stare at Madeline, who delivers her speech with drama and flair. Like a Shakespearean play, this has been studied and blocked for the stage. She continues, "If you've been to Temple Bar, you've never been to the Odeon. If you've been to the Tunnel, you've never been to the System. You may have been to an art gallery opening once, but only because a friend invited you. Everyone is after that same illusory feeling—the feeling that he or she is a part of it. Part of New York. We're all trying to collect New York experiences." She looks around the funky, gothic-industrial Yaffa Café garden. "What are we doing here? McDonald's is cheaper, and the coffee is just as good." She pulls out another cigarette.

All of us, under direction, look around. We take in the crowd, their hairstyles, their pierced faces, what they eat. We take in the waitresses with pretty teeth, the lights hitting the mural. Bits of conversation hit us like fumes from a car. Words. Nothing really makes sense.

"Most of us are choosing," I begin to say, "an environment that safeguards our own eccentricities and—"

"You know," Madeline cuts me off, "what's with you? You love it here; you hate it. You wanna move and set up house with a colander; you want to be in a place that caters to your intolerable behaviors that would drive most Midwesterners crazy. Are you staying, or are you going?" She glares at me, quite literally. There's brutality in her stare. "Sometimes you act as if you're on the next bus out. And then, in the very next breath, you'll defend Manhattan as if it were part of your identity. Someone needs to call you on it already." She looks to Rob and Jeff, who seem to be staying out of this discussion. Their mouths are tightly shut, and their arms are crossed. "What are you doing, Sybil?"

I feel a mild hot flash. "I don't know," I say with embarrassment. "Maybe I'm just one of those people who likes to talk about leaving."

"Talk is cheap." Then her eyes soften. The sharpness of her voice fades. She takes a sip of water and blows air out of her mouth. "Sorry."

I look first at Rob, then at Jeff, and finally at Madeline. I pause on their faces, each very different from the other. The rocker boy, the businessman, the iconoclast. A cheap suit, Polo and taupe, and a negligee number over a rainbow-colored bathing suit. That's what Madeline's wearing. Yaffa's backdrop does do something to me; it does frame my scenes, block my actions, shape my dialogue. I admit this. New York is not wholly who I am, but it's a part. "Maybe it's a matter of whether or not you want geography to play an important role in your life." I'm feeling profound. "Do you want a mere background, or do you want something invasive? New York can be a comfort."

"What? Do you talk to it sometimes?" Madeline shuts her eyes. "I always look at menus as I walk by restaurants," she opens her eyes and continues, "I'm always thinking I should try this or that place. I'll literally stop and peer into windows. They're like pet stores in small towns. And you know what?" She lights her cigarette and shakes out a match. "I never will." She takes a drag. "And, even if I attempted to, the restaurant will soon close." Her eyes flash. "We get nervous because we've never eaten authentic Vietnamese or authentic Cuban. We feel left out—we think everyone is having more fun than we are." She blows smoke through partially closed lips. "Well, I will not live my life trying to go to all the new restaurants that will eventually close—I won't do it."

Rob and I are speechless. Jeff looks proud.

Madeline adds, "I'll be damned if I do."

Jeff lowers his head. "You make me want to go too."

Huh.

"But it can be a lot of fun," I say, startling even myself. "We're having fun."

"Yeah? How?" Madeline leers at me.

I'll make something up, quickly. The same way I write my columns. "Well—"

"The music," Rob says helpfully. "Can't beat the music."

"Yes," I nod my head, continuing, "folk, acoustic, jazz, rock. We've got music."

Madeline waves her hands around. "Myth. Mythology. Art flourishes elsewhere too, my friends." She flicks the ashes off the tip of her cigarette. "Same with the food—you can eat great food in the backwoods. I once had a terrific steak in Carbondale and fantastic shrimp scampi in Greer. You New York people convince yourselves you can only eat a decent slice of pizza within the five boroughs. It's a lie—"

"Once, at a party, a guy was hitting on me." I look around proudly. Guys have actually hit on me! "Then a Rockette came in, and he dropped me like a lead balloon." I snap my fingers. "Just like that. He saw the Rockette, everyone started whispering about her, he said, 'Excuse me for a minute,' he left me alone, and I never spoke to him again." I scrunch up my face. "They left together too." I nod my head up and down. "I was dropped for a Rockette! Where else can you say that?"

Madeline looks disgusted. "Why would you want to?"

"Ethnic diversity." Rob raises his eyebrows. "We're taking a stand against racism."

Madeline leans forward. "Look around, kiddies." She whispers, "Count the white kids."

This isn't completely fair, but we don't say anything.

"Madeline." I stiffen. "We stay here for the same reason we stay anywhere. We stay for the people, not for the place. After a while, you figure this out. It's the people."

We all fidget uneasily, since I've unintentionally said how we feel about each other.

"We have choices," she says, "about the people who determine our geographies."

"You'll write us," I tell her.

"I will." She lowers her eyes.

"You'll visit us," Jeff insists.

"I will." She looks up with a smile.

"You'll make yourself useful," Rob suggests.

"I'll try." She wraps her arms around her body and hugs herself.

We leave Yaffa after eleven. Madeline and Jeff leave together. They stroll away, arms wrapped around each other, disappearing into the East Village night. "I'll walk you home," Rob tells me, even though he lives right around the corner.

"No, it's okay." I shake my head. "I'll splurge and take a cab."

We wait together on the sidewalk. A five-minute silence ensues. "Syb, I'm still not wearing the ring." He shows me his ring finger.

"And I still haven't binged or purged." I jut out my chin. "Not gonna do it."

What an odd way of speaking.

I see a cab and hail it. Getting into the backseat, I say, "Well, call me, if you want. Really."

FORTY-FOUR

ANTIBIOTICS 9

FROM *NEW YORK SHOCK*

From Friday, September 29, 1995

Next time you have out-of-town visitors, take them to a Broadway play and be done with it. Don't get crazy.

—Bill, Flatbush

You've got this vision in your head about the way New York City is. Somewhere there's Mr. Hooper on Sesame Street, peddling fantasies. In your Edward Hopper painting, your nighthawks are James Baldwin, Bobby De Niro, and that Guggenheim chick. Maybe Lou Reed is pouring the coffee.

—Tyler, Bed-Stuy

Sybil, friend, talented writer-person. I've never missed a column of yours. I have an issue, though: you seem to equate intelligence with wittiness. We often hear you insisting upon your own intelligence. I'm a fan, but I'm not so sure we're actually convinced that you're really all

that smart. We just know you're witty. Be smart. Don't be so idealistic. It can be, well, *crushing*. Romantic idealism can be the very thing that leads to stuffing your face with pancakes.

—Dice, SoHo

FORTY-FIVE
ACQUITTAL

Tuesday, October 3, 1995

Fuck Dice.

I'm at a temp job on the fourth floor of a Manhattan high-rise with an uneaten cinnamon roll next to a cold cup of coffee on my proxy desk. Listening to AM radio, I stand by the window looking at the street below. A group of mostly black women, possibly the same women I ride the subways and walk the streets with but rarely speak to every single day of my life, is watching color TV in a TV-shop window. All sets are on the same channel, so the world seems like a techno-music club. Like me, the women wait. I wonder if the waiting is the only thing we have in common. Though these women are always cast in my story, I imagine separate lives elsewhere, in places like the Bronx or Brooklyn; I imagine *Porgy and Bess*; I imagine stereotypes and family life and music I don't understand. I think of myself as decidedly not racist, but I'm ashamed that I don't know these women at all. We wait together—it's all we have. They're anonymous to me, faceless. There's no real sense of racial harmony or human equity if only a verdict unites us for one split second. We have nothing in common.

And then we know: O. J. Simpson is acquitted in the murder trial of the century. The century!

This is what I do.

I put my palms flat against the glass; I lean my forehead against the pane. The women jump around, shouting victoriously. I turn and go back to my chair.

The phone rings. Madeline: "*Now* can I leave?"

She flies out tonight, so this is only partially ironic. We make plans to meet at Michelangelo at seven.

Rob hasn't called. Without him, I dread everything from climbing stairs to grocery shopping. Routines are punishment. Nothing's funny anymore. I'm like one of those inflatable dolls you punch and it bounces back up with that stupid, silly, lifeless smile on its stupid, silly, lifeless face. Right now, minus Rob, I'd commit suicide if I were suicidal. But I'm not. I miss him, plain and simple. However, there's my pride, his rejection. I can't go back to *just being friends*, one of the dumbest ideas ever. Well, life without him is just like it was before we met in that Laundromat when he was wearing those ridiculous orange pants. At least, that's what I bet any money-sucking therapist would probably say. I need to remember that. I lived without him for years and years. During those fucking years, I read many good books, saw many good movies, and had a couple good conversations. I don't need him.

This is what I do.

I leave work early, feigning illness, and go to the *Shock* offices.

I rush inside and close the door to Fred's office.

He looks up from his desk, not really surprised. "Did you hear about O. J.?" he asks. Fred's desk is cluttered with files labeled things like "Foreign Film Fest" and "Organized Crime" and clippings about NPR listening habits and possible Led Zeppelin reunion tours. His walls are plastered with Eric Clapton posters. I nod and sit across from him. He swivels his chair around the desk and rolls toward me. "I see a column in it, Weatherfield." He weaves his fingers together. "That name—can't you change it? Get a real one?" He opens a wooden treasure chest he keeps. "Wanna a cigar?"

"No O. J. columns, Fred." I pick lint off my temp dress and scowl at the cigar.

"It's right up your alley." He starts moving his hands wildly, the cigar between his fingers. "That whole *depravity*, *injustice*, *the-world-is-screwed* thing."

"Fred, I'm thinking of leaving New York." My voice is matter-of-fact, direct. "In January." Yes, today Manhattan is out. Today I envision a move back to San Diego, pet ownership, possibly a Ph.D. Maybe career fulfillment. Definitely houseplants. If not a man, a kid. I'd like a child. I could do it alone; I know I could. I just need money. If I wrote a book or won the lottery or hung out at an old people's home till someone had mercy on me and wrote me into his or her will.

Fred, who's worked on *New York Shock* for thirteen years, stares doubtfully at me. "Sybil." He puts an elbow on his desk and holds his chin in his hand. "Sybil Weatherfield." He scowls. "I don't know what's bothering you, but maybe you need a rest. A break.

Some time away." He wheels backward, rolling behind his desk. When he gets there, he puts on bifocals. "I can spare you for a month, maybe two. Why don't you take a trip to Europe or the Bahamas? You could continue to write 'Abscess.' We'll call it 'Still Bleeding Abroad.' If you found the writing therapeutic, that is."

I squeeze my temples, cross my legs, and flare my nostrils. "I'll think about it."

This is what I do.

I grab the past issue of *Shock* and head to Michelangelo to meet Madeline, who leaves for Guatemala tonight on a red-eye.

The Village is a comfort. I stop performing and move with ease from my life as temp to my life as failing writer, in which my legitimacy is less questionable. I feel better already—having removed my nylons, having given up small talk for the day. With *Shock* under my arm, I walk into Café Michelangelo off Bleecker and see Madeline waiting.

After all these years. Madeline Blue, an *Annie Hall* presence, a pitted face, a lackadaisical frown, a charm and a wit that slays and stuns and knocks people over. She's a disease. She leaves scars. Madeline Blue, fleeing after cappuccino.

"Jeff will be here soon—he's coming to the airport with me," she says when I sit. From here, she leaves—no wasting time.

"In less than a year, you won't be pop-culture-savvy," I say. She won't know singers, celebrities, movies—props we use to determine cultural sophistication and level of worldliness. I reach for her hand over the marble table. "We've always been so *good* at that."

Madeline was the first person I met who hung up on student-loan officers when they called, smoked cigarettes and took daily vitamins, pierced her navel but scorned artifice. She'd hop tall fences with *Beware of Dog* signs, kiss beautiful boys she'd never see again, and buy *Charlie's Angels* memorabilia. Madeline co-opted clichés. She did so lavishly, voraciously.

I'm not sure I can live without her clichés.

"Begging you to stay seems unbecoming." I order a piece of cake, not counting calories. Also unbecoming. "But I'd really like to beg."

You love a woman one way. You love a man another. I miss Madeline Blue before she's gone. It's a thoughtful, dull pain—like a headache you do your work through. I miss a man after he's gone. It's a gut-wrenching living hell that requires drugs or sleep. Right now, Madeline increasingly evanescent, I *ache*.

She picks up the bill. "My treat."

"Is that it? Do we meet for long weekends in Florida?" I say, flinching.

Madeline smiles. There's nothing left of her. "Remember that time I won fifty bucks in an Atlantic City slot machine and you couldn't keep me from hunting for quarters on the casino floors?" she asks.

"Yeah." I barely smile.

"Remember that time we went to Boston and you made me walk that insane historical trail with all the fading red footprints?"

"I remember." I look up at her, her eyes not watery. I'm about to be Robless and Madelineless. It only takes a few hours.

"On Newbury Street, I asked, *Where's the truth in Boston?* Remember?"

Anything we do together from this point on will be in commemoration, out of respect for what has been. We will never be germane to each other's lives again. "I remember," I say. Then I add, "Didn't we used to want to save the world?" I pause. "Isn't that what we once wanted?"

Madeline exhales, and her voice is a whisper. "You'd have to start recycling, Sybil."

Jeff walks in. He shakes my hand before sitting!

"What time's your flight?" I ask Madeline.

"Eleven-eighteen," she answers.

"Always those weird, imaginary times." I smile.

For twenty minutes, we say very little. Then it's time to go. "I'll write you the moment I know where I am." She means it; I don't doubt her.

We make our way onto the street with her bags. On the curb, she reaches for my hand again. "I'm leaving now."

There's a breeze, making her hair balloon. Nighttime in Manhattan. Bleecker is busy, filled with body postures I recognize—electric, edgy, sad, trendy. Madeline's hand is damp like the sidewalks.

After a taxi stops, the cabbie parks and gets out to help Jeff load Madeline's bags into the trunk. Jeff, wordlessly, kisses my cheek and crawls into the taxi. Madeline and I stand there. She puts her hands on her hips. "Well, Kitty." Now her eyes fill and she blinks rapidly. "You have a good life, you hear me? I'll see you around."

We hug on Bleecker in front of Café Michelangelo on an October night. When she's in the car, next to Jeff, I close the door for her. She arranges her body in the seat, pulling at her skirt, mouthing, "Wedgie." Then she sticks out her tongue at me and yells, "Love you, Kitty!" The taxi drives away.

This is what I do.

I turn down familiar paths, familiar Village streets, routes like routines, and I love her, but there's something tailor-made about our friendship. There will be no tomorrows with Madeline Blue.

She is, most tragically, disposable.

FORTY-SIX

Binge and Purge

Monday, October 16, 1995

Rob hasn't called, and it's been nearly a month.

And Madeline is gone.

A column is due tomorrow at midnight, and I'm faced with the ubiquitous blank page, scrambling for ideas. Soon I'm driven by a singular desire. Bodiless, my mind tours the kitchen. It enters, careful to be quiet in the unsettling of hinges. It rounds corners and scrutinizes the offerings of my plastic shelves, taking in dry cereal without any added sugar, flakes that can be measured into healthy portions and served up with skim milk. It caresses instant oatmeal (baked apple and cinnamon), uncooked pasta in more than one shape since variety is the spice of life, ripe bananas tipped and veined in green, canned black beans, and low-sodium vegetable soup. My mind opens the knee-high fridge, with drudgery, with resignation—its contents are dull, unappealing for any true and decisive binge. After all, what kind of deprivations can be cured with canned beans? What kind of demons expunged with uncooked pasta? Must the bananas turn yellow and be freckled in brown before sorrows are fully absorbed?

The knee-high fridge makes a suctiony sound when it opens, the rubber lining pulling away from its kiss with the chilly interior. My mind is disappointed. Yogurt cups, all announcing low-fat ingredients. Skim milk for cereal. Grapes, which could work in a pinch—though it would be a remarkably unsatisfactory binge. Of course, all binges tend—in the final analysis, the final *fucking* analysis—to be remarkably unsatisfactory. But who sits around and thinks these things? A lone stalk of broccoli. Doesn't this girl eat?

My mind slams the door, disgusted, returning to my head.

Obviously, if there's going to be a binge, someone has to get off her fat ass and head to the store for a pint of Ben and Jerry's.

But then.

I notice there's a message on my answering machine: "We're playing at the Fedora on the sixteenth. Please come."

Rob! I love him! I do, I do, I know I do!

We haven't spoken since September. Will we remember each other's names?

With insides splintered, I arrive at the Fedora at 8:30 p.m. Ten people sit around a rectangular table—a hodgepodge of individuals I've met at shows, seen around town, shared Cheez Whiz with at parties. Dave is on a corner next to Lynn, who waves cheerily when I come in. Rob sits by Dave. Rob is wearing a gray suit; Dave wears red.

Suddenly I'm embarrassed. I see him and our eyes meet and we both know we need to talk and he doesn't look away but, dear

Lord, he *blushes*. The Fedora is lively and crowded and noisy despite the fact that it's a Monday night. Everyone reaches his or her hand out to me in greeting. So I say hello to this great big noisy Fedora table, stooping to kiss cheeks, making my way around its edges. My heart beats fast as everyone pretends not to watch my kissing patterns around the table and that's just what everyone does. They watch; they *stare*.

Arriving at Rob, I bend to kiss him on the cheek. He lifts his hand to the back of my head and applies pressure. He says nothing, and I say, "Hi, Rob."

Then I continue my ballet down the table till I've kissed everyone. To be honest, I don't know what happens next. When I return to my seat, appetizers are ordered. I have mini-heart-to-hearts with several people. Rob and I have a few embarrassing instances of eye contact. I sweat and eat fried mozzarella.

The members of Glass Half Empty excuse themselves after the opening act, Sarcastic Reply. After five minutes, I say, "I'll be right back."

Frankly, I've got to talk to that man, or I may have to slit my throat right in the Fedora on top of one of these rectangular cocktail tables.

A guy with frizzy long hair and a crazy thick extension cord in his hands stops me as I move toward the backstage area. "May I help you?"

I point behind the stage, as if I'm surprised to be averted. "Oh, I—I—I need to see Rob. *I'm with the band*."

"What's your name?" he asks, looking me up and down.

"Sybil," I hesitate. His face is blank. "Sybil Weatherfield."

"Oh, you." He winds the extension cord into a loop. "Okay. You know where they are."

Which, of course, is a bitter lie.

I step over wires, moving with confidence, and keep my eyes peeled for signs of a man in a gray suit. After five minutes of serious wandering, I find a room with two big, overlapping tinfoil stars on the door, presumably announcing the presence of Glass Half Empty inside. A crude green room of sorts.

I knock on a tinfoil star. When the door opens, Dave's eyes widen upon seeing me. "We're playing in about ten–fifteen minutes. I'll be around." He shuts the door marked with stars.

Rob Shachtley and Sybil Weatherfield, alone at last.

"Hello, Rob," I say, sounding like a girl in a romantic comedy.

"Hello, Sybil."

I look down. "You didn't call."

"No, I didn't."

"Rob." I look at him, hoping to see that familiar thing in his eye—a gaze that resembles desire. I don't see it. "Rob," I repeat.

Rob shuffles his feet, puts his hands in his pockets. "What was I gonna say, Syb?"

This is the part where we're supposed to fall against one another with resolute bodies, famished lips, greedy mouths, Harlequin-romance hands. We're supposed to kiss like Paris is *burning*, like the Berlin Wall is coming *down*.

Instead he says, "I'm sorry." And it's only then that he kisses me, softly, politely, a kiss without promise. "I'm so sorry." He holds my shoulders and says, "Can't we go back to how we were? Such great friends. We were such *great* friends."

I say nothing, nothing at all.

He adds, "I wanted you to be here tonight for the public announcement. It's official. Glass Half Empty is over. Dave and Lynn are moving after the new year."

FORTY-SEVEN

BRAINSTORM

Tuesday, October 17, 1995

Alas, a column and a temp job are before me. This is how it goes.

First, Michelangelo.

I sit alone in Café Michelangelo, three days after my thirty-first birthday. The day is bright and chilly. I pull out notebook paper and pen for a little artless meandering.

The trial of the century, I write. There may be possibilities; perhaps I can make Fred a happy man.

The trial of the century. Inversion. Inversion. *Inversion of what?* Of expectation?

Madeline had expectations, Rob had expectations, I had expectations. Madeline and her fairy tales—her white-picket-fence fairy tales. Me and my romantic idealism—my sexy and somehow sustainable rebels without cause; my coup d'état against conformity, rendering me chic and artistic. Rob and his dead wife—so young, so tragic, so perpetually beautiful. Ah, so beautiful!

Disappointment coupled with displacement (spiritual/geographical), disillusionment, dead wife. The failure of romantic idealism, a temp ethic/aesthetic, a lack of permanence in our sinews.

Madeline, maybe the most hopeful, leaves. Rob simmers, hopelessly. Sybil. What does Sybil do? Hmmm. *What does Sybil do?*

What, in truth—is there *Truth?*—is the trial of the century? *What* is on trial?

Yes, this is how the writer's mind works. At least, this writer—this one who wanders the seditious streets of Manhattan—who writes, most articulately, about the noble freak, the good freak, the freak with a stack of pancakes tattooed onto his or her shaved skull.

Ah, the trial! Is it Truth with a capital *T* that is on trial? I am but thirty-one. Give me till forty for *that* trial.

Is it hope? Disappointment? Displacement? Disillusionment?

How eighties. How Gen X, prior to balding and mortgages that will inevitably be ours. How Earth Day, how Aung San Suu Kyi, how Desmond Tutu. Oh, our woe! It's on trial? It's passé. It's over. We're five minutes ago. So five minutes ago. *I'm* five minutes ago?

No!

How'd it happen?

Romantic idealism is on trial in the Trial of the Century?

These are the things I write.

I take a deep breath and look around.

Today Manhattan—hot spot of my romantic idealism—is *out.* Today Manhattan is the crux of my troubles, the vortex, hub, focal point of all despair. Beyond Bleecker, the Village spreads. Across the street, Horny Toad Used CDs with deliciously underground bands advertised on cheap color copies in the front window is situated next to Freddy's Boots with bodiless mannequin legs in fishnet stockings and big black boots lined up in a can-can assembly, ready to burst through glass and onto the street. Nearby, Souvlaki by Sid with specials handwritten in red Magic Marker on the backs of paper plates hanging from exposed pipes like mobiles above baby cribs, serves as a backdrop for girls clomping by in gold tights with gaping holes in platform heels. Boys on bikes cuss. Dogs on leashes pull. This veritable, unstoppable rush of *cool* passes by.

Around me, this buzz, a messy cacophony, a wild cross-section. The hip and the thin and the exceptionally ugly stroll by, using hands to speak in loud gestures, carrying plastic bags with commercial logos, whistling, mumbling, saying nothing. It's a movement in an orchestra, a point on a map.

I think of the smell of hot garbage and honey-roasted peanuts. I picture bums and beautiful women, drug addicts and singers. I think about having hope beyond Pearl Jam tickets, beyond pancake platters. I think about how everything is blown out of proportion when there is no expectation for a future. New York, too, is blown out of proportion. I look out into the Village, my true mecca.

I've made a silly bohemian division—thinking my liberation, my identity could be mapped, geographically defined, subject to east and west, upper and lower. My Korean launderer with his Anne Murray tapes, my pierced and tattooed neighbors—how foolish I've been in wanting to pinpoint their whereabouts, in wanting to localize and tie them down. I squint and face Bleecker: busy, trenchant, a slap in the face.

Crazy things flash through my mind. The Museum of Modern Art and a Bruce Nauman exhibit called *Clown Torture.* Throwing up dim sum from Chinatown in a Trump Tower restroom. Accidentally rollerblading down Central Park's expert trail instead of the amateur one on a Saturday afternoon because I couldn't remember what *novice* meant and I was pretty sure that wasn't me. Cowgirl Hall of Fame for BBQ with Madeline, oh, Madeline. The view from the top of the Empire State Building, how everything changes from high above and all you can see is beauty, dazzling light, like the shock of tropical fish in clear ponds. Flower shows, because New Yorkers love flowers in bloom. Small clubs, small bands, small audiences. Cheap books, expensive wine. I think of James Dean, dead; I think of the subway running in my basement walls and the homeless men asking me for spare change. I remember all the Ben and Jerry's pints I've stowed away, dipped into, with sly eyes and sad resolve—my Chunky Monkey retreats and regrets. I think about my writing, how a fine line is drawn between a sense of self-importance and an awareness of insignificance. I think about art and love and the dogs in Washington Square Park. I'm torn up and put back together again. I think of New York City, of all it is to me: a finger against my chest, an allegation. I have cast sad, sad eyes on this small, small island and called it deadly.

Drawing Gotham air into my lungs, I feel foolish.

I go to work. The temp assignment is simple. Answer five lines that barely ring, have full access to Microsoft Word, drink an endless supply of bad coffee. And so it begins, me and my blank page.

From here, I write my column. That's enough to get me going. That and the bad, bad coffee.

FORTY-EIGHT

LOVE SLAVE

ANOTHER TRY

SYBIL WEATHERFIELD FOR *NEW YORK SHOCK*

From Friday, October 20, 1995

I was thinking about salmon. Salmon swim upstream. We learn this as children. Then we're offered a few words of advice: *Do not tap on Walter's bowl! Leave Thelonious Monkfish alone! Give poor Crystal Gill some space!*

Salmon swim against the current to breed. There is no contact—mating involves a little fertilization, a little egg-laying: no fondling, no caressing, nothing to get excited about.

These salmon swim for dear life; they do their business; then they die. That's right, they *die.* Salmon mate, then die. And the mating isn't exactly *beguiling*.

So I'm thinking that salmon are the epitome, the heroes—if you will—of *romantic love.* They're scaly Romeos and Juliets, aquatic tragedies. They meet their fates head-on; they do it for love.

Can't you relate? All that work, that upstream shit? The instinct

to mate? The desire for that magic moment, that consummation, that supposedly earth-shattering union of bodies and souls that turns out to be nice, even really good, but for some enigmatic reason fades after a while like perfume on a pulse? Aren't they just wishful thinkers, the Jay Gatsbys of the fish world? Salmon are romantics, my friends. They struggle; they mate; they die. They pave the way, forge the path, show us the pratfalls of romantic love.

Truth is, I believe in love. But I don't want to work my way upstream, fail even to lay a *hand* on my lover, do my *business,* and then drop dead. Forget *that.* I'd like to live, thank you very much. No matter how noble or quixotic the plight of the salmon seems to be, I think I want my love in another flavor.

A wise friend once said to me, "Love is a decision."

I guffawed: not very feminine. I thought, *Whatever happened to roller coaster rides and honeymoon periods and making out on Blueberry Hill?*

I want Blueberry Hill.

The metaphor for my life in Manhattan has always been temping. *I'm the temp.* People know it, and they expect nothing less and nothing more from me. I do the minimum, but I do it well. And I always get more from *them* than they get from me—whether it be free printing on the laser printer or a dozen extra copies of my résumé on the Xerox machine while everyone's at lunch. I don't steal supplies; I just use the equipment. Not to mention the fact that there better be a paycheck at the end of the day. And free coffee is a *must.* But you can always count on me to be polite when answering the phone.

Temps don't stick around. When temps want off the roller coaster, they simply leave the amusement park.

Commitment, therefore, has always been shunned. Making long-range plans has been like making promises I can't keep. I don't have a career, a profession, and my love life has been, well, *tempestuous.* A temp "loves" tempestuously. I enjoy saying this. Especially to my mother.

Last time I was home in Cali, I went for breakfast with a friend from grade school. She's my age and divorced. Despite these notable disadvantages, she has a sweet face. And a six-year-old kid. We don't really live in the same worlds anymore. You know, lots of dichotomies: West Coast/East Coast, single mother/ ovaries drying up, maternal instinct/blind ambition, pleasant facial expression/frown lines and crow's feet, office job/ undiscovered artist, etc. The two of us barely keep in touch. This was just a holiday thing.

In a San Diego coffee shop this single mother and I, a temp and a New Yorker, met for breakfast. She told me how she worked two jobs, participated in carpools, fixed lunches, and slept when she could. Baffled, I fondled the rim of my coffee cup as if it were a sleeping lover's lips. I couldn't begin to imagine the scenario. I wondered when she had time to read, when she got to go for walks alone, if she were ever able to listen to Barbra Streisand or Steely Dan on a Walkman.

"But are you *happy*?" I asked after hearing her saga.

The single mother, sweet roll and orange juice before her, looked earnestly at me. "It's not a matter of whether or not I'm happy, Sybil." She folded her napkin and placed it on the table. "I have a son. I take care of him. Happiness isn't something I have the luxury of thinking about."

While *I* was thinking about self-fulfillment, *she* was thinking about picking up her child from first grade. She loved him. She wasn't trying to figure out what was in it for *her.*

This may have been one of my first lessons on love: if you approach love like a temp job, like a diversion, if you think it's all about personal happiness, you're doomed to upstream swimming.

If love is a decision, it's not unstable or subject to whim and fantasy. Blueberry Hill isn't left behind. Rather, you commit to staying up there. Even when the weather sucks. You kiss the salmon's fate good-bye. You forget futility. You blow off death.

Rob Shachtley, my decision is to love you. I won't measure my days by you, but I'd like to measure them with you. Let me be your love slave. Just let me.

FORTY-NINE

CHOICE

Saturday, October 21, 1995

And it is only then that he calls. I pick up and he says, "You leave me without a choice."

I'm caught off guard. "I do?" This seems so sudden.

"Yeah, let's commit." He stops; he breathes.

"What made you change your mind?" I ask. I think that's what he's doing—*changing his mind.*

"The salmon. The salmon did it. I don't want to be like salmon."

"Oh." It's all I can say. I dump my cup of cold coffee into the sink.

"I'm coming over. I'm wearing sweats."

I stand up, untangling my toes from the phone cord. "Now?"

"You okay with that?" He jangles something—keys. He's at his door already. "Are you ready?"

I look around. I haven't showered; there's no food in the

apartment. I haven't even filed my nails. "Am I ready for *what* exactly?"

"Love slaves, let's be love slaves." He stops again. "That's what we gotta be. Okay? Is that okay with you?"

"Yeah," I say. "Come on over."

And that's it.

FIFTY

EPILOGUE

Monday, January 8, 1996

A new year and the white snow falls, covering car tops, blanketing parking signs, muffling catcalls and door slams and unassigned shrieks—nothing can be heard on this snowy January day when a blizzard stops Manhattan, saying enough *is* enough. No one works; no one goes to school; people stay home, quit smoking, play Solitaire. The city is hushed, held in icy repose. My basement is an igloo; the streets are the Arctic. Some venture outside, for one minute only, to snap a picture of a vacant and fair Manhattan rendered frozen and mute on this uncommon day.

We spend slow and spun-out minutes bundling up in down coats and bulky scarves, clothing my mother sent and I forgot I had. Earmuffs. When the door opens, we step out like astronauts testing the surface of the moon. We hold the railing to climb my three steps to the sidewalk, which is ice-packed and crunchy.

We join mittened palms. I think how silly it is to imagine that love is something like snowfall, a change in the weather, a simple storm. He pulls me into the street, wanting to walk down its center since there are no cars, since there are no legal restrictions. We can venture out, walk in the middle where usually there's traffic, saying nothing, bypassing the hollow, the idle, the noisy. We walk, tracing a thin vein down Sixth, turning onto a surreal and spacey Houston.

He stops dead, right in the snowy heart, and he turns to me. I halt, stiffly. I'm a snowman. We move our heads with our bodies. He takes off a mitten, tugs at mine. Our fingers are exposed; they'll burn or become icicles. He clasps my hand and jams both of our extremities into his pocket so we hold hands in the storm.

We walk, seeing what it's like, touching flakes, opening our lips to feel them on our tongues. We aren't ghosts; we're alive. If I reach out to touch him, my hand hits his body. It doesn't pass through. There's something there. We step carefully, slowly, with deliberation. Our hands link, and our bodies work through thick snow. We sense our membership, our bond, to that world of disposability, of takeout coffee and the latest rock 'n' roll. We smile faintly, both happily and mournfully, both committed and troubled. We're made uneasy by the nature of reprieve, made so sharply clear in a Manhattan blizzard, but we walk forward. This is what I do.

ACKNOWLEDGMENTS

Less is more? I could name so many people to whom I'm most grateful for their *Love Slave* contribution, but I'm going to keep this relatively short. Please know that there are others. I would particularly like to thank Arizona State University's Creative Writing Program for the education, deadlines, and professionals. Thank you to Tim Bell for our life together. Thank you to the following individuals—friends, writers, publishing folk—who have been encouragements, have said or done something so funny and magical I had to use it (if not here, elsewhere), and/or have shown me unwarranted kindness and wisdom: Matt Bell, Kelly Fitzsimmons Burton, Anastasia Campos, David Duhr, Steven Gillis, Julie Hensley, Susan Huber, Scott Hyder, Robert Johnson Jr., Kate Kindred, Scott MacDonell, Kyle Minor, Sean Nevin, Rory O'Neill, Siobhan O'Neill, Adam R. Stephenson, and Dan Wickett. Thank you especially to those at Unbridled Books. Thank you to Penelope Krouse, who has always managed to do a close reading and edit of my stuff at a moment's notice—even after having twins (with a toddler already home). Thank you to Fred Ramey at Unbridled for taking on *Love Slave* and calling it "electric." Thank you to Marilynn Spiegel and the late Harvey Spiegel for being great parents.

Dedicating this book is necessary. At first I was going to dedicate it to my mom because she's been so supportive. It's not easy to hear that your daughter wants to be a writer. It's not easy to read her weird stuff. There's a certain unorthodoxy she's stood behind, and I am most thankful for that.

Then I was going to dedicate this to my husband, Tim Bell. Craziest love story I've ever heard.

I decided, though, to dedicate this to my daughters, Wendy Ireland and Melody Prose. They probably won't read this for years and years, but this is for them. May they be real love slaves, slaves to a pure kind of love. May they be good like their father and witty like their mom. May they inherit their father's blue eyes and their mother's unbelievably fabulous taste in art and movies. Wendy and Melody, this is for you.